MURDER
with
ALOHA
at the
COCO PALMS HOTEL

By

David Penhallow-Scott

Second Edition

My entire life has been a search for a funny side to that very tough life out there. I developed a kind of an eye for scenes that made me laugh to take away the pain.

---Blake Edwards, Director of The Pink Panther (1963)

TO THE READER

This mystery is a work of fiction. However, I could not have written a story about the Coco Palms Hotel without including Grace and Lyle Guslander, Big John, Mrs. Nakai, Elsie, and the neighbors, Gladys Brandt, Anna Bishop, Kathryn Hulme, and Lou Habets. These people were so well embedded into the fabric of Coco Palms' history that it was impossible for me to write the mystery without including them. Sadly, all of them have passed away. The situation and people that make up this mystery come from my imagination and solely my imagination.

Enjoy the ride!

THIS BOOK IS DEDICATED TO:

The employees and guests of the Coco Palms Hotel

Barbara, Willie, and Nan--all living relatives of Grace and Gus

Gabrielle (Alice) James

Jim Ogdan

Vivian Nickerson

Colleen Kelley

Jane Lasswell Hoff

Glenn Lagman

Randal McEndree

Jackie Pualani Johnson

Cynthia Sorenson

Charles Rice Wichman

And especially Grace Buscher Guslander – She *was*
the Coco Palms Hotel

ISBN: 978-1-48358-606-9 (print)
ISBN: 978-1-48358-607-6 (ebook)

CAST OF CHARACTERS

COCO PALMS STAFF AND ADMINSTRATORS

Big John – Assistant Manager of the Coco Palms

Elsie – Secretary to Miss Buscher

Grace Buscher – manager of the Coco Palms

Lyle (Gus) Guslander – President and owner of the Coco Palms

Mrs. Nakai – Seamstress and best friend of Miss Buscher

Percy – Employee of the Coco Palms

GUESTS FROM HOLLYWOOD, CALIFORNIA

Alice Downes von Bismark – Lizard Lady from Pasadena, California; wife of Eric von Bismark

Eric von Bismark –Film director known for his legendary appendage

Gretchen Yamashita –Lillie Russell's friend and make-up artist. Married to a famous cinematographer

Granny Myers –Lillie Russell's old friend, from her San Francisco days

Herbert Nutt Trescutt – Physician known for his tainted needles; husband of gossip columnist Heidi Fleishacker

Lillie Russell – Megastar movie actress

Tilda Francis – Stand-in for Lillie Russell

Tommy Twinkle – A wannabe movie star and a friend to everyone who walks the red carpet, especially Heidi Fleishacker (former Hollywood gossip columnist)

Tony Pinto – A western movie actor; Lillie Russell's lover

Raul Pasqual – Lillie Russell's husband

RESIDENTS OF KAUAI – FRIENDS OF GRACE BUSCHER

Anna Bishop – Third grade teacher

Gladys Brandt – Educator

Kathryn Hulme –Author of *The Nun's Story*

Lou Habets – Nun of *The Nun's Story*

PROLOGUE

Later Summer, 1959 – West Hollywood, California

A home on Hilldale Avenue.
The cottage, two blocks up from Santa Monica Boulevard, built in 1930, was constructed of stucco and designed to resemble a small Mexican hacienda found on the cobbled streets of Cuernavaca.

Gales of laughter was heard through the walls of the cottage. The hysterical laughter was coming from an elderly man sitting in his living room, drinking a rum and coke. Tears ran down his cheeks. Overcome with giggles, the old man could not hear that an intruder had entered by the back door into his kitchen. The intruder carried a long, chiffon green-blue-and-yellow scarf.

Silently, stealthily, the intruder crept up behind the old man, mumbling, "I've got you now!" With a sudden thrust, the scarf was bound tightly around the man's neck and wrenched until all laughter was silenced.

Pouring gasoline around the living room, the intruder cried out, " I NOW HAVE THE LAST LAUGH!"

The cottage burned to the ground.

Two weeks later in a mansion in Beverly Hills.

Heidi Fleishacker, a gossip columnist and the most hated woman in Hollywood, sat in her mansion –it was once the home of the tragic, silent-movie star, Mable Norman.

On a late afternoon in August, Heidi sat in her sunroom, drinking a dry martini with an olive. As the sun caressed her face, Heidi dozed off dreaming of all the scandals she had stored in a vault. She did not hear that an intruder had entered into the sunroom, wielding a hypodermic needle. Bending over Heidi, the intruder was about to plunge the needle into Heidi's arm, when she suddenly awakened and cried out, "YOU!"

"ME!" The intruder plunged the needle into Heidi's arm.

Heidi died

In December, 1959, as the year closed, the Beverly Hills Police Department still had on its books two unsolved murders. The only clue to the identity of the killer came from an anonymous phone call made to the head of detectives at the Beverly Hills Police Department. A muffled voice said, "The killer behind the two murders is either visiting or working with Paramount Studios and is about to shoot the film *Blue Hawaii* starring Elvis Presley at the Coco Palms Hotel on the Island of Kauai . . . Hawaii! Later, the Chief of Detectives sniffed and was quoted saying to his staff, "I've heard a lot worse!"

Grace Buscher Guslander

CHAPTER ONE

February 9, 1960 – Joanne Woodward, actress and wife of Paul Newman, receives the first star on the Hollywood Walk of Fame.

In the state of Hawaii.

I'm Percy the Fat, born on Oahu. During my teenage years, my family and I moved to the Island of Kauai, the fourth largest island in the Hawaiian chain.

So that you may understand the teller of this tale, I forthwith provide snippets from my authorized autobiography: The day I left my mother's womb and hit the bright lights of the operating room, the doctor dropped me on my head. (That should explain tons.) I screamed to the doctor, "Buster, the world is now in big trouble!" My prophecy came true.

After Dr. Mansfield snipped off my umbilical cord, I goo-gooed sweet things to my precious mother, giving her the impression that I was going to be a fabulous, fantastic gasser. I proved my point by farting the smell of violets. Until today, after I eat a bowl of chili topped with mayonnaise, winds blowing from the south, my fat body transports to the world the fragrance of a florist shop that sells violets.

My first years on earth. I was a spoiled brat. I annoyed the hell out of my family singing loudly "Over the Rainbow" while doing number two sitting on the pot. A dreamy kid, at five, I wore a kimono at home, playing Madame Butterfly. I'd confide to my mother's friends that I served drinks in Mama-San's bar on King Street in downtown Honolulu. Mama-San's was known as a seedy joint that reeked of wet floors, cigarette smoke, and the strong aroma of bourbon, scotch, stale beer, and poppies.

Why Mama-San's?

Fusako!

I adored our Japanese maid, Fusako. Her father owned Mama-San's bar. Fusako and I made frequent visits to see her father—it was our designated pee stop. Fusako was my whole world, because she was all mine—my very own Japanese mama-san. Since the day she walked into my life, smelling of Sen-Sen, Fusako treated me like her very own precious baby boy. Because of Fusako at the age of two, I could count to ten in Japanese. At three, I recited Japanese love poems.. After I learned to walk, Fusako and I began our afternoon excursions to see movies, catching the bus on Punahou Street. Movies were our favorite pastime and we saw every feature film that we could cram into our precious afternoon hours. We knew well the Waikiki, Hawaii, Palace, Princess, King, Queen, and Pawaa movie palaces. Inside those ornate castles, we held hands as we cried, laughed, and swooned watching our favorite stars under contract at Warner Brothers, Twentieth Century Fox, and Universal Studios. Nelson Eddy, ZaSu Pitts, Alice Faye, Cary Grant, Fred Astaire and Ginger Rogers, just to name a few, became my best friends. These actors became my only friends other than Fusako. I especially adored *The Thin Man* murder mysteries starring William Powell and Myrna Loy.

At the age of seven, Fusako broke my heart. She left me to marry a sailor stationed on the battleship, Utah, anchored in Pearl Harbor. Despite Fusako's desertion, I grew up without killing anyone, more to the point, without anyone killing me. I graduated from high school by the skin of my teeth, and remained a lifelong cinema addict, a movie fan who constantly searched for a happy ending.

I never got over my childhood passion for movies. I adored the movie stars of the 1930s and 40s and ached to be one of them. I felt that I had been born too late and had missed out on all the glamor of Hollywood's golden age. Perhaps, this is one of the reasons I chose to write this story.

1960 in Kauai.

After failing my driver's test on Kauai twice, I finally passed. On my first try, I rammed the fender of my license-testing officer Waialeale's police car trying to back up. After I assessed the damage that I had caused his car, I gave the police officer a good scolding. I told him that he had parked his car illegally in front of Lihue Department Store. Waialeale answered my complaint with a thump on my head and a kick in the pants.

Now being of age, able to drive, I bought a Model A Ford. Without money to buy Best Foods Mayonnaise or to see a film at the Royal movie house on Rice Street, I was forced to get a job. Imagine! Through the good offices of my mother, I was hired as a waiter to work in the main dining room of Kauai's fabulous Coco Palms Hotel. Within weeks, I earned the reputation of being the most incompetent waiter to ever work in the hotel main dining room. For instance: I mixed up food orders and sloshed ice water onto hotel guests' laps more times than they or I care to remember. I blamed each mistake on the poor lighting in the dining room because the ceiling lights were covered over with coconut hats. In truth, I was just plain incompetent because I was a big snoop. I loved to tune into the gossip that the guests exchanged while I took their orders. I could always remember the gossip but never their orders.

After enduring two weeks of disasters, Honey, the dining room manager, threatened me with dismissal if she heard one more complaint against me. The day after I had ruined the dress of one of the hotel's directors, I was strictly forbidden to be within five feet of the tables allotted to "people of importance," POI. The hotel manager created the acronym POI after the much-loved gray mush that Hawaiians ate with their fingers. Honey exiled me to the outskirts of the Lagoon Dining Room and she prayed that I could do no more harm serving food to the tourists who came to the hotel on the cheap.

I was thrilled with my new assignment because every night live Bette Davis-style soap operas were performed in front of me. Some of the dramas were so damn exciting that my toes tingled, my bellybutton itched, my ears rang, and all the loose stuff in my pea brain rattled. I became addicted to these crazy foibles of human beings who wore flowery aloha shirts, flashy *muumuus*, and paid $28 a day on the American Plan (three meals were included). I could hardly wait to get to work waiting on tables at the Coco Palms as it was better than a double bill of Joan Crawford, Irene Dunn and Clark Gable movies at the Lihue Theater'

Here is the real skinny about the Coco Palms.

The hotel was a Petri dish of human shenanigans, a movie extravaganza featuring a combination of Joan Crawford coffee-and-cigarette dramas, Buster Keaton kick-'em-in-the-pants comedies, and tropical, romantic, Technicolor, MGM musicals starring swim-star Esther Williams.

The Coco Palms movie was brilliantly directed by someone who could have been a clone of Cecil B. DeMille - the great director of epic movies like *Ten Commandments* and *Cleopatra*. She not only directed the Coco Palms movie but was the star of the extravaganza. I found her as theatrical and mesmerizing as any of the movie stars of the 1930s and '40s, all the movie stars that I loved.

The "she" was Grace Buscher.

Grace acted like a movie star and had a larger-than-life persona. She was an original. Not being a clothes horse, abhorring the dictates of Harper's Bazaar or Vogue or the tyranny of racks upon racks of dresses hanging at Liberty House, Grace brilliantly wore the same fitted white *muumuu* every day. This original costume was created and hand-stitched by Mrs. Nakai, the Coco Palms fashion designer and hotel seamstress.

Mrs. Nakai was not only in charge of Grace's costumes but she created and sewed the hotel's red cloth napkins. the table cloths and employee's red and white uniforms, not to mention the skimpy red *malos* (jock straps) that Hawaiian men wore every night when they ran through the coconut grove, dipping their torches into cans of kerosene.

Mrs. Nakai was a tiny, tiny Japanese person—barely four feet two inches tall—but according to everyone who worked at Coco Palms, she was a towering six-foot dowager empress who sat on a golden throne in her airless, cramped basement sewing room. When wet, she weighed not more than an eighty-pound bag of rice. I kowtowed to Mrs. Nakai and was tempted to bow and call her Nakai the Great, especially, after I had been reprimanded for doing something stupid. Thankfully, good sense prevailed, as Mrs. Nakai was one of Miss Buscher's best friends and a stupendous source of information.

Let's talk about Grace Walters Buscher, the extraordinary hotel manager who was born to brighten people's lives—people whose lives had been colored in grays and browns. Without Grace's magic touch, the Coco Palms would have appeared as a cluster of drab cottages thatched with droopy coconut fronds, a riptide dirty beach across the street, and multiple army barracks looking so much like a World War II Army camp, The buildings were set in rows next to a busy highway with a murky lagoon that stretched the length of the property. A coconut grove was etched in the background that had lost its purpose as a copra plantation in the year that the Titanic sank.

Through Grace's wizardry, the barracks were transformed into frog rooms and Hawaiian canoe suites. The thatched cottages became palaces furnished with seashell beds fit for a Hawaiian chief and his queen. The frosting on the cake was the honeymoon suites that Grace created for those who wanted to be treated as Hawaiian royalty of old. Under the Buscher reign, the murky lagoon sparkled blue in the ancient fishpond and splayed with Monet's pink and purple water lilies. No one dared to drown across the highway at her pristine, white sandy beach —except once in a future time Frank Sinatra did try. On holidays, two of the staff members volunteered to be Santa Claus and the Easter Bunny and were paddled down the lagoon by stalwart Hawaiian men. Santa and the Easter Bunny, directed by Grace, waved and blew kisses to the hoi polloi who screamed to them from the banks of the lagoon. Every night, the coconut grove was lit up by torches and was turned into a magical Disney fairyland. On New Year's Eve (Grace's favorite event), the grove exploded with fireworks unequaled anywhere in the Hawaiian Islands, or in China for that matter. Grace's Coco Palms was all about romance and under her guidance, it became a Hawaiian tropical dream come true, especially, for people living in the freezing snow places like Switzerland and North Dakota.

Forty-five, five-feet-four-inches tall, blond, slim, and pretty, Grace exuded more charm than God ever possessed. She spoke in a Lauren Bacall baritone voice that rose up from the bottom of a barrel of molasses. Her vowels had the same intonations as the ladies who chaired meetings at the Daughters of the American Revolution and Philadelphia Main Liners who she admired. After Grace became famous, the corseted ladies who inhabited the city of Benjamin Franklin claimed the Coco Palms manager as one of their favorite daughters.

Grace was the queen of all the hotel managers in the Hawaiian Islands. Travel writers gushed after meeting Grace. They wrote that meeting Grace was like having an audience with the Empress of the Pacific. The travel writers exclaimed in all their columns that Grace, as a hotel manager and creator, was not to be surpassed."

Since the year 1953, when Grace opened the hotel doors, she operated her kingdom from inside a tiny, cluttered office. Her closet-sized war room was stacked with reports, unpaid bills, and Hawaiian kitsch—all scattered on the floor orderly disorder. Sitting at her desk, she glued a telephone to her right ear and pasted the fingers of her left hand around the handle of a silver cup brimming with hot coffee. She frequently refilled the cup from a red thermos bottle set on the floor, to the left of her chair, so that, by noon, she would have drunk a gallon of coffee. Whenever Grace's cup of coffee rested on the desk, her two fingers elegantly cradled a cigarette. Grace chain-smoked two packs of filtered Viceroys a day.

When holding court from her desk, Grace wielded a ruler in lieu of a scepter to make a point. Her employees regarded her ruler as a magic wand.

Grace never looked back. She always plunged forward into uncharted waters to devise her next creations at her Coco Palms Hotel. Her guests regarded Grace as Glinda, the magical witch from the *Land of Oz*. That notion came from watching Grace glide fairy-like around the hotel grounds picking up rubbish.

In reality, Grace's feet were firmly placed on the Coco Palms grounds. She was a sharp businesswoman who developed the most lucrative hotel to ever have been operated in the Hawaiian Islands. Ever! Beyond that, the Coco Palms offered the only authentic Hawaiian experience to be found in any hotel in the Hawaiian Islands; and to this day, no one has ever come close. As a result, Grace became a folk hero to the native Hawaiians.

For historians, in 1969 Grace married Lyle Guslander, her boss, and co-owner of the Coco Palms. *In my story*, Grace and Gus are not married, but are business partners in bringing tourists to Hawaii and the Coco Palms. When the murders occurred, Gus worked full-time in Waikiki managing the parent company, Island Holidays, Ltd.

Grace thought Gus walked on water, not because he wore shorts on all occasions and had great legs but because he was a brilliant businessman in creating his hotel empire.

What endeared Gus to the Coco Palms staff was the fact that he loved his boxer dog, Happy. When Gus visited the Coco Palms, he and Happy flew together side by side, always in first class on Hawaiian Airlines. As far as Gus was concerned, Happy was his Tonto to his Lone Ranger. In those innocent and romantic days, Hawaiian Airlines flew dogs as passengers, doled out free tiny packs of cigarettes, and served Kona coffee complemented by small paper packages of C&H

sugar. Sitting inside those smoggy cabins, the flights to Kauai were heaven on earth to nicotine and caffeine addicts.

In 1954, Happy was voted Hawaiian Airlines' favorite passenger. The airlines presented Happy with a pair of tin wings—one for each ear—and a travel bag to carry his Skippy Dog Food.

Gus ran his corporation from Coco's coffee shop on Kalakaua Ave in Waikiki. Seated in his favorite booth, Gus—built like a football fullback—handled important, lucrative deals while scarfing down honeyed ham, crisp bacon, two fried eggs, and a stack of banana pancakes drowned in hot butter and topped with homemade coconut syrup.

Always to bed early, like clockwork, Gus phoned Grace every night from Honolulu at 7:30 sharp to check on the day's receipts. He kept a bottle of Bayer aspirin within easy reach in case Coco Palm's expenses had exceeded its revenue. Gus growled like a lion every night, making sure that *his favorite cub* wasn't taking him to the poor house. But by 1960, Gus knew his cub was a rare breed. He also believed that if he didn't give Grace (his eccentric manager with her cockamamie ideas) stern fatherly advice on finances, he, Grace, and the Coco Palms could easily become extinct.

Gus lived to eat and nightly advised, "Doll Face, serving bad food, no matter how beautiful your Coco Palms is, will cause your guests to leave in droves. And I promise you, Grace, these guests will never return to your beloved Coco Palms if they eat one lousy meal in the Lagoon Dining Room."

Taking up his challenge, Grace nightly chanted, "Food, yes, but my Hawaiian ambiance is the key to Coco Palms' success."

Gus swallowed two aspirins, because he could only hear his manager say, "Spend, spend, spend." In Gus's mind, Grace went on crazy wild buying sprees, ordering "crap" he thought was mad, crazy, and frivolous for his hotel. Gus envisioned that all the loan money that he and George Shipman, his treasurer, had wheedled out of the skinflints at Bishop Bank had gone down the drain. Gus ate three huge helpings of cherries jubilee the day he heard that Grace ordered 500 cases of toilet paper. Checking with Albert Teraoka, Grace's comptroller, he learned that there wasn't an epidemic of Montezuma Revenge at the hotel - it was far worse. Grace had bought 500 cases of toilet paper as torch wicks to light up the coconut grove. In the end, the toilet paper idea didn't work out, but now Grace was fully prepared for a hurricane, tsunami, or an outbreak of Montezuma's Revenge.

From the day Grace first stepped into the Coco Palms Lodge, she thought of nothing else but her dream of a Hawaiian Renaissance at the hotel. If anyone doubted her vision or got in her way, damn the torpedoes, and that included Gus. In the years to come, to Gus's amazement, Grace's dreams and her "crap" brought him a pot of gold.

In Gus's defense, he was once a poor twelve-year-old boy from Alameda, California, who sold newspapers to support his mother and baby sister. He too, dreamed big and of faraway places. All his life, (till the day he died), he kept his foot pressed down on the accelerator to create deal after deal. He could never stay in one place. It wasn't in his DNA. It is a loving legend that he explored the entire Louvre Museum in fifteen minutes.

Grace's greatest fear came to pass; Gus put Coco Palms on his back burner and began to take away Grace's precious profits to create his hotel empire—on Maui, Hawaii Island, and Oahu. These hotels soon became Grace's competition and because of that, fierce arguments erupted nightly on the telephone.

Grace, speaking on the telephone, reprimanded Gus, "Don't forget, Mr. Lyle Guslander, without my Coco Palms profits, there wouldn't be a King Kamehameha Hotel in Kona or a Maui Palms. So, lay off taking money away from my Coco Palms. Remember, I have a hotel to operate and I have to pay bills and my employees."

After reading an invoice for two dozen koa, canoe-styled king-sized beds custom-made for the Wailua Kai rooms, Gus screamed into the telephone, "You're sending me to the poor house, Doll!"

"I am not. Tell your treasurer, George Shipman, to ship to me on the next barge to Kauai two dozen giant clam shell basins for the bathrooms in the Wailua Kai wing!"

Gus gulped down two more aspirins.

Grace never lost a battle with Gus. Ultimately, Grace's dreams made Gus a millionaire twice-over. Coco Palms was always Gus's cash cow and, in the end, Gus gave Grace free reign and let her be the queen of her domain. And, for you historians, in 1969 Gus sold his entire hotel empire for $30 million to American Factors in Hawaii.

As my mystery progresses, Gus recedes into the wings. He worked on Oahu all week, meaning, he was separated from the island of Kauai by a thirty-minute airline flight and the fierce, stormy seas in the Kaieiewaho Channel. At that time, 1960, Gus stayed away from Coco Palms for weeks at a time working on his new hotel projects. However, he remains a strong force in this story because he took up so much of Grace's energy just to keep him out of her hair. Had he been on Kauai at the time of the murders, Gus would have screwed it up for Grace when she assumed the role of a detective. Volatile Gus hadn't an ounce of patience and when he was on Kauai he charged around the hotel like a bull in a china closet delving into Grace's latest projects. Gus's kinetic energy would have spoiled everything for Grace because being a good detective took finesse.

Might I say here, and modestly write, that Grace and I reeked with the finesse that Gus lacked.

The reason that Grace brought the movie star Lillie Russell and her party into the Coco Palms was because the wealthy actress brought needed revenue to pay off the hotel's mounting debts. The Russell money, Grace secretly planned to keep the Russell money out of Gus' grasping hands.

———◆———

More about me and Grace.

In 1960, at nineteen, I tipped the scales near the obese end of 200 pounds, all because I was a mayonnaise addict.

A mayonnaise addict?

I craved Best Foods Mayonnaise every waking moment of my life, and *only* Best Foods Mayonnaise.

Definition: A mayonnaise addict smears the white goop on anything edible—white bread (yum, yum), canned Coral tuna, beef stew, hot chili, and steamed white rice are just a few examples. Mayonnaise on peanut butter with sliced bananas topped with caviar was an all-time favorite for Marie Antoinette at Versailles. Albert Einstein believed that mayonnaise lubricated his gray cells. On his deathbed, a mayonnaise addict told me that Einstein's final words were, "Best Foods Mayonnaise helped me discover the Theory of Relativity."

I give warning to all those who value their lives: a mayonnaise addict can turn into a saber-wielding, whirling dervish at the mention of Miracle Whip Salad Dressing.

Putting mayonnaise aside, but only for a moment, I pride myself in being a great detective - better than Charlie Chan, the well-known Honolulu Chinese detective celebrated in the movies and in the Earl derr Biggers mystery book, *A House without a Key*. Believe it or not: Charlie Chan ate mayonnaise with his egg foo yung.

Here are some of my characteristics that I believe made me a great detective:

I am curious. I sniff into every hole I can find.

I was born with a motor-mouth. It is a recessive gene from the Waterhouse side of my family. Waterhouses can never stopped talking—not for ten generations. Because of my yapping Waterhouse mouth, I made murderers confess.

I keep secrets, have courage, and persevere in all my causes,

I keep my word,

And I am completely delusional.

———◆———

The Coco Palms' coconut grove of more than a hundred trees, was not, itself, sacred to the ancient Hawaiians, only to Grace. The coconut grove was planted by a German copra grower, Mr. E. Lindemann, in 1896. Being a German, he planted the coconut trees in symmetrical rows. Here is a truth about the coconut grove: ghostly spirits wander through the grove every night because it was once the site of an ancient Hawaiian burial ground. There wasn't a watchman at the hotel who didn't personally witness the ghostly night marchers that after midnight, roamed the grove.

The most memorable experience for guests staying at the Coco Palms Hotel was Grace's nightly pagan torch-lighting ceremony. The ceremony was performed in the coconut grove at 7:30 p.m., sharp. Young, handsome Hawaiians, nearly naked, wearing their *malos*, zigzagged throughout the grove holding up lit torches. Number eight tin cans placed on the ground were stashed throughout the grove.

Men filled the tin cans with kerosene, then stuffed the tin cans with shredded coconut husks and when lit; the cans created a luminous magic. Coco Palms, every night, metamorphosed into a thousand starry lights. Before the hotel was a year old, the torch-lighting ceremony became the signature experience for anyone who visited the Garden Island. The viewing of the Waimea Canyon had slipped into second place.

After the torch-lighting ceremony and Grace's nightly cocktail party and the meal service were completed, the hotel manager relaxed in the Palms bar and shared her dreams and philosophy with favored guests.

Grace whispered mysteriously to her guests: "Here is something, my dear friends,

that is most important for you to remember—everything at Coco Palms, from the ground to the trees, has life . . . in fact, all around us is sacred So, please respect and treat everything here at the Coco Palms with reverence—even to the smallest stone. I was told all of this by a lovely Hawaiian lady of great importance. That meeting happened when I first arrived on Kauai and it is how I have lived my life at the Coco Palms and on Kauai ever since."

One added thought I'd like to mention about Grace and how she lived her life: Grace's Chinese astrological sign was that of the dog. "A dog is loyal." Loyalty was Grace's greatest strength of character. Her loyalty and her friendship saved not only my fat *okole* (the gluteus maximus) a thousand times, but also the okoles of the housekeepers, the bellmens, the cooks, the bartenders and Assistant Manager Big John, Andrew and Sam in the grove and the guests, whenever they hit a wall of troubles. Grace was a rare breed in the hotel business - in fact, in the world of business. She treated the people who worked for her and the hotel guests like family and never, in my experience, were they treated as servants or strangers.

Another thought: Grace loved Hawaiians and the island of Kauai to the depths of her soul but Coco Palms was, far and beyond, Grace's passion. Night and day she did everything possible to ensure Coco Palms' existence. Her daily challenge was to keep the hotel doors open, even under the most adverse conditions that hit the hotel: floods, hurricanes, tidal waves, mounting bills and shipping strikes that kept necessary supplies from sailing on the barge to Kauai. She prayed in the Chapel of the Palms for God to keep Coco Palms from going down into the drink. Coco Palms' financial survival was Grace's main motivation to solve the murder mystery.

Let me begin the tale.

My story began when Coco Palms was at its peak of its popularity—overbooked every night of the week. The killer was shrewd and clever, thinking he or she could get away with the murders, especially when Coco Palms boasted it had a full house. But it happened. Gory things can happen to people on vacation. Tourists visiting hotels anywhere in the world, sitting around a swimming pool, out for a good time and not thinking about bad things in life, do become targets for the unhinged.

Because Grace loved movies (as I did). she advertised weekly in the *Hollywood Reporter,* trying to attract motion picture studios to film a movie on Kauai. Grace understood a movie made at the Coco Palms was worth thousands of dollars of publicity and hundreds of thousands of dollars in room and food revenue.

Grace underlined in her advertisement that Coco Palms made a perfect location for a musical or a drama. For example: "Rita Hayworth filmed *Miss Sadie Thompson* for Columbia Studios at the Coco Palms Hotel."

Grace embellished her pitch, "Coco Palms is the most romantic hotel in the world and has the largest and oldest coconut grove tree in the Hawaiian Islands. This coconut grove is situated on Kauai, an island, where movie star Hedy Lamarr ravished men to exhaustion and Clark Gable, of *Gone with The Wind* fame, chased Marilyn Monroe up a coconut screaming for mercy." (Here Grace went a trifle overboard.)

Grace wrote letters to the movie moguls, promising them that Coco Palms could be a filmmaker's delight because it could save the studios millions of dollars to film at her hotel. She added that Coco Palms offered reduced room rates, great meals, hot water, warm beds, a sky brimming with heavenly stars, full moons, and a bright blue sea. Grace emphasized: "Every day, a sunny beach sand glimmers as diamonds, no rain, and the smell of romance and musk hangs in the air all year long." Continuing: "Imagine Adam and Eve languishing in a canoe feeding tilapias in a tropical lagoon. Coco Palms is the earth's forbidden fruit, the original Garden of Eden. Coco Palms is ready and waiting for all of Hollywood's great producers and directors to film their romantic exotic movies on the Garden Island and only at the wonderful Coco Palms Hotel." The Eve of Kauai placed phone calls and messages to Hollywood every month and waited patiently for studios to bite of her apple.

Hollywood bit.

Hal B. Wallis of Paramount Studios, taken in by Grace's promise of a romantic Kauai, phoned the hotel manager to say that he wanted to film *Blue Hawaii,* starring Elvis Presley at her hotel and to please reserve (and confirm) a hundred rooms needed for the shoot.

The murders that happened at the Coco Palms was the week before Presley, the producer, the stars, and the film crew were about to descend on Kauai. Grace was afraid that if Paramount heard about the murders, the studio would cancel the film.

More problems: Myrtle Lee, Gus's assistant, had already booked money-making, big travel groups into the hotel at the same time as the Presley film. With finesse, Myrtle offered new dates to these travel groups and solved the problem. The problem solved, Grace confirmed an ironclad contract with Paramount but also certain that people from La-La Land were known to bolt from their commitments at the merest excuse. What made it even more scary for Grace was that she took a chance, unbeknownst to anyone, by personally blocking out her pricey King's Cottages for Lillie Russell and her party. These were the same Kings Cottages that were reserved for Hal Wallis, Elvis Presley, and his co-stars Joan Blackman and Angela Lansbury. If the Russell party extended their stay one hour beyond their confirmed dates – huge dust-up would occur.

The potential publicity about the film was a colossal gift for Grace. Elvis had signed a multi-million-dollar contract with Wallis and was committed to make a film each year; one of the films was to be *Blue Hawaii*. Paramount Studios spared no expense. They hired the best film crew in Hollywood to accompany Elvis to the Coco Palms Hotel for the month's shoot. The extravaganza was to be filmed in glorious Technicolor and many of the millions of dollars spent on the production would be left behind on Kauai. It was a huge financial windfall for Grace.

Helpful for Grace. The locals on Kauai were so distracted by their Presley frenzy coming to Kauai, they overlooked two murders that happened right under their noses at the Coco Palms Hotel. The people on Kauai didn't care one whit that an over-the-hill, temperamental Lillie Russell, a well-known movie star in Hollywood and one of the oldest movie stars living and a true-to-life crazy from Tinsel Town, had arrived at the Coco Palms to celebrate her birthday. You would have thought that Kauai denizens would have noticed the great star's arrival on Kauai because Lillie stormed off of her Hawaiian Airlines plane looking as deranged as Gloria Swanson playing Norma Desmond in *Sunset Boulevard*. She stepped onto the tarmac wearing high heels and a full-length mink coat. She dripped with Van Cleef jewels, and carried with her enough luggage for a year's stay. People on Kauai should have also noticed Lillie's entourage. They were all well-known Hollywood eccentrics of whom everyone read about in the Hollywood gossip columns. These cuckoos had one thing in common: they hated Lillie Russell.

Little did these Hollywood furies know that they were about to star in a Greek tragedy at the Coco Palms Hotel directed by Lillie Russell. Lillie had invited these furies to her birthday party for hidden, mysterious and devious reasons.

Her financial coffers empty, Grace gave thanks to God she had booked the Lillie Russell party at full price into her hotel for three days. Russell's three-day stay in the King's Cottages and an elaborate birthday dinner party guaranteed to pay off the entire costs of the Elvis Presley renovations on the King's Cottages.

Empty coffers? Weeks before, Gus had grabbed Coco Palms profits away from Grace to complete the construction of the King Kamehameha Hotel in Kona on Hawaii Island. In addition, Gus desperately needed to take away more profits away from Coco Palms' to open his prestigious Hanalei Plantation Hotel on Kauai's North shore. The luxurious Hanalei Plantation hotel boasted to have fifty luxurious cottages, the House of Happy Talk bar, and in the dining room from the ceiling hung twelve crystal chandeliers from Czechoslovakia. A one night's stay at the Hanalei Plantation was to be priced for two people at the exorbitant price of fifty dollars a day and that price included all three meals. Poor Gus, by his accountant's last tally, Gus building his two new hotels, headed into a debt of over a million dollars.

While Gus was building his hotels, unpaid bills plagued Grace, one being, Otsuka's honey wagon pumping out breakfast, lunch, and dinner out of the hotel's cesspools and the other being Esaki's produce of fresh vegetables and fruits. These and many other outstanding invoices preyed on Grace's mind from morning to night. Tired of the pile of bills growing taller than Jack's beanstalk, desperate, Grace called in a Hawaiian *kahuna* to wave a ti leaf over the bills and then instructed the *kahuna* to chant the damn bills into her cesspools. So, worried was Grace over her lack of money, she had doubled the number of Stingers she drank after dinner. When she was about to add a third Stinger is when kahuna's ti leaf intervened in the form of two phone calls—one from Hal Wallis and the other from Lillie Russell.

Interestingly, Grace was in good company in 1960. Most hotel owners in Hawaii were in the same financial boat as Grace, and being in debt was a normal part of the times. Now, Grace was the envy of all hotel owners in Hawaii because the lucrative *Blue Hawaii* was to be filmed at the Coco Palms.

Instinctively, having the Russell party at the Coco Palms, Grace knew though Lillie Russell brought her hotel money, but because of Lillie having an unsavory reputation of being a diva, Grace could head into a spider's web of deceit and treachery. Grace also understood clearly, though she needed the Russell money badly, but at all costs to keep her eye on the Elvis Presley movie being filmed at the Coco Palms. Through it all, Grace never regretted having Lillie Russell at her hotel. The three days that Lillie Russell and her guests stayed at the Coco Palms, Grace lived as if she was written on the pages of an Agatha Christie murder mystery. Above all the murder and mayhem that was about to happen to Grace at the Coco Palms, her one purpose for her hotel held firm: Coco Palms changed people's lives for the better by the magic of staying at her hotel. Changing people's lives for the better at the Coco Palms was one of Grace's reasons to exist - to be.

Then arrived an unexpected bonus, Grace solved a murder mystery.

CHAPTER TWO

February 13, 1960 – France tests its first atomic bomb in the Sahara.

More people for you to remember.

One Wednesday night out of every month was sacrosanct for Grace. It was a night to play hooky from the hotel dramas. Instead of dining with celebrities in the Flame Room, extolling Chef Jiro "Jigs" Okamoto's lobster bisque and hearts of palm salad, Grace played mahjong with close friends who lived in the neighborhood. She needed a moment of sanity from the demands of the hotel world. Grace's closest women friends, were full-time residents on Kauai. They shared girl talk with her—the same local gossip that women chattered sitting under the dryer in Mrs. Shinseki's beauty salon in Lihue.

Grace chose these women friends because each one had integrity, was loyal to her and, most of all, kept their mouths shut. Surprisingly, each woman brought out a raucous genie that Grace hid underneath her *muumuu*.

Holed up in a corner of the hotel's library and museum, Grace's "round table of talk" drank scotch on the rocks and each of them were knighted by Grace as her Five Golden Palms of Womanhood.

To Grace's right sat the regal, beautiful, tawny-brown skinned Gladys Brandt, Grace's first friend on Kauai. With Gladys, you first noticed her black hair swept high off her forehead and held firmly in place by tortoise shell combs. To underlings, it formed, and rightly so, a Hawaiian crown. Gladys was queenly from head to toe and was one of the most revered women on Kauai. She spoke with a slight English accent as many of the Hawaiian royalty did. Gladys was Hawaiian to her very core and played many roles on the island: a high school principal, an activist for women's rights, and was regarded as one of the most influential leaders for the Hawaiians. Gladys Brandt was a force of nature, a hurricane wind, a woman not to be trifled with, and there was a consensus among many influential men and women in Hawaii, Gladys should have been elected governor of the state.

Seated to Grace's left was Kathryn Hulme, author of a best-selling novel, *The Nun's Story*. Kate was another force of feminine nature. Her inspired, Book-of-the-Month Club novel, was captured on a Warner Brothers film, starring the rapturous Audrey Hepburn. Kate was as bright as an Eisenhower dime. One of her proudest claims, Kate had been a welder in the Kaiser shipyards during World War II. She sported a French nose that she likened to Cyrano de Bergerac and was as proud of her flagship as she was of France's gift to America, the Statue of Liberty. Kate bragged that she inherited her schnozzle from a French aristocrat who had escaped the guillotine. This aristocrat brought Robespierre to his knees and helped Napoleon to become Emperor of France.

Lou Habets sat opposite of Grace. She was a former nun and the protagonist of Kate's run-away best-selling novel. Lou had jumped over the convent wall during the middle of the Second World War being she was a nurse first. She decided to follow her inner voice. She left the convent, defying the Pope. Anyone who thumbed her nose at the Vatican in 1942 and worked in the underground in Nazi-occupied Belgium was not a shrinking violet.

The last of the group was Anna Banana Bishop. She was born on Kauai and sat next to Lou. Everyone on the island included Anna in their lives, not because she was rich, famous, or powerful but because she was the kindest and most amiable person on the island. She was a single mom, and earned a living as a third (turd as her students called it) grade teacher.

At eleven o'clock on Wednesday nights, "the girls" laid down their Mahjong tiles after punging, konging, and chowing. After two hours of drinking, hooting, and hollering, they called it quits. "The unwashed," as they affectionately referred to themselves, were all working gals. When the Hawaiian sun rose, each working gal rolled out of their bed at 5 a.m. and embraced the morning with gratitude.

On those Wednesday nights, Grace learned more dirt about the people living on Kauai than from any cub reporter writing gossip found on the front page of the local rag, *The Garden Island* newspaper. Their raucous laughter at the tales told was heard in every nook and cranny of the hotel. Even out in the coconut grove, especially, the laughter, when Gladys described how the hunky firemen, Likeke and his crew, rescued ample, nude, pigeon-breasted Aunt Rose stuck like glue in her bathtub. Although unlikely, it was rumored that after that incident, one of the local firemen proposed marriage to Aunt Rose.

The Wednesday night before the murders, I had served the Golden Five their drinks and, of course, eavesdropped. I hid behind a cluster of cymbidiums with my ear cocked. I was in luck because I overheard Grace whisper to her confederates, "Keep it under your hats, girls. Gus is going to fire me for what I am about to do."

The next part I couldn't hear because the late plane from Honolulu was off course and flew directly overhead, silencing what

Grace said next. But after the plane landed at the airport, what I heard brought out the curiosity in my cat's nature.

"You haven't the guts!' Kate exclaimed.

Grace's voice rose in fierce opposition, "You wanna bet? Just watch me, Katie. If I do it, Kathryn Hulme, you will give me every first edition of all of your books for my hotel library."

"You're on, Witch." (Kate Hulme nicknamed Grace "Witch," because she felt that Grace conjured magic at the hotel.)

Without as much as a glance behind her, Grace yelled, "Percy, get out from behind those orchids and, if you are not out of my sight within three minutes, you can skedaddle all the way down to the Kauai Surf and tell Brad, the manager, that I sent you with my love and compliments."

I skedaddled to my room with a tingle in my toes for what I had just overheard. From that moment on, I planned to be on the alert because.....

Something was definitely up!

Note: What I didn't know then but Gladys, Kate, Lou, and Anna would figure prominently in assisting Grace to catch the killer

CHAPTER THREE

February 13, 1960 – Winter Olympics open in Squaw Valley, California.

Sundays and Secrets.

Because Grace didn't graduate from Cornell's prestigious hotel school, it was absolutely no mystery to me why Grace's was so successful in the hotel world. It was because she worked harder than any employee and hardly left the hotel grounds except on Sundays. On Sundays, she'd crawl on all fours on deserted beaches wearing an old muumuu, picking up shells of every size, shape, and color. Sundays, she'd meditate, breathe in the salt air, and thrill to find rare shells. These discoveries rejuvenated Grace's imagination and the energy she needed for the coming week.

Grace's sea shells were stored by the thousands in old ice cream cartons in her bedroom. In moments of inspiration, she'd scatter her precious shells on the Coco Palms' walls, lamps, and furniture.

Shortly, after I was hired by Grace, I went shelling with her on Haena beach. She instructed me as I handed her a shell that if I was to be a part of the Coco Palms staff, I had to be as dedicated to the hotel as she was. Otherwise, she implied, tapping her fingers on my head, I would be hauled in a tumbrel like Marie Antoinette, guillo-tined, and then fired.

Unfortunately, my interests and attention were on movies or somewhere over the rainbow, but not on Coco Palms. Actually, my mind's thoughts were as scattered as the shells on the beach. My mind went this way and that way and never seemed to go Grace's way. So, I felt I had to speak to Grace, truthfully, and in confidence as we left the beach.

I confessed to Grace, looking at one of the shells in my hand, "You have to understand, Miss Buscher, my mind is like a Mexican jumping bean, drunk on Spanish Fly. I can't help myself. My interests go this way and that way and, mostly, I just love to pry into other people's business. I love to unearth people's secrets."

"That's well and good, my boy, and for those reasons, you are truly made for the hotel business. But Percy and this is big but, my secrets I keep locked in my bedroom and don't you dare go into my bedroom without my permission or meddle into any of my affairs while you are working for me. I repeat, my bedroom is strictly off limits to you and everyone else, but I am not going to worry about you because your mind operates only on two pistons."

Wow! Oh baby! When I heard that I felt I was going to have to find a way to get into her bedroom. Two pistons, my ass?

By luck, not long after that, I got clued into one of Grace's secrets. One night, after she had drunk two Johnny Walkers, feeling mellow, she whispered to me that she had longed since childhood to be an amateur sleuth or, at the least, a murder mystery writer. She craved since she was a teenager to be a wannabe Agatha Christie.

She never told that secret to anybody but me.

Grace continued to say, "In high school, I received an A for writing a twenty-page murder mystery in Mr. Bart's sophomore

English class. And for your information, Mr. Smarty Pants, I have a collection of first editions of every murder mystery that Agatha Christie ever wrote."

That night, I understood everything she had said. Other times, she annoyed me because she'd whisper important instructions to me that I needed to hear and I couldn't hear or understand her. On those rare occasions when I did hear her, what she told me sometimes made no sense to me at all. Many the times, she'd walk briskly down a walkway, me, following near her, and she'd spew out baffling instructions. Not able to hear her clearly, what I'd think I heard, I was later to find out that I had been completely wrong and made a mistake. But I'd be damned if I was going to ask her to repeat herself because I felt it would have been folly on my part. Grace believed that I acted only on two pistons, if I had asked her to repeat herself, I would have been sent to the bottom of the lagoon eating stale bread crumbs with the tilapias. I tell you this because Grace gave me instructions to help her catch the killer and I goofed! She almost died because I couldn't hear her.

Weeks later, being my most annoying self, and determined to the very fiber of my nosiness to find a way to get inside Miss Buscher's bedroom, the opportunity presented itself. Without having to use a screwdriver, I entered her bedroom with her permission.

CHAPTER FOUR

March 3, 1960 – Elvis Presley returns home from Germany after being away on duty in the Army for two years.

The fateful day I sleuthed into Miss Buscher's bedroom was the day the murderer arrived at the Coco Palms. I walked up from the swimming pool to the lobby to schmooze with little, old Japanese ladies who carried umbrellas and waved little Nippon flags. At the entrance, I saw Miss Buscher talking to tourists. She noticed me at the door, and wiggled her finger. I marched over to her, stood to attention, clicked my heels, and played Fritz, a Nazi storm trooper in an MGM movie. If looks could kill, I would have been dead. Grace then ordered me to run into her bedroom to fetch the keys to hotel station wagon car. On a whim, she had decided to make the mail run into Lihue. Most times, that chore she assigned to the hotel bellmen.

Kauai's main post office was a twenty-minute car drive from the hotel. Looking at her wristwatch, Grace estimated that she had just enough time to make the mail run before the morning plane arrived from Oahu bringing to Coco Palms "fresh meat" (a word Gus used for new check-ins).

In 1960, Kauai operated as a third world country. Mail delivery to the hotel by an attractive postman or lady was not an option.

"Run, Percy! My car keys."

"Gadzooks!" I cried as a thrill struck into my left testicle. I was now being permitted to enter her inner sanctum.

Whoopee!

Rumor had it that Grace's bedroom was cluttered from floor to ceiling with "crap," another word I learned from Mr. Guslander. He used that word to describe anything, and everything, that Grace bought in auction houses and fire sales from old, kamaaina estates that had gone bust during the Depression.

I remembered back to a "don't-tell" story, told to me by Chuckles, the night clerk. I worked with him at the front desk: Story: Halloween, who was once a bellman, was ordered to get the car keys from Miss Buscher's bedroom. He had vanished from the hotel without a trace.

Grace's door was unlocked!

I stepped carefully inside the inner sanctum, and peered up at the ceiling, and searched for Halloween. Halloween wasn't hanging from a chandelier. I was very disappointed.

Damn!

I was in! I was in!

Rubbing the goose bumps down on my arms, I gave a second look around, and this time I yipped. I knew the meaning of the cliché, a needle in a haystack.

Where the devil did Grace put the car keys in all this mess?"

Grace's haystack was a colossal clutter of crap. Floor to ceiling, she had stacked mountains of ice cream cartons filled with her sea shells. I sang to myself, looking at the mountains of ice cream cartons, a little off key:

Grace's sea shells are from her sea shore.

In my sight were light fixtures that were twisted into Picasso sculptures. Pillars of Hercules—fabrics from the Mainland with air freight tags attached to them itched to have Mrs. Nakai's rusty sewing machine swirl them into drapes, uniforms, and bedspreads, some would be embroidered with the Hawaiian coat-of-arms.

Before me lay a twisty path lined on either side with odd-sized cardboard boxes. Cardboard boxes were chockablock filled with gewgaws to spruce up Grace's hotel rooms.

I deducted that the lethal land mines, the cardboard boxes, were to keep the Percys of the world from Grace's forbidden secrets.

Grace's entire bedroom seemed to me more dangerous than a World War II minefield. As I meandered down Grace's yellow brick road of danger, more hazards loomed ahead. Floor to ceiling, high rolls of woolen carpets designed with tropical flowers lined the walls, each threatened to crush and kill me if I made one single false move. Cautiously, I sneaked past the carpets as they swayed above me back and forth treacherously.

Gadzooks, an intruder could hide out in this bedroom for weeks, months, years, and no one, not even Grace, would be able to find the suspect.

I continued my hunt. Shoved against the east wall stood a queen-sized bed piled with mountains of "crap" on it, under it, and beside it. On the bedspread, hidden under old newspapers were catalogs that advertised bathroom fixtures, hotel dining room accessories, and stainless steel kitchen pots and pans waiting for Chef Jiro's stamp of approval. Against the wall was a vanity table adjacent to a window that overlooked an alley, the exit, and entrance to the hotel kitchen. Garbage cans nestled under her window that released the smell of rotten cabbages. Two painted blue bureaus bookended on either side of the vanity table. The tables revealed that Grace "cock-roached" the bureaus from the renovated Lagoon Lanai hotel rooms.

I saw Aphrodite sitting among the ruins (her vanity table) on a faded cloth stool. The stool featured a deep indentation on its faded, flower embroidered pillow. The indentation indicated where Grace sat contemplating thoughts about me—thoughts I didn't wanted to know about. Above the vanity table hung, precariously, an oval mirror. A crack on its left corner created the illusion of antiquity, though Grace had purchased the vanity table at the Lihue Salvation Army Store. Set in a disarray on the vanity table were her elixirs: a bottle of Chanel No.5, two jars of Elizabeth Arden cream for the face and arms, a dented silver hair brush from Shrives, Avon lipsticks in different shades of red, pink, and orange, a Gillette razor, Tiger Claw red nail polish, and Zip Off Hair Remover as advertised in July's *Town and Country* magazine.

Two reasons for this lengthy description: First, to let you understand that at first glance, I thought my assignment to find the car keys was not going to be a simple one. Second and more importantly, Grace's bedroom played an important role in catching the killer.

I dropped and peered under the double bed where I discovered a treasure trove of Grace's secrets. "Oh my God!" I gasped. I peeled away a wad of paid bills and found that Grace had spent hundreds and hundreds of dollars of her own money at auctions in Honolulu, London, New York and Los Angeles. She had bought Captain Cook's original journals, Hawaiian calabashes, rare books about the Hawaiian Islands, and feather capes. Some of the items were once owned by the finest families of Hawaii (the Ward sisters for one). Most of the items came from families that had gone bust during the Great Depression of 1929.

Large hinged Chinese screens stood in the four corners of the room. I shivered thinking of what she hid behind them—more secrets?. Painted on the four oriental screens were ferocious dragons that blew red flames out of green mouths. The dragons' razor-sharp teeth were painted a bright orange to keep intruders from venturing behind into the screen's hinterlands.

I had the notion that one of the screens hid the mummified body of Halloween.

I discovered that the screens were bought from an estate sale in Hong Kong. The. Provenance: "Stolen by eunuch, One Hang Lung. The treasures came from China's Empress Dowager's palace."

Further under the bed, I inhaled clouds of dust. Strangely, it brought back memories from my eighth grade world history class. I fantasized that Grace was once an Egyptian princess who collected all this stuff to take with her to heaven . . . to bargain with God for His Presidential Suite with View."

Queasy in my stomach, I felt claustrophobic. Another vision arrived. I was in an underground tomb surrounded by a thousand curses, curses that was out to kill a two-piston fat man under a bed. Next, I was suddenly reminded of my favorite gory film, *The Mummy's Ghost.* Thinking of that film, my arms pimpled with chicken-skin. I knew for certain that something awful was going to happen in this bedroom.

Squiggling further under the bed, I spied a stack of Agatha Christie mystery books. Next to the books, lay two scrapbooks of unsolved crimes in America and Hawaii. Opening one of the scrapbooks, I spied Grace's handwritten notes written in the margin where she had attempted to solve one of the mysteries. On her own, Grace had underlined, slashed and circled in red ink a sentence that intrigued her . . . a lethal poison that killed one of the victims in seconds.

Oh boy, seeing her interest in lethal poison, I knew I had better keep my good eye on Grace!

Squiggling out from under the bed, I took in a deep breath and thanked God that Grace had placed a Bible next to her bed and had laid *The Daily Word* on her vanity table. *How to Be a Better Spiritual and Kinder Person* by Swami Kitagunda, she positioned on top of her stool.

Oops! I couldn't believe it. My name was written down in today's *Daily Word* message. Grace underlined it. It read: "Forgive Those Who Vex Thy Soul."

At very least, no poison for me today.

I've lied. I had spied the car keys the moment I stepped into the room. The keys to the station wagon were in plain sight all the time. The keys were positioned carefully on top of today's *Daily Word*."

Just so you know, I always vexed myself.

Grace had a stroke waiting for me to deliver the car keys. The furrow in her brow sent me a message loud and clear: I had spent too much time on her errand and she was frustrated that she couldn't come after me. Two guests had trapped her and she couldn't escape their chatter. On and on they went on how much they loved their stay at the Coco Palms.

I pretended to be out of breath.

Not fooled, Grace gave me her famous feared look of death. I felt that if the guests hadn't been standing next to her, Grace, without hesitation, would have grabbed me by the scruff of my neck, throttled me and thrown me to the sharks.

I responded to *the* look by giving her a great big smile and dangled the car keys in front of her face. She grabbed the car keys out on my hand and with her angry, blue eyes rayed another deadly look of death into mine. I wanted to throw up. Her underlying message to me was that my fragile, thin piece of thread that suspended me from heaven to earth, that kept me alive, her look told me that the thread was about to snap.

Grace never missed a trick. By her witch's magic, she detected the guilt in my eyes, the lint in my hair, the dust on my clothes and performed her first Coco Palm's Jane Marple—Agatha Christie ace detective deduction. Without the slightest doubt, she knew I had snooped under her bed. Seeing her make her deduction, fearing that I was about to be buried alive, a goddess rescued me. The goddess came in the guise of Elsie, her secretary. Blessed Elsie distracted Grace from killing me.

CHAPTER FIVE

April 24, 1960 – 32nd Academy Awards ceremony held; Ben Hur wins Best Picture.

"Miss Buscher," Elsie interrupted, "something important has come up. It's urgent!"

Elsie waved a piece of paper in front of Grace's face and informed her what the message read: a mysterious Mrs. Brown had booked all the King's Cottages for today. The reservations were made by someone at the hotel, but not by the pretty Chinese–Hawaiian secretary reservations manager.

Elsie paused before she stressed twice that the reservations were for all of the pricey King's Cottages. "There is more to the message, Miss Buscher: Mrs. Brown and her entourage were arriving on the next plane from Honolulu. In fact, if Hawaiian Airlines is on schedule, Mrs. Brown and her party were collecting their bags at the Lihue airport and would be arriving at Coco Palms in minutes." Looking at her watch, Elsie cried, "Did you make those reservations, Miss Buscher?"

Grace blustered indignantly, "I did not. I don't know anything about these reservations. How dare you accuse me of such treachery?"

Dramatically taking the paper, looking at it, Grace informed Elsie that the party of eight will not be staying beyond the time that the Presley and Paramount Studios entourage were to arrive from Hollywood.

Taking back the paper, Elsie reminded Grace that Mrs. Brown had demanded all the King's Cottages that Paramount Studios had booked weeks ago. "We want those cottages in pristine condition when the Elvis group arrives!"

A pregnant pause followed before Elise cried out. "MOREOVER, WE ARE OVERBOOKED!".

Calm as the waves that lapped across the street, Grace whispered to Elsie: "Well, maybe, I did know about the Brown party reservations, but they will be out of the hotel the day Elvis arrives. Not to worry, Elsie, the cottages are protected for the movie people and I will see to it that they will be left in pristine condition. Here is something you don't know. Mrs. Brown is actually Lillie Russell."

"Lillie Russell? The movie star? The one that has had more lovers and husbands than Elizabeth Taylor, Zsa Zsa Gabor, and Lana Turner combined. The LEGEND!"

"That's the one!" Grace nodded knowingly.

After Elsie heard the name Lillie Russell, she calmed down. As far as Elsie was concerned, Lillie Russell was one of the greatest movie stars in all of Hollywood's history.

"Lillie Russell must be over a hundred years old!" exclaimed Elsie.

"Now, now Elsie! She's only been out of films for a few years. Didn't you love her sexy lisp?" Without letting Elsie respond, Grace continued, "Elsie, tell the staff that Miss Russell doesn't want anyone to know that she is staying here. She's traveling incognito as Mrs. Brown. She wants to be addressed only as Mrs. Brown and is here to celebrate her birthday."

Elsie was one brave dish. She's was the only one who could speak up to Miss Buscher and really take her on. Elsie, I was sure, knew all the time that Miss Buscher made the reservations.

Born stupid, I raised my hand and marched into the cannon's mouth, and spoke, "I'm an avid Lillie Russell movie fan, Miss Buscher."

Before Grace could erupt me, I rattled to Grace gossip I remembered by heart from an article written by the notorious, evil gossip- columnist, Heidi Fleishacker. I spoke to Grace as if I was giving a speech to Lillie's fan club. and commenced, "Lillie Russell is known for her lisp. She can't for the world pronounce her *r* or her *l*'s. Speaking her name is her greatest challenge. Many of her lovers and fans thought the lisp was sexy, but it was her *r*'s and *l*'s that killed her film career. Jack Warner at Warner Brothers wanted her out of her expensive contract, because she made more money than he did as head of the studio. Eating lunch at the studio commissary, Jack, daily, complained loudly for everyone to hear him that Lillie Russell was an over-the-hill has-been and her films were a pile of junk, and losing money for the studio. Jack Warner, a known skinflint, misogynist having an ego larger than the Hollywood sign, did everything in his power to jettison Lillie from the Warner Brothers' contract'. When Lillie was the golden girl at Warner Brothers, making the studio millions of dollars, Jack ordered his writers to extricate all the *l* and *r* words from her scripts. When her films lost money, Jack Warner ordered his writers to write dialogue using every *l* and *r* word in the dictionary: "Rita ran little steps while reeling lightly regularly off of the lighthouse railing!"

I continued on talking without taking a breath. "Lillie grinned and bared it. She stayed at the studio, and took Warner Brothers to the financial cleaners. She hung around the Warner Brothers lot until her seven-year contract expired. In her last film at Warner Brothers,

Lillie received fifth billing in a Bette Davis drama. Lillie didn't care a whit, because her Warner Brothers contract made her filthy rich. Her wealth was partly due to her mother who had invested a major chunk of her money in real estate that fronted Wilshire Boulevard in Los Angeles. A tip from Cary Grant made her even wealthier and Lillie acquired two mortgage free townhouses on Park Avenue in New York City. Because of actor, Edward G. Robinson's advice, she made more millions in art and had one of the greatest French expressionist painting collections in America. She was also known for amassing jewelry that rivaled movie-star, Paulette Goddard's stash."

Grace under my spell, I continued, "One of the most retold stories by wags at Hollywood cocktail parties was about Lillie's last day on the Warner Brothers lot. Lillie took all her thousand-dollar Orry-Kelly gowns and everything she could unscrew or pry open with a crowbar from her dressing room and with her beloved crew (grips, electricians and make-up men, who adored her) hauled her stash out of her dressing room and stuffed it all into her yellow Rolls Royce."

"Lillie, a known clotheshorse, on her last day at the studio, dressed to the nines, wearing nothing underneath a full-length mink coat, sashayed into Jack Warner's office. She threw her dressing room key on Jack's desk, gave him the finger, flashed him, and said sweetly, lisping, "Fuck you Jack, you rlllittle llrrrrat.""

Seconds after delivering my spiel on Lillie Russell, the star and her entourage sped into the Coco Palms' driveway in two rented white limousines.

What an arrival it was!

Car horns blasted from the two Lincolns as soon as they zoomed through the front gate. Down the driveway the limos raced into the porte-cochere and screeched to a halt, one behind the other. The limo driver who had won the race, maneuvered his Lincoln into the middle of the front entrance of the hotel, while the other limo stopped suddenly, scrunching the first limo's fender. Their spectacular arrival happened in a millisecond. After the first limo braked, out of the first car's door, whirled a human cyclone swathed in a full-length mink coat.

Grace gathered her wits, threw the station wagon keys to a bellman, and ran down the front stairs, thrusting out her hand, and gushed, "Mrs. Brown welcome to Coco Palms."

The star tipped down her dark glasses, squeezed Grace's hand. "I'll need two more rooms for my clothes, dinner for eight at seven in your private dining room, and who the hell is Mrs. Brown?" Blinked her eyes, and said, "Oh, forget, dear, what I wrote about calling me Mrs. Brown. My name is *Lilih Rthsell.* Now, whoever you are, take me to my room. NOW! I've got to pee!"

"I'm Grace Buscher, the manager of the hotel."

Grace grasped a hand that wore a huge yellow solitaire diamond ring on its third finger and pulled Lillie up the steps into the lobby.

Lillie took the steps two at a time and moaned, "Not so energetic, dear. Let go of my hand, my rings, dear. God, it's stifling. I can't breathe. You're going too fast, Miss Bushwhack!"

Inside the lobby, Lillie, sweating like a horse, threw her mink coat on the floor and scurried behind Grace out of the lobby, over the lagoon bridge, and made a beeline for a King's Cottage to sit on a pot. When Grace and Lillie raced over the lagoon bridge, a bystander on the bridge was pushed aside. The bystander felt he had been hit by a tornado who wore a lavender chiffon dress. What lingered behind: was the scent of lilies from an expensive French perfume—one that Madam Du Barry splashed that kept Louis XV under her sheets.

As an afterthought, Lillie yelled in a voice that reverberated out into the coconut grove, out to sea, and into the lobby, "Pick up my mink and get ahold of my vanity case. Twinkle, if you lose my jewels, get the next plane back to Los Angeles."

Coconut Grove

CHAPTER SIX

May 1, 1960 – A Soviet missile shoots down an American Lockheed U2 spy plane over Russia; the pilot, Francis Gary Powers, is captured.

I imagined I was behind a one-way mirror looking at suspects in a police lineup, and that is how I observed Lillie's guests as they hoisted themselves out of the limos. They were under my Charlie Chan magnifying glass.

So you know I was up to speed on the latest Hollywood gossip and an expert on the smarmy things written about Lillie's guests, I was a student of Hollywood history. Here are some of the things I filed back in my mind about other denizens in Hollywood. I knew what Paulette Goddard did under a table at the Mocambo night club; about the murder of movie producer and director Thomas Ince on William Randolph Hearst's yacht anchored off Catalina Island; and why brokenhearted Lana Turner, the sweater girl of MGM, divorced Lothario Artie Shaw. Artie Shaw who was a known a celebrity, sex crazed, intellectual clarinet player band leader. To make my points on the Lillie's guests, I had relied on the gossip columnists, Hedda Hopper, hearsays in movie magazines, Louella Parsons, William Randolph Hearst's gossipy venomous viperish chitchat, and my once favorite columnist, Heidi Fleishacker's (now deceased) gossipy files to make these first impressions on Lillie's guests:

First suspect, a rodent-looking man weaseled out of the backseat of the first limo. I recognized him immediately as movie director, Eric von Bismark, aka Sylvan Seltzer, from Toledo, Ohio. Eric wore a black patch over his right eye. He had the reputation of turning into Hitler the moment he sat his big fat ass down in his director's chair. He yelled at his actors speaking in a fake German accent using a used Eric von Stroheim megaphone. He used the megaphone even in his close-ups. Inside this Nazi Hun's bully soul, he had the persona of a scared, skinny rat. What made him so popular, rumored by those who knew him intimately, was that Eric had the biggest bratwurst in Hollywood, one that rivaled comic Milton Berle's. His enemies spread the rumor that Eric once entered his bratwurst in a sausage contest and ran a strong sixth. His leading ladies were known to squeeze his gigantic appendage for luck before they spoke their first lines on camera. The *squeeze* was the most meaningful direction he gave to any of his leading ladies or men. Every day, the Hun thanked God for his big bratwurst and his rich wife for keeping him grinding out B pictures at Warner Brothers.

Alice Downes von Bismark, Eric's wife, was the next to slide out of the limo. Her fish-net stocking legs appeared first—skinny legs that quivered in the air searching for a landing. Her legs looked like two poisonous prongs of a centipede. (Alice was a Scorpio, born on the cusp.) When the whole of Alice's body unraveled, she stretched her arms skyward. I looked at her and understood the meaning of unfortunate. Since her birth, family and friends called her "alligator." Alligator was the kindest thing one could say about Alice. She had the most unfortunate leathery skin and her jaw snapped when she spoke. If Eric the Hun was a slimy rat, Alice was a reptile, but a sweet one.

Alice came from a well-to-do banking family from Pasadena. Her money, her wealthy conservative Republican connections had attracted Eric to her. Need I mention what attracted sweet Alice to Eric? Dear, dear Alligator Alice was overheard six months into her marriage sighing to a blue-haired, family friend at the beauty salon. Lifting the hood of the dryer, she moaned, "Darling, it just isn't worth it—big is not necessarily better. Take it from me."

Alice's money kept Eric from straying into greener pastures. She, on the other hand, had become weary of Eric's dictatorial posturing, but, when she looked in the mirror, she felt she had few alternatives.

Alice was respectful of Lillie. In fact, Alice admired Lillie because Lillie played a diva on Eric's movie sets and made Eric jump through her crazy hoops. Lillie didn't take shit from Eric and laughed, to his face, especially, at his fake Germanic accent.

Standing at last, Alice groaned, "Goddammit Eric, take my purse. I need a shower from sitting next to Dockie. I smell like a rotten cheese tostada from Lucy's."

On cue, the man who next staggered out from the Lincoln smelled like a human three-day-old tostada from Lucy's. (Lucy's was a restaurant across from Paramount Studios, where mega-stars ate power lunches.)

"Dockie" Harold Nutt Trescutt was born in Boston, Massachusetts. He was a graduate from Harvard Medical School and was voted by his peers as the man who had the sleaziest bedside manner. Legend had it that Dockie approached every nurse during his internship, playing the masked Lone Ranger showing off his Tonto. His Tonto, not much to look at, was well known to the nurses, kitchen help, and, unfortunately, to some patients. Everyone in the hospital came out from hiding when Dockie headed for home. After hearing him yip, "High Ho Silver, away!" nurses felt safe to take their patients' temperature. Dockie was kept out of jail because of his rich Boston Trescutt-family connections.

"Dockie Wockie," as he was known to his classmates, thought the word *sleaze* under his name in the Harvard yearbook was a term of endearment. After he graduated from medical school, Dockie left for Hollywood to make his fame and fortune, not believing the prophesies of his Harvard professors: "He'll give Harvard Medical School a bad name that we will never live down." Dockie Wockie might have been handsome, had it not been for his nose. It pointed out of his face like a needle.

After Dockie choo-chooed across country on the California Zephyr, he found that no respectable hospital in Los Angeles would hire him. In job interviews, he was judged by other doctors as delusional and weak. These interviews resulted in no offers to work in a major hospital, and so he went into private practice and married Hollywood's premier ball-breaking gossip columnist, Heidi Fleishacker. Years of marriage were not kind to him or to Heidi, there were too many drugs and drink before and after dinner. He earned the reputation in Hollywood as "easy" because he prescribed, on command, a cocktail of barbiturates and vitamin B shots. Most of his patients were aspiring actors who schlepped their way up the ladder looking for their names to appear above the title. Alas, most of the patients he had injected with joy juice fell off the ladder and were never heard from again.

Nevertheless, Dockie earned the repute for having a kind heart. When Hollywood wannabe starlets were retreating back home to Omaha, Dockie offered them two free valiums: one for the plane ride, the other one for when daddy and mommy met them at the airport.

Other than that, if serious medical attention was required, one would have a better chance with a veterinarian to get well. The more Dockie broke the Hippocratic Oath, the more he took Quaaludes and drank double martinis with Heidi, who *Variety*, the Hollywood trade paper, deemed the most hated woman in Hollywood. A few months prior to the trip to the Coco Palms, Heidi died mysteriously. Rumor on Rodeo Drive was that Heidi died from an infected needle. The gossip around Tinsel Town was that the lethal needle was wielded by Dockie Wockie; a natural mistake after a five-martini lunch. Dockie Wockie wasn't prosecuted; in fact, he was treated with kid gloves after Heidi's death by the Beverly Hills police, studio brass, actors, producers, and directors. Heidi, the Hellcat from Hell, had bequeathed to her husband her entire explosive files containing incendiary gossip about all the celebrities living in Hollywood and Washington D.C. She kept her venom locked up in a vault in a Westwood bank near their Beverly Hills home. Heidi's files contained every secret she had amassed since her arrival in Hollywood in 1922. The contents were rumored to be greater, more potent, and far more incendiary than the one J. Edgar Hoover stored in his Washington D.C. bedroom, under the double bed he shared with lover Clyde Colson. Lloyds of London estimated Heidi's stash of venom was worth more than all the gold stashed in Fort Knox.

Dockie, a certifiable drunk, climbed unsteadily out of the limo, holding the car door for balance. He blinked his red eyes in the tropical sun's bright ultra-violet rays and farted. Bits of breakfast, lunch, and Bird's Eye frozen dinners were sprinkled on his brown, rumpled tweed jacket. Dockie's farts and body odor were at the top of his characteristics that I observed. I could see that anyone who had any common sense and needed medical assistance kept their distance from his pointy nose, tainted needles and probing, yellow nicotine-stained fingers.

Suspect number four and next out of the limo was Tommy Twinkle. Tommy was rumored to be the offspring of one of the greatest film directors Hollywood had ever produced. It was a Hollywood lie. But the director in question was dead, so no one could disprove Tommy's rumor, which he had spread himself. The tale was started as a lark by Tommy and the gossip columnist, Heidi Fleishacker, while having their regular Wednesday lunch eating a Cobb salad at the Brown Derby, on Vine Street. Heidi and Tommy had been best friends until her mysterious demise.

Caffeinated Tommy sprung out the limo like a jack-in-the-box. Twinkle didn't talk; he twittered as he sent his hands flying into the air going in every direction. Everyone in Hollywood knew Twinkle's name because Heidi, who loved him like a son, regularly placed his name in her column. Twinkle and Heidi laughed hysterically and said they were spawned from the same evil caviar egg. Heidi loved Twinkle-toes to death. She was the only one who called him Tommy; most people maliciously referred to him as Twinkle. According to one of Heidi's press releases, Tommy could have been as important a child star at MGM as Mickey Rooney. Another rumor was that Tommy Twinkle wasn't his real name.

Tommy was never cast in a movie that called for a mature human being. Heidi once red-flagged in her column that Hitchcock had Tommy in mind for the Norman Bates role in *Psycho.*

"Tommy, baby," Hedda Hopper wrote maliciously, was one of those people who would look and act like an adolescent until the day he died.

Small, insecure, out-of-work Tommy made a concerted effort to be pals with anyone who could help him be a part of the "in" group in Hollywood. He sucked up to everyone and did everything he could to be indispensable to any celebrity who walked the red carpet. I read in *Photoplay* magazine, a Heidi plant, that Tommy kept all of Heidi's confidences, because he was once a Boy Scout leader who took the oath to be physically strong, mentally awake, and morally straight. Another lie.

Tommy Twinkle squeezed into the same tight pants he wore as an extra in one of the Hardy Boys films. His day-to-day costume was a red baseball cap worn on the back of his head and a UCLA football sweater that motivated him to tap, jump, and leap around as an energetic UCLA cheer leader.

Tommy Twinkle had flitted in and out of Lillie's life since the end of World War II, but he never became one of her regular suck-'em-up sycophants. Twinkle, recently under Lillie's employ, directed the Hawaiian bellboys to sort out the bags. Former Hawaiian cowboys, the bell boys were ahead of the game and had the task in hand.

Lillie hired Twinkle to be her temporary gofer-majordomo. The aging cheerleader had a most unfortunate brittle way about him and thought it cute to call everyone, male or female, working in a menial task, "Mary." Of course, that was only when Lillie wasn't present. When the former Hawaiian cowboys, Coco Palms' bellmen, were called Mary by Twinkle, if looks could kill, Twinkle would have been tossed like a football across the road into the sea for the ravenous sharks to gobble him up for breakfast, lunch, and dinner. By mutual consent, the Paniolos, after hearing the third Mary, the former John Wayne looking Hawaiian cowboys, conspired silently to lasso him and bake this mainland *haole* alive in an *imu* (underground pit layered with hot stones), if given the chance. A second inspection of Tommy, the bellhops rolled their eyes upward and gave up that notion. Tommy Twinkle was made of fairy dust. There was not one piece of solid fat, meat, or potatoes attached to his bones.

Speaking of Tinker Bells, Gretchen Yamashita, the limo's last occupant, burst forth like a beam of light. By actions and speech, Gretchen gave the appearance of being a gossamer pixie found on the pages of a Grimm's storybook tale. All she needed to confirm that impression was to wear a tiara on her head and flutter a gold wand in her right hand. Instead, Gretchen chose to wear a blue polka-dotted farm dress for her arrival. Instead of purchasing a new expensive dress on Rodeo Drive in Beverly Hills, Gretchen borrowed "her treasure" from Western Costume, next to Paramount Studios. The gingham was a fussy farm creation designed for a chorus girl to wear in a road company of *Oklahoma*. Gretchen was known to save her pennies.

As Gretchen nimbly stepped onto the pavement, I felt that Dorothy had left Kansas and arrived in Oz.

Gretchen was Lillie's assistant and make-up lady. She was rumored to be a childhood friend from San Francisco. Both Gretchen and Lillie came from the same side of the tracks—the other side—the same side of the railroad tracks as Julia Jean Mildred Frances Turner, Lillie's rival and sex symbol at MGM, the unforgettable Lana Turner. Gretchen had recently undergone plastic surgery on her face. Again, saving her pennies, Gretchen hired a doctor on the cheap in Tijuana.

Yamashita was Gretchen's married name. She was hitched to one of the most celebrated cameramen in Hollywood, Sam Yamashita. Sam was a cinematic magician. Sam's camera could turn Bela Lugosi, the *Dracula* actor, into Clark Gable by softening an overhead light and using a special lens that he had invented for his camera. His pink gels and homemade crafted camera lens, smeared with a light coat of Vaseline, made him the envy of every motion picture cameraman in the world. All smart, aging Hollywood leading actresses had a clause in their contract that only Sam could film them. Sam was considered to be one of the true geniuses in Hollywood. Since 1939, Sam had signed a very lucrative and exclusive contract with Jack Warner at Warner Brothers.

I watched Gretchen with admiration as she stood next to the limo acting calm as a Hindu priestess. Eyes shut, a clipboard pressed to her chest, she hummed, *Om Na Ma Shiva.*

Her chant transported me to a Zen temple in Japan. I waited for her to unfold a prayer rug, kneel, bow, and ask me for a bowl of rice.

I admit I knew little about Gretchen, more about her extraordinary husband. Hearing her chant, I remembered my Aunt Sophie's warning: "Beware of the sweet-acting people in the world. Sweet-acting people, Percy, are the most dangerous people you will ever encounter." And Aunt Sophie knew her onions. After sweet Aunt Sophie spoke her piece, she hit me with her cane to make sure I got her point.

One last comment on Gretchen's looks: Gretchen was Danish, once a look-a-like Madeleine Carroll—an Alfred Hitchcock beautiful blond. Now, whatever angle you looked at, Gretchen had a crooked smile that never left her face—it couldn't. When she opened her mouth to speak, the secret was revealed. Her mouth! The plastic surgeon, who practiced in Tijuana, an alcoholic, zagged when he should have zigged.

When Gretchen stepped into the Coco Palms Lobby, the second limousine crashed into the first limo and honked annoyingly, signaling for the first limo to move his ass. A voice inside the second limo growled: "Move your Mary ass, Tommy. Get those fucking goddamn bags out of our fucking way before we run you over, a-hole."

Speaking his "Mary's" to the bellmen, Tommy whisked Lillie's make-up kit/jewelry bag into the lobby. Someone screamed like a lunatic. It was the driver in the first limo. He shoved his gear stick into drive and sped from the hotel without so much as a backward glance. By his actions, the harried driver drove directly for "Park Place" onto "Go" without as much as collecting a tip.

The driver of the second limo, watching the first driver abandon ship, gunned his limo, and jammed the brake, screeching his killing machine to a sudden halt smack in front of the lobby. The sudden movement caused the occupants in the backseat to fly in every direction as if being swooshed up in a Waring blender.

A voice from the floor of the limousine screeched: "I'll have your fat Hawaiian ass fired for that little maneuver." An add to the confusion, Tommy grabbed a conch shell out of one of the bellmen's hands, blew it badly. Dockie Wockie inhaled on his cigarette butt, hiccupped, opened his puffy, tortoise eyes, and slurred to no one in particular, "Central casting has arrived, folks!"

How right he was. More oddball character actors stepped out of the second white Lincoln. As if a director had called, "Action," on cue, Tony Pinto scrambled his lanky body out of the second limo. He was Lillie's latest squeeze. Out in daylight, Pinto stretched his arms up to the sky and lifted his legs as if he was about to mount a horse and drawled, "Damn, that was one helluva ride!" In the latest *Photoplay* movie magazine, gossipy Louella Parsons wrote that Tony Pinto had been dropped from the B list to a supporting player, the same day, Lillie had dropped Tony to the rank of a supporting player.

On route to Kauai, Lillie and Tony had a slapping fight in the Los Angeles airport. After Lillie slapped Tony, he stood tall and took it without saying a word. Lillie screamed at Tony that he was making whoopee behind her back.

As the lovers' war raged in the Pan American terminal, reporters came out of the men's room and photographed the lover's spat. They salivated, clicking their German Leicas at the embarrassed Tony. When they arrived at the Honolulu Airport, Tony and Lillie's fight had made the front page of the *Los Angeles Times* and *The Honolulu Advertiser*.

Tony wore shiny cowboy boots adorned with silver buckles, and stood tall and firm as Gary Cooper. It was as if the real Coop had planted his size fourteen-foot shoe size on Coco Palms Terra Firma. He brushed the red dust off his spangled cowboy shirt, and spoke slowly, "That was a pisser!"

Tony Pinto looked slightly shopworn in the bright sunlight, but fit his cowboy outfit as if he had been born on a horse. Pinto presented to his faithful fans a rugged face that had met a couple of flying horseshoes. He named himself after cowboy actor, Tom Mix's, horse, Tony. "It sure wuz the right thing to do, after all you all, Mix's horse, wuz a Pinto." Tony's baptismal name was Herbert Hazzelfat the third.

Before anyone could shake Tony's hoof, he'd inform you right off the bat that he was the actor who was almost cast as the lead in the *Hopalong Cassidy* TV series. "That damn rascal Billy Boyd must have been sleeping with someone I hadn't met or who hadn't met me or my horse. That good-for-nothing rascal plumb cheated me out of what should have been rightfully mine."

But Tony did all right. He was typecast in all cowboy actor Joel McCrae's westerns as the bad dude. McCrae and the producers made certain that Tony was shot dead in the middle of the first reel. On the second week of shooting when Tony drew his gun for the climatic showdown, the script supervisor had to remind Tony to reach for his gun, not for the gin bottle. His legendary gin at ten in the morning caused his eyes to slit by noon, making a puffy-eyed iguana make love to his horse and leading lady. Tony would have been one of those lost souls of movie-land, a somnolent who, after midnight, wandered up and down Hollywood Boulevard, but after admiring his attributes, Lillie took him under her wing and he dried out.

Tony wore dark glasses to hide his faded "long-lashed" Gary Cooper blue eyes. Middle-aged women still admired his black Clark Gable "brush" mustache and swooned on cue when he shot them his "I-don't-give-a-damn smile. What really turned Lillie on to Tony was a trim waist and firm, small, round butt.

Tony leaned against the limousine and stared at the fans looking at him. He curled his lip and, on cue, as he did at his premieres, he tilted the cowboy hat forward and shot at them with his fingers. He practiced that move for hours by standing in front of the mirror, trying to perfect a mean, deadly, ugly movie actor Jack Palance look.

Tony Pinto was known in Beverly Hills social circles as a man's man. There was nothing sissy about Tony. Being on tap, night and day, living with a movie star like Lillie—a manipulative controller with an insatiable sex drive—hadn't hurt his macho reputation.

Celebrity-breakfast-eaters at Nate and Al's on 414 Beverly Drive, especially radio and future TV personality, Larry King snickered to his friends, jealous of Tony's reputation as a cocks-man, winked as he said, "Yea, Tony may be a man's man, but he's now turned into Lillie's lapdog."

Deep down, Tony was one of the sweetest he-men in Hollywood. Another thing that drew Lillie to Tony—the thing that bound them together like peanut butter and jelly—was not only his firm butt; they both had the smallest bladders in Hollywood. On camera, before Tony snarled, "Hello, Pardner" or "stick 'em up," the cowboy wet his pants on cue.

Next, scrambling out of the limo, walking on all fours, swearing in a voice that sounded like a hung-over, five-pack-a-day Lucky Strike smoking Marjorie Main (the Ma Kettle character actress), entered into the mix, voilà—Tilda Francis!

"Fuck that sucker, he almost killed me. I'll have his brown ass fired for this!"

Her toilet mouth had the reputation of being as randy and foul as the late Carole Lombard's, comedienne movie star and Clark Gable's love of his life. To be perfectly candid, Tilda's toilet mouth was not to be compared with anyone else's. Many believed that Tilda invented the word *fuck*!

Looking down at the crawling creature from Mars, Tony drawled: "Calm down, Tilda darling, if it wasn't for your foul mouth, scaring the driver, we might have arrived without an accident.

Assuming an upward position, standing erect, pointing out her tits, Tilda cooed sweetly into his face: "Alright. Alright, I get your point. Oh Tony, Jesus Christ, you wet your pants."

"You spilled coffee on me."

"Cover it up with your hat. You embarrass the hell out of me."

Looking down at her bruised leg, Tilda moaned: "Ow! You hurt me. You dumb ass, you pushed me on the floor of the car."

"Saved your life, Tilda darling."

Tilda lifted her skirt and gently touched a red cherry mark on her knee. Tony shook out a blue-and-red handkerchief from his pocket and dabbed her wound gently.

"That fucking hurts!" Tilda peered into the limo. "Come on you two fudging warhorses. Get the hell out of that death trap. I need a swim to cool me off."

Tilda thrust her arm inside the car and tried to pull out one of the occupants out. That someone resisted.

Tilda yelled to the occupant, "I'm not going to bite you."

From inside the limo, a voice screeched, "Take your cotton frickin' hands off of me, Tilda."

The guests in the Coco Palms lobby were frozen into popsicles as they watched Tilda Francis from Hell perform her foul mouth craziness in front of all of them. Ladies and gents from Middle America had paid good money out of their meager savings to come to Coco Palms to taste the tropical nectar that Grace had promised them; not to observe Hollywood at its worst. Against their will, they watched a mid-morning shoot of *Creatures from the Black Lagoon*.

Even though Tilda was the most off-putting woman God ever created, what made her a real oddball, was that she was as pretty as Doris Day—no, prettier. No, no, Tilda was drop-dead gorgeous! Tilda was blond, curly-haired, blue-eyed, had big tits, with Shirley Temple dimples on both cheeks, and looked as angelic as the Virgin Mary in a Titian painting. But long ago for some perverse reason, Tilda had turned herself into a smoking, fire-breathing Lucifer's henchwoman.

Tilda Francis was Lillie's stand-in, and a longtime friend. The employees and hotel guests watching Tilda's antics each thought: "Run for the hills when that gal's around" In front of them stood a man-eating termite.

Inside the limo, before she exited, Tilda had threatened death to the limo driver, Hairy Aspic. Fearing for his life, pulled on the brake, thrust the car door open, abandoned the limo in the porte-cochere, and ran down Coco Palms driveway as far from Tilda as he could run. Once on the highway, he screamed for his mother.

When the screams died down, Raul Pasqual and Granny Myers appeared out of the backseat, holding hands.

Raul was a Mexican actor and Lillie's husband. He was as handsome as Ricardo Montalban He was dressed all in white and wore a white polo shirt, short white pants, and appeared as if he was about to call out to Cary Grant, "Tennis, anyone?" Raul kept his figure by eating raw vegetables and exercising at the Beverly Hills Athletic Club. The handsome actor worked in films but only acting in minor roles. Although he was Lillie's husband, Lillie and Raul hadn't shared a bed, according to *Confidential* magazine, since the first night on their honeymoon in Puerto Vallarta . . . decades ago. According to a rumor spread by the hated Heidi, the reason for the abrupt honeymoon was that Raul had a skin problem; a rash that ran all over his body in splotches. Speculation was that the rash increased in size when Raul was aroused. Lillie's friends, who wished not to be quoted, divulged that despite the unseemly rash, Lillie kept Raul around for luck. The handsome Mexican stayed in Lillie's orbit because he received a large, monthly check that Lillie deposited into his Bank of America checking account on one condition: part of the money was to be spent weekly at a discreet Beverly Hill's dermatologist.

Next. Granny Myers was not Lillie's grandmother nor had she any semblance of being a grandmother straight out of central casting. In plain words, there wasn't a smidgen of a grandmother found anywhere inside or outside of Granny's body. She earned her dissipated pudgy face from late night cocktails. To keep her gray pallor from blotting out her features, Granny dabbed spots of red rouge liberally on her cheeks, her chins, and a third eye as if she had one. Her dyed-orange hair was brushed into a tall pompadour which gave Granny the appearance of being a whore from Nero's ancient Rome—a profession that Granny actually knew quite well.

From the lips of Sally Stanford, a notorious madam in San Francisco, Granny's whores named her Granny for being the oldest in the oldest profession and the ladies of the night needed someone to go to for council, advice, and comfort. Granny was never felt comfortable in the role of a mother hen, because she couldn't tell a fairytale to a child if her life depended on it. Her scrawny appearance, orange hair and witch's cackle, invariably sent children to hide behind their mothers. Granny reminded the wee ones of the bad witch in *Snow White,* especially when she offered them an apple. Children instinctively understood that deep inside the depths of Granny's soul, she hated children. The only was exception was Lillie. According to the gospel of Heidi, Granny gave Lillie her first job. It was an unsubstantiated rumor. However, Lillie was known to never forget a kindness or a stab in the back and kept Granny on her payroll for reasons she never divulged.

Now with their bags sorted, Lillie's guests stood next to each other, in the middle of the lobby, perspiring profusely. The morning became a typical, muggy Kauai day causing the group to quiet down from the humidity and lack of sleep. The eight-hour flight from Los Angeles to Honolulu, followed by a long layover in Honolulu, and the forty-minute flight to Kauai had fogged their sense of time and place. As the group waited impatiently to hop into the electric carts to be transported to King's Cottages, I gave them another once-over. In my mental notebook this is how I would remember them:

Lillie Russell – the star

Eric von Bismark – the rat Nazi director

Alice Downes von Bismark – Eric's lizard wife

Herbert Nutt Trescutt, Dockie Wockie – a doctor once married to Heidi, the gossip columnist; yellow fingers and a needle nose

Tommy Twinkle – a flit. Mary is a grand old nam

Gretchen Yamashita – a Swedish Zen monk with a zig-zag smile

Tony Pinto – "friend" of Lillie and a cowboy with a pee problem

Tilda Francis – Doris Day with a sewer mouth

Raul Pasqual – Lillie's husband; a Mexican white knigh

Granny Myers – a cackling, orange-headed broad

One thing that stood out: all Lillie's guests had one thing in common: they were not bosom buddies.

Woosh! Lillie's party disappeared. Two electric carts carried them across the lagoon toward the coconut grove where King's Cottages were lined up in a row. They came alive and screamed hysterically, as the driver drove like a wild man down the gravel path. While screaming, Lillie's guests yelled to each other they wanted a hot shower, a martini, and a crawl into a soft bed – alone.

Hearing their words and screams echo throughout the coconut grove, reminded me of the witches in *Macbeth*—the same witches who warned Macbeth of dire things. Hearing their shrieks should have cautioned everyone at the Coco Palms that unspeakable things were about to happen at the hotel.

Woosh! Next their luggage vaporized. A squad of bellmen raced each other barefoot to squeeze their belongings into the King's Cottages with only moments to spare before the roar of the witches arrived. Room service ladies stood outside the cottages, holding bamboo trays of complementary Mai Tais: six lethal ounces of dark rum, orgeat syrup, and other high-octane liquors, garnished with tiny, delicate Japanese umbrellas—a gift that Grace had hoped would send her new arrivals to Never-Never Land.

The spectators back in the lobby, solid citizens from the hinterlands of America's red, white, and blue, righted themselves into standing positions, paled, and looked at each other, aghast at the bad behavior they had just witnessed. There was a silent agreement to steer a course far away from these Hollywood types. One couple was already at the desk checking out and moving to the Royal Hawaiian Hotel on Waikiki Beach.

A Mormon from Cedar Rapids, Iowa, whispered to her husband, "These are truly God's step-children."

A deaf shoe salesman from Toronto, Canada, screamed into his wife's ear, "I now know

what happened to *Baby Jane*."

I shoved my hands in my pocket and drawled to the man next to me, mimicking Tony Pinto, "That was a pisser!"

A middle-aged lady from Tucson, wearing an off-the-shoulder purple *muumuu* and a pea-green straw hat tilted on the back of her head, glowered and sniffed, "If those weren't the dregs of humankind, I'll eat my hat." I longed to offer her Best Foods Mayonnaise to make the hat digestible.

The Tucson pit bull glowered at me as if I had orchestrated the whole debacle and snarled, "If you keep people like that keep coming to this hotel, my family and I will never return to the Coco Palms. You tell that to Miss Buscher. Tell her that Mrs. Dinwiddie in Room 202 from Tucson, Arizona sent her that message with aloha."

CHAPTER SEVEN

July 4, 1960 – Because of Hawaii's admission as the 50th state the previous year, the 50th star flag of the United States debuts in Philadelphia, Pennsylvania.

It was a good half hour before Miss Buscher flew back through the lobby riding on her broomstick. I waved my arms to get her attention but she whisked past me, not, however, before giving me a slap on the head. "Not one word. Not one word, Percy. Not one word out of you. Not one word!"

"But…"

Heading towards her office door faster than a Japanese bullet train, Grace spotted Elsie sitting behind her desk: "I have seen cuckoos in my lifetime, but these Tinsel Town rejects take the cake. Such vulgarity! I will not stand that kind of behavior at my Coco Palms. Before she checks out, I'll make sure that blond creature stops swearing if it's the last thing I do. Imagine speaking those awful words in my sacred coconut grove. Guests at my Coco Palms are never crude, rude, or impertinent! I can't believe it. All my friends in Hollywood have class."

"There is good in everyone," I called out to Grace. I repeated something Grace had admonished me with when I had trashed one of the guests. Just so you know, I just can't help the things I say and do. I laugh at the most inappropriate times. I am sure I would have giggled while the Titanic sank, giggled being swallowed up in a crevice during the San Francisco earthquake, and shrieked with laughter going down in flames on the airship, Hindenburg (May 6, 1937).

Grace stopped in front of her office door. She put her hands on her hips and snapped, "That's not funny, Percy."

I started to protest.

"Not one word, Percy!" She zipped into her office and slammed the door.

Seconds later, she yanked the door open and yelled for Elsie. Knowing her boss, Elsie had a pencil poised in midair, prepared to record the wisdom of the Coco Palms god.

"Only three days here, not five. Three days at the most. Three days and those people WILL BE OUT of the Coco Palms. Do you understand me, Elsie? Why in heaven's name did you book Lillie Russell into Elvis's cottage? You're fired!" She slammed her office door.

Elsie sighed, and said quietly, "You're the one who booked them, Miss Buscher."

The door opened again, "Elsie, you're fired for only two minutes." Then she turned to me, "Percy get in here . . . RIGHT NOW!"

I would have rather been ordered by General Patton to jump out of a plane without a parachute, or to climb over a barbed wire fence, nude, fight the entire Nazi army single-handedly holding a flame thrower without a flame rather than to enter Miss Buscher's inner sanctum, especially now that she was in such a foul mood.

When I walked in, my imagination saw the macabre actor Vincent Price's dungeon decorated from floor to ceiling with leather whips, hanging chains, and a stretch rack to squeeze all the poisons out of me.

"Close the door."

"I . . ."

"Not one word out of you, young man. CLOSE THE DOOR!"

I glanced longingly out into the outer office, where freedom had once existed. What greeted me were the terrified eyes of the other employees, frozen to their desks, each saying a prayer of thanks that it wasn't them going on the chopping block. I felt that I was about to sail down the river Styx into Hell and burn for eternity.

I closed the door carefully and stood ramrod straight, ready to meet Grace Buscher's firing squad. I wanted to pee as I waited for her to command the rifle squad, "Ready, aim, fire!"

Instead, I heard, "Do you know what today is?"

I squeaked, "The thirteenth?"

"Don't squeak. Just listen."

"Yes, the thirteenth. In my astrological chart, the thirteenth is a very, very, bad, bad luck number for me and for the Coco Palms."

Everyone who worked at the Coco Palms knew that Grace ran her life and the Coco Palms according to her two lucky numbers, five and eight.

Grace took a breath before she spoke again. "The thirteenth day of every month should be eradicated . . . eliminated . . . extricated from all the calendars in the world. Listen to me! We have a problem that is none of your business."

Grace confused me to the very depths of my soul.

"Tonight, I am directing you to be a busboy in the main dining room. You are to wander around all the tables where Lillie and her guests are sitting." She pulled out a Viceroy cigarette from her pack, lit it, and inhaled. "I am certainly not inviting those Hollywood types to my cocktail party. If I did, all my other guests will check out before sunrise, especially, if anyone has any more contact with Lillie's "goof balls." Grace exhaled smoke out from her nose, coughed, and looked at me intently. "Your mission is to listen to all that is being said at the Russell tables . . . remember every word and don't be obvious about what you are doing. This mission will call on one of your most annoying skills—prying into everyone's business. For God's sake, for once, keep your mouth shut. After dinner, you are to report to me in this office and tell me word for word what you overheard."

"May I ask a question?"

"No, you may not. I want you to remember that you are the worst waiter I have ever employed in this hotel. I have yet to hear from any of the guests that you took their orders without you messing up. Not once has a meal you served resembled what the guest ordered. Beef for fish, fish for lamb. Tonight, you are to only fill the water glasses and serve the coffee. You can do that, can't you?"

I nodded humbly and said I would be her best Bengal Lancer, Musketeer, Robin Hood, even better than George Washington freezing at Valley Forge.

Grace groaned: "Whatever goes on in that two-piston mind of yours remains a mystery to me. I have told you numerous times that you're too much, too, too much into everyone's business . . . and, I might add . . . MINE included! You are the most annoying busybody I have ever known. Against my better judgment, I am giving you this mission of greatest importance to me and the hotel. Here is a piece of information to help you understand how important your mission is: Lillie Russell is giving an exclusive birthday dinner-party for herself, tomorrow night in the House of Flames. There may be big trouble at that birthday party"

"May I ask..."

"No, you may not ask. That is all. Scoot. Get out of my sight. Tell Big John I want to see him."

Hearing Grace speak Big John's name, I knew she meant business.

Big John was the King Kamehameha of the Coco Palms, the Arnold Schwarzenegger of Kauai, and the Charles Atlas of all Hawaii, rolled up into one big brown, Hawaiian laulau.

Big John had a handsome, movie star face topped with a full head of wavy, black hair. He was a full-blooded Hawaiian and built like a Russian tank. With one hand, Big John could crush a human head into a messy pulp and, with the other hand, his grip turned my hand into mush. I often felt I deserved the Purple Heart for shaking his hand. More often than not, he'd rescued a damsel in distress or saved the life of a little bird that had fallen out of its nest. Big John did most things in his life as gently as St. Francis of Assisi. He was politeness itself but I knew to never make him mad.

Grace beamed with pride and devotion whenever she talked about her assistant manager to guests at her cocktail party. "When Big John roams the hotel grounds at night, I sleep like a baby."

His reputation around Kauai: "Big John mad, he geeve you one look, one eyeball to one eyeball, den he press da finger in da middle of da stupid's forehead. Den you hear one beeg growl start from his beeg toe and den he say, "Excuse me Brah, you outta step around here."

When Big John presses his finger to the forehead, give his eyeball look, the white-eyed stupid, if smart, ran like hell, yelling, "Please, Big John don't hurt me!"

"When that damn fool had crossed-over-the-Big John-line, that stupid buggah could never step one foot back on Coco Palms grounds ever again."

Yes, siree, bringing Big John into Grace's office meant that dark clouds were looming over the hotel. I'd bet a tuna sandwich heaped with tons of Best Foods Mayonnaise and layered with two slices of tomato and cheddar cheese that the dark clouds were presently unpacking their duds in the King's Cottages.

I had a momentary urge to eavesdrop on Grace and Big John. My guardian angel blew some sense up my ass and cautioned me that if I valued life and limb, I wouldn't take the chance of being caught by Big John, with having my ear glued against Grace's office door.

Howard Keel and Esther Williams

CHAPTER EIGHT

July 11, 1960 – Harper Lee releases her novel, "To Kill A Mockingbird."

Thoughts short-circuited into my crafty, little brain. The one thought that caught my attention was that I was about to become the best busybody spy ever. I was about to become a male Mata Hari, a Scarlett Pimpernel, and a Sherlock Holmes/Charlie Chan extraordinaire all in one package. I wanted desperately to make a great name for myself and become a five-piston mind.

To do that: First, I planned to sniff around the King's Cottages to spy on the cuckoos. Today's bar inventory could wait. This assignment was far more important than adding up numbers. I gathered my wits about me and walked out of the lobby, holding in my hand a list of who was staying with whom in the King's Cottages. I would use my innate snooping instincts to discover important information for Grace even before the dinner witching-hour. I salivated at the possibility of overhearing Hollywood secrets that even Heidi the Terrible didn't have hidden in her secret vault. What a fantastic idea!

I crossed over the lagoon bridge and took a sharp left, wandering down the cobbled path that fronted the King's Cottages. Inadvertently, my nose twitched like a bloodhound but, playing it cool, I plastered a nonchalant look on my face. I didn't want to stand out like a sore thumb more than I did, so, I decided to skip down the path and pretend to be a gardener. As I skipped, I considered all the racy stuff that was hidden in dead Heidi's files and imagined all the sordid things I was about to hear inside the cottages. Many thoughts blossomed in my head coming to me as naughty sugar plums. One thought, the Hollywood types were probably unpacking their suitcases and doing kinky things to each other. By the time I reached the last cottage, my imagination had gone into a sewer. To regain back my focus, I stopped and pulled weeds by Cottage Five's front door. Kneeling down to pick yellow weeds, I hoped to overhear what was going on inside that cottage. This brilliant ploy, I deduced was a Sherlock Holmes ploy. It would keep the occupants inside the cottage clueless to my sneaky presence, thinking that outside their front door was a gardener, not a wannabe Charlie Chan, master sleuth, sniffing for clues.

My two-piston brain remembered: *Picking yellow weeds is a brilliant ploy for detectives. Movie stars Joan Crawford and Fred MacMurray, playing spies, picked daisies to outwit Nazis chasing them through a park. I read in July's* Life *magazine that to keep an undercover agent from being exposed, a spy picks flowers. It is one of the first lessons a spy learns at the FBI and that's the truth!*

Second ploy: to catch evil people off guard, act like a silly twit. I was born to perform that role to perfection. *Actor Leslie Howard in the movie,* The Scarlet Pimpernel, *played a twit. Using his sissy act, he outwitted bloodthirsty Frenchmen who guillotined aristocrats in Paris. I, too, playing a twit will save the innocent and eliminate evil from the Coco Palms.*

Oh, boy I am about to be a real authentic twit!

I will sneak around the cottages, acting as the Scarlet Pimpernel. If I discover bad doings, I will eject the evil from the Coco Palms with the help of Big John faster than you can say...

"Percy, where are you?".

Oops. My name was called. Damn, someone at the Coco Palms is always looking for me especially, when I am not where I am supposed to be. It was the bartenders, Alex and Chunky.

Gadzooks! I should be in the bar doing inventory.

I am going to dismiss them out of my mind and continue on with doing my spying faster than I can say,

"We seek Percy here, we seek Percy there.

We seek Percy everywhere,

Is Percy in heaven or is Percy in hell?

If you want to find Percy, just follow his smell ...."

Aw, to hell with Alex and Chunky! I have more important things to do for Grace.

After those silly meanderings, I began to read from the list in my hand I that had copied from the hotel check-in register.

King's Cottage 5: Lillie and Gretchen were bunking together in the cottage where I was presently picking yellow weeds.

King's Cottage 4: The von Bismarks had a connecting door to Cottage 3.

King's Cottage 3: Dockie roomed with Tommy Twinkle.

King's Cottage 2: Raul and Tony had a connecting door to Cottage 1.

King's Cottage 1: Granny and Tilda occupied that cottage unhappily. I knew that because as I passed their cottage, Granny screamed at Tilda.

Carefully listening for mouthwatering gossip in Cottage 5, my mind meandered. I was reminded of Miss Buscher's romantic blockbuster idea—her clandestine connecting doors from one King's Cottage to the other. By Grace's personal direction, Coco Palms' carpenters had constructed hidden doors inside the large walk-in closets. Hidden doors made for midnight trysts. The hidden doors were constructed for naughty guests who shouldn't be sharing the same bed.

To keep the unwanted out, each connecting door had a protective stainless steel bolt, which meant the occupants on either side of the door had to be mutually agreeable, mutually compliant, and mutually horny to slide back the bolt and take a trip to paradise. I later learned one couple in Lillie's party, unbeknownst to Lillie but known to Grace and the housemaids, had stepped over the Primrose Path . . . more than once.

Grace loved gossip. While doing my spying by Cottage Five, I daydreamed that I was about to receive a medal of merit, brownie points, and a raise in salary from Grace for what I was about to perform.

The King's Cottages, the Queen's Cottages, the Deluxe and Standard rooms all held many secrets at the Coco Palms. Illicit tales of the goings-on behind the doors in all hotel rooms figured prominently in all the early morning gossip by the Coco Palms' staff. Lurid tales of who slept with whom was spread out as smooth as butter around the employees' table at their early morning briefings. Their gossip began two hours before the honey wagon arrived, an hour after the sun rose, and a half hour before Chef Jiro fired up his stoves. Hotel gossip was orchestrated by the toilet brush section maids and Mrs. Nakai. Mrs. Nakai was the first violinist and Grace was the orchestra leader.

During these early morning roundups, gossip was put first on the agenda. It was their shot of vitamin B12 to start the morning work. Sitting around a wooden table, knee pressed to knee, down in the bowels of the kitchen, the salivating bloodhounds (the house-maids) described in lurid detail all the telltale signs of what former occupants had scattered around the hotel rooms. The most interesting bits of tittle-tattle were the tools that the creative lovers fashioned out of Grace's shells to frolic with on a royal Hawaiian king-sized bed. Grace was thrilled at hearing the house maids' lurid tales of how her shells were being used. These romantic trysts were in keeping with her Coco Palms modus operandi. Studying the romantic chapters of British romantic novelist Barbara Cartland first fired Grace's imagination to the many possibilities of the affairs of the heart at the Coco Palms. Grace transferred Cartland's kitsch into the hotel rooms, and made it Hawaiian style: red velvet bedspreads appliquéd with the Hawaiian-coat-of-arms and palm trees etched on the mirrors above the bed. From chapter three of a Cartland book, Grace copied and embellished one of her ideas—midnight servings of raw oysters in a coconut bowl to the weary. That touch kept a millionaire surfer returning to the hotel two dozen times, paying hundreds of dollars for a suite, and each time bringing with him a different *kumu* (girl of the moment). This surfer tycoon went on to build grandiose hotels, and credited Grace and the two dozen oysters on the half shell served in a coconut bowl, cooled in a refrigerator, for the nexus of all his hotel creative ventures.

When Grace's day was over, thoughts of the Coco Palms put aside, looking for new ideas, she snuggled in bed with a Barbara Cartland novel and then devoured an Agatha Christie mystery; for Grace, that was heaven on earth.

Back to the problem at hand, crouched down next to a window of King's Cottage 5, I was anxious to hear tales about Hollywood romps on Sunset Boulevard. With my ear pressed to a wooden shutter—bingo—I heard Lillie on the telephone talking to Grace.

Lillie was changing instructions she had given to Grace for tomorrow night's birthday dinner party. The table was now to be set for fifteen.

"Miss Buscher, I do not plan for more people to join my party . . . that are alive, that is."

Gretchen interrupted, "Lillie."

"Hush, Gretchen, I know what I am doing"

Back to Grace.

"My plans are final. I will not change my mind."

Silence.

"Miss Buscher, I am not accustomed to explain anything to anyone. Just remember what we talked about and follow through. I am counting on you to follow my instructions to the letter."

Lillie slammed down the green cricket-sounding telephone that Grace had installed for Elvis. The telephone was shaped like a green candle—another one of her romantic touches. These phones miraculously chirped like crickets when they rang—a plaintive sound of a lonely locust calling for its mate in faraway Shanghai.

"Gretchen, close the shutters tight so we can talk in private. And Gretchen, dear," Lillie spoke in her steely voice—a voice she used when she played Elizabeth I sending Mary Queen of Scots to the chopping block—,"I don't like being interrupted while I am talking on the telephone. I know what I am doing . . . *dear.*"

"Ouch!" The wooden shutters slammed in my ear.

On to the von Bismark cottage.

Pretending to prune a bush outside the von Bismarck's cottage, I didn't have to cup my ear to hear the onslaught that raged inside this cottage.

The Hun screamed at Alice, "YOU ARE A DOLT!"

Alice spoke back to Eric using a voice brimming with annoyance, "Darling, before I take my bath, please order me two gin slings for your dolt: one for my headache and the other to blot out your irritating voice from my head. Make it heavy on the gin, dearest, and light on the slings." There was a pause. "We're in our room now, darling, so cut out the German accent crap. I can't abide that phony accent of yours. Cut it out. You know, honey bunch, Lillie is up to something and I think you better watch your silly ass. She's after you for what you did to her on her last picture and I love it because Lillie never does anything without having a conniving motive behind it. She's dangerous, dear, especially, now that she's been kicked out of the studio. She hates you, so, I'd watch my step, honey bunch."

"Forget Lillie, she's history now. I need more money, darling!" screamed Eric.

"More money? I gave you ten thousand just last week. No more do re me from ME this week, sweet nuts!"

A sound of a slap.

"You bastard. Hitting me isn't going to do you any good. No more dough and that's final."

Another slap.

"YOU BASTARD!"

"Quiet. Lillie is next door to us. Whisper, you ugly little bitch!"

"Ouch." Slam, crash, shut went their wooden shutters in my face and that was the last I heard of the von Bismark's fight.

At King's Cottage 3, I scrunched as low as I could behind a coconut tree and peered into the living room. Dockie and Twinkle couldn't see me, because a coconut tree stood next to one of the windows of the cottage.

The same tweedy voice that rivaled the myna birds fighting above me in the coconut trees twittered inside. Tommy Twinkle flitted about the living area changing the décor. I couldn't see Dockie, but from where I stood, I could hear his voice. I imagined Dockie in the bedroom, flat out drunk on the bed in a semi-comatose state.

"Dockie," twittered Tommy, "this joint is right out of a road show company of *Sadie Thompson*. Tacky, tacky, TACKY. You're a goddamn mess. Dockie, you know, I loved Heidi more than my precious Pussy."

Dockie mumbled something back to Tommy under his breath that I couldn't hear.

"Stop saying that, Dockie! I am speaking about my cat. Heidi saved my ass ten times ten. Now, I'm going to save your ass because of her. Keep your wits about you, Dockie. Don't say squat to anyone about anything, especially to Lillie about the files. Give me your pills and all your morphine vials. I know you hid them in your suitcase somewhere. You know, dear one, everyone in Lillie's party wants you dead, because everyone thinks that you read Heidi's files and you know too much, too much, about all of them."

In a slurred voice, Dockie responded, "I never read her files. Her files never interested me. Leave me alone, Tommy. Go order me a double gin and tonic."

Tommy disappeared into the bedroom. "Get up, Dockie. Let's get with it. I want the truth. Do you have Heidi's files or don't you? Oh, this hotel is hopeless. Hopeless. Come on, Dockie, let's get your smelly carcass off that bed and into the shower. Come on, Dockie, let little Tommy lift you off the bed. Little Twinkle is here to help you get cleaned up. Let's get stinking fat-assed Dockie smelling like a rosebud again. I'm going to sober up nasty-smelling you before dinner. Off we go to the shower, clothes, and all. Tell me about Heidi's files . . ."

The bathroom door shut.

I slithered out from behind the coconut tree and headed for King's Cottage 2. The shutters were closed; not a sound came from inside the room, but my nosy antenna quivered, because something naughty was going on inside there. I crept alongside the cottage, kneeled on the ground, and I saw in-between one of the wooden slates a shocking sight. As my eyes adjusted from the bright sunlight into the semi-lit room, I discovered a real secret to tell Grace. Yippee! Tony and Raul were nude, clasped in a passionate kiss, and headed for the bedroom.

"Oh, my darling!" Raul whispered to Tony.

Wouldn't you know it? Just as I was about to watch a pornographic matinée, a gust of wind flipped shut the wooden slats, erasing it all from my prying eyes.

At King's Cottage 1, I found another coconut tree to hide behind. This cottage had a connecting door to the romantic goings-on in King's Cottage 2. I crouched as low as I could to peer through the bottom wooden slats and saw another shocking sight: Tilda was whipping a nude Granny on the sisal carpet with a wet towel.

"Beat me harder. Harder, you fool," cried Granny.

Gotcha!

You are going to be annoyed with me. I warned you that I am not reliable. The last two sightings were entirely made up by me. I couldn't spy on the last two cottages because Rattle, one of the bellhops, headed for the von Bismarks' cottage carrying two gin slings on a tray, caught me spying behind the cottage. Rattle had been gifted by his girlfriend with a set of identical Clark Gable false teeth which didn't fit his mouth, therefore, he was the nicknamed Rattle. He shaked, rattled, and rolled whenever he talked.

As Rattle was first cousin to both bartenders, Alex and Chunky, I hopped, skipped, and jumped for the bar. (Everyone on Kauai is related, you know). Heavens to Grace, the last thing I wanted was for Rattle to squeal on me that I wasn't doing my inventory job in the bar. Rattle, given the opportunity, would clack, clack, clack to Grace, to Alex and Chunky that I was not where I was supposed to be. He was a squealer.

Clacking Rattle, the sneak, kept tabs on me. Being a wiz at math in high school, he coveted my inventory job in the bar. Behind my back, he'd re-check my math, making sure I correctly counted the empty liquor bottles I had thrown into the trash can.

I want it on record that I hated the inventory job passionately. My main task was to measure the amount of liquid left in the liquor bottles from the night before using a twelve-inch ruler and making sure it tallied exactly with the receipts smashed on a spindle next to the cash register.

A bee had buzzed in Gus's bonnet that some hotel employees, given the opportunity, pinched money out of the till, or at the very least, without Gus's controls in place, would guzzle up all the hotel profits after work. Doing the bar inventory stressed every one of my mathematical "two-plus-two-equals-five" piston brain. I am dyslexic.

I learned fast at the Coco Palms University of Hard Knocks to become creative with my numbers. I learned shortcuts by doing my made-up creative math. With new skills in place, I could have graduated cum laude from Harvard Business School and been hired after college as a crafty bank president or a Morgan Stanley stock broker on Wall Street. Bit I could have been one of those wizards whose crooked math landed him behind bars at Sing Sing. According to the *Honolulu Advertiser*, the financiers on Wall Street used the same smoke, whistles, and imaginative numbers to balance their books as

I did. I always pleaded foul to Grace when she found my numbers had collapsed on her inventory sheet. My excuse was that I was a two piston, dyslectic moron but, I said on the other hand, "Miss Buscher, you have a future genius Wall Street broker doing your inventory."

After hearing my excuses, Grace always threw my inventory reports back in my face and said I was not to return until they were correct and honest.

I confided, before I left her office, that I really wanted to be an honest person. Deep down I was not cut from the same cardboard as those crooks who ran our financial institutions. Because, and this I shared with her, I had a fear that kept me honest: I didn't want to share a cell with a tattooed bodybuilder who hated mayonnaise. One of the reasons I was not fired was because I kept Grace amused.

I didn't share with Grace that, if I became a broker for Morgan Stanley, I would have advised all my clients to put all their life's savings into the Best Foods Mayonnaise stock. Since I had eaten over a thousand mayonnaise sandwiches and was about to eat more, they'd all become billionaires.

On and on and on I go, don't I?.

Back in the bar, I reflected on Lillie's cast of characters in the King's Cottages, clamped a pencil in my mouth, looked down at the inventory list, and fell asleep.

Rattle woke me up!

CHAPTER NINE

August 17, 1960 – The newly named Beatles begin a 48-night engagement, residing in the Indra Club, Hamburg, West Germany.

After the last rays of the sunbaked Georgia peach skins into the color of Maine lobsters, after parents screamed at their kids to abandon the swimming pools, and after slimy, green frogs swam laps in the hotel pool, Coco Palms' began its second act.

In the blink of a minute, the Hawaiian gods lowered the curtain on daylight and announced that it was the time for the pungent odor from the kerosene torches lit alongside the lagoon to fill the air. The smell of kerosene mingling with the scent of beef sizzling on an open spit was Coco Palms' unique perfume. It was that scent that welcomed guests as they walked down to the Main Dining Room. The odor of musk, kerosene, and fat burning on a spit was a strong aphrodisiac. It was so strong that monks squatting in Tibetan caves would have thrown their vows into the wind. That fragrance certainly stirred up the juices in all of Grace's guests. The aroma was so invasive, even nuns went cuckoo and did crazy things. It was rumored that nuns who had stayed at the Coco Palms drank poi cocktails and one even guzzled a gin sling. I might add, blushingly, some tourists ran amok in the coconut grove and did things that innocent Thoreau in nineteenth-century New England didn't even know about camping alongside Walden Pond.

Under the gaze of a hula moon, this was the night the Lizard Lady, Mrs. von Bismark, faced death. It was a night so surreal that it had the feel of a Humphrey Bogart bête noir film. Shadows flickered ominously in all the hidden corners of the hotel as silhouettes spawned silhouettes. It was a night when the adventurous had permission to slither as snakes into the grove, looking for romance and intrigue, all hoping to experience the unexpected.

Here is something odd to think about: God had to be living it up on Maui. I had my own theory about God. He went on vacation when bad things in life occurred—like the Holocaust. How could a loving God be present when terrible things happen to us here on Earth? I think He would be ashamed of Himself to see what we humans do to each other . . . or is it fate? Is it God's Purpose? I do know God was spending a wet weekend with Liz Taylor and Richard Burton in Puerto Valletta when I learned to masturbate.

Alas, what was about to happen here at the Coco Palms, was it all part of God's plan? Destiny? It remains an age-old universal question.

Nightfall at the hotel was timed to the second by Grace's wristwatch. Real time no longer existed when the stars came out at the hotel because. Coco Palms time was orchestrated by the wave of Grace's baton.

At six, on the dot, not yet under the control of Grace's baton, squadrons of mosquitoes flew in from an abandoned secret War World II base. Mosquitoes flew in formation into the dining room. It was told that they were retired Kamikaze pilots that attacked the unwary without mercy. These little devils sucked blood from the juicy, pink flesh of the recently arrived. Especially delicious were the check-ins from the wheat fields of Iowa. These fleshy succulents were the mosquitoes' appetizers, entrees, and dessert. These bitten guests received a badge of honor—red dots all over their bodies. They all had the same look of Gus's famous Flaming Cherries Jubilee dessert. These mosquitoes performed their nightly tasks without humor, in precision, and were all registered Republicans.

At 6:10, guests, famished from a day of sightseeing, abandoned their hotel rooms in twos and threes for what they hoped was to be a night of Hawaiian debauchery—a night of romance, promised in bold green letters on the front page of their Coco Palms brochure. A Vanda orchid lei accompanied the brochure and was placed with delicate finesse on their pillows by the housemaids.

These travelers from all over the world, who arrived on Kauai, all looked for a fantasy experience—the same experience they had seen on a movie screen. For example: *Hurricane,* a black and white film starring Dorothy Lamour, who wore a sarong, and promised sex with Jon Hall who wore a jock strap. These travelers never forgot the image of those beautiful actors making whoopee under a coconut tree.

For myself, I wasn't out to make "whoopee." I was prepared for a night of spying. My ear was cleaned and cocked, ready to hear Lillie's party spill out their guts in the dining room. I crossed my fingers, hoping against hope that I wouldn't mess up my spying by spilling coffee and sloshing water on the unwary guests. I was determined to be a better detective than Charlie Chan.

I even dressed as a spy by wearing a red aloha shirt with designed large, white ginger flowers splayed on it, and white Chino pants. I wanted to look like a Chinese detective who walked his beat down on River Street in Oahu's Chinatown. I slicked back my hair with Vaseline to make me look like Humphrey Bogart without his toupee. In my enthusiasm, I had missed by a mile the Sam Spade-Bogie look in *The Maltese Falcon* and Charlie Chan look. Instead, I appeared as Humpty Dumpty, fat Percy, smelling of Old Spice aftershave. I ambled bowlegged down the path to the dining room, hoping to have had the John Wayne walk perfected. Upper-most-in-my- mind, I was eager to report to Honey, the dining room manager, looking shiny as a dime.

Honey reminded me of slinky-looking Gale Sondergaard (the femme fatale in the Sherlock Holmes film, *The Spider Woman Strikes Back)*. Honey was a grande dame Hawaiian lady, whose mother was a royal. Her mother, an alii, waved a peacock feather in Queen Emma's court. Queen Emma was the wife of Kamehameha IV, a founder of the Queen's hospital, and known to speak with an English accent. Queen Emma was a royal favorite of the Hawaiian people. I felt being in the presence of a Hawaiian with alii blood was big stuff!

Honey was a tall, dark, beautiful Hawaiian who spoke with a tinge of an English accent. With a slightest wave of her finger, she dominated me and all the other underlings in the dining room. I wanted to genuflect in front of her because she ran the dining room as if she were Russia's Catherine the Great. Like the Russian empress, she took no prisoners. Every night, Honey operated her kingdom as if she was entertaining nobility. Those of us who served under Honey were treated as lowly serfs but all grateful to do her bidding. Coco Palms never had in its history a worthier person to run its Lagoon Dining Room.

As I walked down the path to the dining room, thinking detective Charlie Chan thoughts, a hand suddenly reached out and shanghaied me into the liquor storage room.

"What in heaven's name prompted you to wear that god-awful outfit. Only Hawaiians wear red at the Coco Palms, and besides, you're making yourself a target for everyone to notice you. That's not what we want, do we, Percy? Run immediately into Mrs. Nakai's and get a proper dining room aloha shirt. Can't you do anything right?"

As Miss Buscher vented her wrath on me, towering over me in her white high heel pumps, I imagined I was a sailor under the command of Captain Bligh in *Mutiny on the Bounty*. A ferocious Scorpio, when Grace was angry always appeared to me seaworthy and in her *muumuu*, was as trim as the *Bounty* (Captain Bligh's ship) having every strand of her blonde colored hair coiffed in place. What got to me was her Chanel No. 5 that mingled with the odor of liquor stored in the closet. That smell made me want to faint in ecstasy. Around her neck, Grace wore a double red carnation lei that hid an expensive double strand of white, Mikimoto, freshwater pearls. Her carnation leis, red or white, were flown in every day by Hawaiian Airlines, fresh from Auntie Rebecca's lei stand on River Street in Honolulu. Minions from the home office on Oahu were assigned the task daily to pick up the lei at Auntie Rebecca's. and to make sure, by threat of being boiled in a vat of poi, that the lei flew to Kauai on the afternoon plane—in time for Grace's nightly ceremony.

Woe to the unfortunate minion, who in charge of fetching Grace's carnation lei, missed the afternoon flight. One never knew whatever happened to that unfortunate minion, as Big John said, "only the Shadow and Miss Buscher knows?"

Further to describe Grace's muumuus. Grace wore a fancier white *muumuu* at night. Grace, a brilliant actress, knew her onions and costumed herself day and evening in the same style garb. Her muumuu marked to the guests that she was the reigning queen of the Coco Palms. Grace's genius for being immediately recognizable gave everyone at Coco Palms a sense of order, place, and continuity. When the sun rose every morning, Grace would emerge from her bedroom the same as she did the day before. Her familiar presence brought comfort to everyone at the Coco Palms that "all's right with the world and would forever be."

Behind her back, some annoying guests speculated that Grace never washed her clothes. Those doubters didn't know that hanging in Grace's closet were thirty or more identical Mrs. Nakai's designed *muumuus*.

Ghostly in her white costume, Grace, that night, glowed. She appeared as a mystical priestess. I had to pinch myself that she was the very same angry person who had moments ago dismissed me with a wave of her hand to get a new shirt.

Garbed in a signature blue aloha shirt, I entered the dining room out of breath. Honey gave me a withering look for my lateness, a look that I actually loved. I happened to be very fond of Honey's withering looks. Her look turned my irises into mush and telegraphed to me that I was a meaningless white man, a lesser being, a lowly ant to be stepped on, and a person of unworthiness that Grace had foisted on her that evening. Don't ask me why but, in spite of all those things, I just adored Honey.

No moon or stars were out that night or, for that matter, for the next three nights at the Coco Palms. God, I believed, was not in His heaven, He had to be visiting on Maui. One clue: there was a Kona storm that loomed ominously out on the horizon, causing dark clouds to blanket away all the celestial lights above the hotel. Except for the few flaming torches on the pathway to the dining room, and overhead light bulbs in the dining room shaded by woven *lauhala* hats, Coco Palms Hotel was consumed in a semi-blackout—a perfect setting for mayhem to occur.

Given instructions from Honey, I wandered about the dining room schmoozing with guests and, incidentally, filling their glasses with water. In minutes, I located where the entire Lillie Russell party sat without having to use my mental Boy Scout compass once. I saw that Lillie's guests were scattered, by choice or design, hither and yon, throughout the Lagoon Dining Room.

Lillie sat at a table alone, next to the lava stone wall that separated the lagoon from the dining room. She was scribbling notes with a pencil on a napkin. Her eyes signaled, "I want to be alone."

Two people were missing: Gretchen and Granny. I overheard Tilda remark to Tony that Gretchen was ironing Lillie's clothes and Granny was tending to the welts from Tilda's beating (just kidding). No, Granny was re-dyeing her hair from orange to fire-engine red. Granny's orange roots were showing.

Tilda bitched to Tony and Raul, "Granny is a pain in the ass. She had an acute attack this afternoon from her bile ducts. I had to run all over the hotel trying to find liver pills for her. It's her damn bile ducts that make her so damn mean and all that fucking red dye is poisoning her."

Gretchen was alone—as far away from Lillie's crowd as she could bribe Honey. Since she was at the farthest end of the dining room, Gretchen—the lady with the perpetual smile—made spying on her a challenge!

Cozy together next to the lagoon's lava wall were the von Bismarks. They were eating dinner while living in their own hell.

Nearer to the stage, Tony and Raul ate with Miss Potty Mouth, Tilda. Two tables over, Dockie sat with his roommate, Tommy. Dockie had cleaned up good. He wore a clean, white suit and blue tie, and was drinking his third scotch on the rocks. His table mate, acting as Twinkle Toes, flashed white teeth around the room, longing for someone to recognize him from a photograph in the June issue of *Modern Screen* magazine. It was his last photograph in any movie magazine since the day Heidi died. In his last photo, Tommy scarfed down a Cobb salad at the Brown Derby holding hands with his beloved, Heidi.

Tommy, fountain pen within reach, fingers crossed, delusional, waited for a fan to ask him for his signature.

The lights in the dining room dimmed. Isaac, Grace's favorite bellman, wearing a red *malo* stood on the bridge over the lagoon. He stretched his lithe body upward as if he were reaching for the top of a coconut tree, placed his fingers around a conch, put the shell to his lips, and blew. The sound of his conch soared up to the stars.

7:30 p.m. "Grace time" had begun at the Coco Palms. The sound of the conch signaled the lights to go out in the dining room, bringing the bar and all meals and drink service to a screeching halt. The waiting staff froze in place. Walter, the bellhop, returned Isaac's call with his conch shell from across the lagoon. The nightly ceremony had begun; it was Grace's summons to dinner.

Standing in front of a microphone, speaking in a modulated voice tinged with her Philadelphia accent, Grace narrated a speech she had written: "A Coming to Supper in Ancient Hawaii." Her narration ended with "tables are laden," and everyone was asked to join her in invoking a remembrance of ancient Hawaiian hospitality and aloha.

A stillness followed her speech and not a creature stirred in the hotel. All the guests fingered their drinks, feeling they had just experienced the breaking of bread in a cathedral under the coconut trees. More to the point, they had experienced a *Pagan Love Song.*

Grace wanted her guests to experience, every night, the same primitive force she had discovered the day she arrived on Kauai. A special force of nature, a *mana,* that had been spewed from the heavens to create Kauai's mountains, valleys, and beaches. This mana was not to be surpassed, nor found anywhere else on earth. On Kauai, if one heeded the call, one could be immersed in a rare breath of primitive life.

There was a deeper meaning to Grace's nighttime exposition. She called out every night to the dead spirits that roamed the grounds, especially to the last queen of Kauai, Queen Deborah Kapule—the royal who had built the fish ponds, while living on these grounds. Grace called to Deborah to assure the queen that all was well at the Coco Palms and that her sacred piece of land would be protected as long as Grace lived there.

No one who stayed at the hotel, especially the returnees who arrived year after year, ever doubted that Queen Deborah Kapule, though dead, roamed the grounds at night.

A final drum beat signaled that Grace's narration had ended. Still seated in the dark, the guests watched as young Hawaiians leapt like gazelles, torches in hand, and lit up the grove into a luminous spectacle of lights.

Grace told me, "After the spiritual, came the ballet."

As Hawaiian men ran through the grove, out of the quietness of the evening came a piercing shriek—a woman's cry for help. The cry came from somewhere near the dining room stone wall.

"A snake bit me!"

A deathly silence ensued.

Diners thought the "snake bite" line was part of Grace's ceremony—the moment when a virgin was sacrificed and tossed into the lagoon. What would be more fitting to end a pagan ritual than dumping a virgin into the lagoon?

A woman whispered, "Isn't that Buscher woman the clever one? She certainly keeps my nerves on edge."

Glued to their seats, everyone waited for the next scream. Those of us who worked at the hotel knew the scream was the real McCoy.

Next, came a moan out of the darkness, "I'm dying."

"Lights on," Grace commanded.

The dining room burst into a blaze of midnight suns.

Looking around, I spied Alice Downes von Bismark prostrate on the ground. Her skinny arms and legs were splayed over the lava wall—the stone wall that kept the lagoon from erupting into the dining room during tropical storms of thunder and lightning.

"Help me! Mit wife is dyink. Bit by a viper."

"No snakes in Hawaii!" yelled Honey, to stop a stampede out of the dining room.

Grace, Johnny on the Spot, was at the von Bismark's table, followed by Big John. Without a word, Big John carefully placed Alice back into her chair and checked her pulse. Grace reached for a napkin to wipe spittle from Alice's face and spotted the culprit. Into a crack in the lava wall wiggled a twelve-inch red, fat, many-legged centipede.

"Is she allergic to scorpions or centipedes?" Grace inquired of Eric who had collapsed in his chair, acting as Eric the Hapless.

Von Bismark uttered weakly, "Any sink that stings like utt bees or even utt centipede would keel her."

Grace found two red-rimmed punctures on Alice's left leg and ordered, "Big John, run to my office. In the bottom drawer on the right side of my desk, you'll find a box labeled as allergic reactions."

It wasn't long before the diners had formed a semi-circle around Alice. I tried to keep the curious away by spreading my arms out. I was pretty successful blocking their view of the Lizard Lady.

Alice moaned like a San Francisco foghorn and bawled to Grace that she was dying. Looking for direction from Grace, at a moment's notice I was ready, willing, and prepared to dump my pitcher of ice water on the Lizard Lady's head, to keep Alice from joining Deborah Kapule in the grove.

Big John, a high school football and track star, ran faster than Jessie Owens (the Olympic track star) for Grace's office and arrived back at the table in a matter of seconds, holding in his palm a small brown box. I anticipated that inside the brown box was something as miraculous as a vial of water from Lourdes. I wasn't wrong. The medicine inside the box provided a miracle before my eyes.

Alice's face had now turned to the color of a purple sweet potato. Her lizard eyes were rolling back and forth into her skull looking like two purple marbles searching for a home. Alice was losing consciousness. Grace quickly opened the box, took out a small vial, and performed her voodoo. Grace's magic worked like a miracle. Within seconds, Alice's alligator skin once again resembled my mother's purse.

Alice held tightly onto Grace's hand, fully conscious, spoke into the hotel manager's ear. Rounding out her vowels, making sounds like a matron of quality from Pasadena, California, and being as dramatic as if she had just been rescued out of the Amazon River swimming with Piranhas, she gasped, "I thought I had cashed in my chips. Thank you so much for saving my life. Whatever did you do?"

Grace smiled like a Cheshire cat.

Alice repeated, "Whatever did you do? I didn't feel a thing. Not a poke, not a prick, nothing, only something wet and cold on my left leg . . . then . . . whoosh! All of a sudden the poison left my body. What happened?" Alice then confided softly into Grace's ear, whispering, "Somebody is out to murder me. Somebody wants me dead."

A dry napkin in hand, Grace wiped more spittle from Alice's mouth, and replied, "Murder you? Murders just don't happen at the Coco Palms. Your murderer, the culprit, happened to be a pesky centipede. The centipede was probably more scared of you than you of it. It was a case of being seated in the wrong place, at the wrong time, and you just happened to make the acquaintance of a very naughty, fat centipede. Karma. Fate. The substance that helped you recover came from a dear Hawaiian friend of mine—a Hawaiian priest, a kahuna. My hunch is it's his pee, but whatever it is, that liquid works like a miracle—one hundred per cent of the time whenever there's an occurrence like this at the Coco Palms."

Grace speaking the word *pee*, Alice returned to Wonderland and fainted.

Big John picked up Alice gently in his arms, held her at arm's length because she smelled like the public men's restroom at Poipu Beach. Dutifully, Big John carried Alice to King's Cottage Number 4. Eric, his head and balls hanging low, followed behind Big John, clasping his hands behind him. He looked much as Napoleon did when Nappy retreated from Moscow in the snow. Forlorn Eric complained out loud and bitterly, to no one in particular, while he walked to the cottage, "I did not get to eat my fresh coconut cake layered with creamy custard." He spoke into the grove without using his accent and sounded like a spoiled brat.

Something was amiss in the dining room. Most of the guests had been out of their seats, curious, and concerned for Alice's welfare. Some searched under their tables to see if a centipede was headed their way. Here's the rub: not one of Lillie's party got out of their chairs. Lillie and her entourage remained seated as if nothing of importance had happened. Each of them found it amusing that Alice been attacked by a centipede.

Back at the microphone, Grace calmed the guests, talking in a soothing voice: "Well, that was a little excitement we didn't expect, did we? I'm going to confide to you a Coco Palm's secret. We love all our croaking frogs. In fact, I am about to dedicate a wing at the hotel in their honor. For you see, those little greenies that keep you awake at night are a true blessing to us. Those darling green croakers eat those pernicious centipedes. So, the next time you see a frog hopping near you, bless him. Also, ironic, Hawaiians believe that when a centipede makes an appearance in our dining room, it is an omen of good luck."

Grace made up legends. She made them up on the spot by the hundreds. I exaggerate but exaggeration, after all, is the spice of life. Exaggeration makes people far more interesting and more likely to be remembered.

"In keeping," Grace continued, "with Coco Palms tradition, I am treating everyone in the dining room to our special goodnight drink, the Coco Palms coconut-lilikoi-go-to-sleep aloha cocktail. One sip and tonight you will sleep like a baby. And by the way . . . is there a doctor in the house? Anyone, please?"

A formidable-looking woman, wearing a lavender *muumuu*, elbowed a bespectacled bald man who sheepishly stood up beside his table. Using the crook of her finger, Grace beckoned him to follow her. This middle-aged man, a flower behind his right ear, ambled unsteadily toward Grace. He sheepishly carried in his hand a Mai Tai. From his outward appearance, he had left his Hippocratic Oath at home in Encino, California. As a doctor, he should have volunteered to assist Grace as soon as Alice cried out, "I am dying."

Grace commanded, "Hand me that Mai Tai and follow me, sir. I want you to check on this guest for me." Looking him square in the eye, she asked, "You don't mind, do you?"

He mumbled an oath under his breath that only the spirits in the coconut grove heard and followed Grace out of the dining room, whimpering, "No, of course, not."

The most curious part of this whole experience was Dockie Wockie. Wasn't Dockie a physician? I saw that Dockie hid his face behind a menu. Tommy Twinkle, having first-hand knowledge of Dockie's dubious medical skills, firmly placed a hand on Dockie's shoulder and kept him in his chair.

Another curious observation: Lillie laughed out loud at Alice's predicament. Her merriment so outraged the honeymoon couple seated behind her, I observed, that if it was possible, the couple would have found the stinging centipede and made sure that Lillie had the excruciating pleasure of making its acquaintance.

Later in the evening, I made my prediction to Grace. At tomorrow night's birthday gala, Lillie and her cuckoos would get drunk, say awful things to each other, and, from what I observed tonight, at Lillie's birthday party, nothing bad would happen because her guests are looney and quite harmless.

Lillie's birthday didn't happen as I predicted—nothing in life is really predictable, is it? Death is! Death comes to all of us and someone was poisoned horribly the next night.

Lobby Coco Palms Hotel

CHAPTER TEN

August 17, 1960 – The Soviet Union sentences Francis Gary Powers, captured American U2 pilot, to ten years' imprisonment for espionage.

The next day was Tuesday the day I described as the most boring day of the week. But on the Tuesday that came after the first night Lillie Russell and her party slept in their King's Cottages, I took it all back and named that Tuesday, Black Tuesday. Since God was on vacation, surfing the waves on Maui, that Tuesday turned out to be a humdinger.

At seven that Tuesday morning, Lillie ordered Itsui, Coco Palms' telephone operator, to place three long-distance telephone calls to the Mainland. Itsui dialed each call to Beverly Hills, California—one collect call was made to the Beverly Hills Police Department.

After completing her long-distance telephone calls, Lillie ordered room service: Breakfast No. 2 (two poached eggs over Portuguese sweet bread, freshly squeezed orange juice, and black coffee). After eating her breakfast, Lillie picked up the telephone receiver again. She commanded Itsui to contact Miss Buscher immediately. Anyone who worked at the hotel knew that command was a big no, no, NO!

Why? When Grace conducted her morning rituals, she accepted no phone calls from anyone until after 8 a.m., and that included Mr. Guslander. It was Grace's sacred time performing her daily morning ritual:

First, Grace gossiped with the housekeepers. Afterward, she walked into the kitchen to meet with Chef Jiro for more gossip, and then she went on to Mrs. Nakai for a recap. While in the kitchen drinking coffee with Jiro, Grace ate her breakfast.

Leaning against a commercial refrigerator, she smoked a Camel cigarette borrowed from Jiro, drank two cups of black coffee and munched on a piece of blackened toast. Caffeine, nicotine, and charcoal were Grace's daily vitamins—drugs that gave her the energy to subdue the anguished piles of reports that begged her attention in the upstairs office. Burned toast? Grace's roughage. Burned toast kept a smile on Grace's face.

Lillie was furious. The once megastar at Warner Brothers was only used to people kissing her ass and was not about to be sassed by a lowly telephone operator—a bit player, in her lexicon—so, she screamed at Itsui, "Put me through to Grace Buscher . . .NOW!"

(For anyone new to Kauai, the first lesson you learn: is if you want to get anything done by anyone on the Garden Island, you don't demand or scream at them.)

Silence. Itsui filed her nails.

Lillie threw a hissy-fit that she once used to beat down Jack Warner, movie mogul, into giving her a raise and one of Bette Davis's juiciest roles.

More silence followed. Itsui concentrated on painting her baby finger Tropical Red.

Ready to tear her hair out, Lillie pulled an old chestnut from her book of threats: "I'm going to commit suicide."

The silence continued. Itsui blew air on her polished baby finger. "Please," whined Lillie."

While this drama was going on, down in the kitchen, Grace dragged on a cigarette, and listened to the end of a story from a housekeeper. The housemaid had spied in Room 206 a nude, tattooed circus performer executing loop-da-loops hanging from Grace's banana-leaf-shaped chandelier. As Grace was just about to find out if the tattooed-nude circus performer ruined her banana-leaf chandelier, the kitchen telephone rang; it was for her. Fire in her eyes, Grace slammed her hand down on the table and walked to the wall phone.

Picking up the receiver, Grace said, "Hello and this better be good, Itsui."

What Grace heard was Lillie's lisp, "Mith Buscher, my table in the Flame Room is now to seat thirteen not fifteen."

Grace rolled her eyes to the ceiling.

Placing her hand over the telephone mouthpiece, Grace whispered to the story-telling housekeeper, "What happened to my chandelier and what happened to the nude, tattooed contortionist? Were the doors and windows wide open for everyone to see her?"

The housekeeper nodded.

"And furthermore," Lillie interrupted.

"And furthermore to what, Miss Russell?"

In code, Lillie hissed, "Remember? Two of my good friends checked out—died, actually; that's what I am talking about. Remember?"

"That's fine but I happen to be very busy at the moment and I haven't the faintest idea of what you are talking about."

Grace slammed the phone back down on its receiver, more interested in her chandelier and the gyrations of the tattooed contortionist.

I am not your everyday run of the mill busybody. I am a busybody who takes his busybody work seriously. I'm an ace at peeking through keyholes at midnight, an ace at hiding under beds while people make love, and an ace at squeezing into hiding places—tiny broom-closets where no one, including Miss Buscher, would ever suspect that I would be spying, considering that I'm so fat.

Up early that morning, I hid inside the hotel kitchen and was fortunate to be present

when Grace received her phone call from Lillie. I didn't miss a word of it.

I had done a little reconnaissance before Grace arrived and I'd found a fabulous new hiding place right in the middle of Jiro's kitchen. Being a fan of John Wayne war films, and looking out for Jiro (or any other cook), I belly-landed like a B-12 bomber and hid under a stainless steel table. Above me, on the shiny stainless steel countertop, were displayed platters of sliced cold cuts and humongous, mouthwatering salad bowls filled with mounds of tuna and egg salad, oozing with Best Foods Mayonnaise. Situated next to those salads, is what I called "trying one's patience." What's more fatiguing in this whole world than a large bowl of salad made of chopped up lettuce leaves mixed with tiny little pieces of carrots and cucumbers and no mayo? Boring!

Lettuce is SO dull!

The spread on the kitchen table was prepared for the Japanese tourists who ate their buffet lunches at the Coco Palms. Booked on the Ginza for a day-long-trip around Kauai, the Japanese would fly in at eight in the morning and leave at five in the evening. The Coco Palms was designated as a major pit stop—lunch and a *shishi* (pee), all for the price of $30 per person.

When the bus tours from the Land of the Rising Sun arrived at the Coco Palms at noon, I gave them a wide birth, all for good reason. White mega-Diesel buses parked in front of the hotel, and out scrambled fierce-looking locusts that stampeded down the walkway to the feed trough. The wild look in their eyes signaled to me they were out to eat everything in sight, all to get their money's worth. Feeling a tickle in my sphincter, my personal warning sign, I knew that if I didn't get out of their way, I'd be their dessert.

Big money for Grace.

Grace espied me while she was speaking to Lillie on the telephone. Putting her hand over the mouthpiece, she hissed, "For God's sake, Percy, what are you doing under that table? Get out of there and don't you dare touch any of those salads!"

Grace was horrified. She saw visions of Best Foods Mayonnaise in my eyes.

After she hung up with Lillie, Grace turned her back to report to Jiro, standing next to her. She talked about what had transpired between her and the star on the telephone.

I got out from under the table and while Grace was speaking to Jiro. Grace being occupied is when I spied a serving spoon, picked it up, and hovered it over the tuna salad. My hand quivered. I was ready to play "bombs away" into the salad.

Grace's second sight, caught me. I swore Grace had eyes in the back of her head, but it was grumpy old Jiro who gave me away by pointing at me.

"Don't do it, Percy or you'll regret it. Grace spoke."

Jiro, the Chef, played two roles in Grace's life: First, he was a superb cook who created unique mouthwatering dishes for the hotel using local foods (poi cocktail being one of his stellar creations). He did it all because of his love and admiration for Grace. Second,

Jiro was Grace's father confessor, par excellence. Jiro listened to Grace's complaints and never once offered her advice. Now *that* is a true friend.

I took a second chance, believing Grace was again being distracted talking to Jiro. I opened my bomb doors and plunged the spoon into the tuna salad. Wouldn't you know it? Grace caught me red-handed. It was too late. My target was met. The spoon was deep into the tuna salad. With a yank, out erupted the spoon, heaped with the mixture of tuna and heaven (mayonnaise) and, damn the torpedoes, I headed the spoon for my open mouth. I closed my eyes. I could taste the mayo in my mouth, when the general commanded, "Don't you dare!"

Her voice hit me like a zap of lightning and I dropped the spoon into the salad.

"Get that spoon out of the salad, Percy, and stand beside me. Look sharp and tuck in your shirt."

Grace announced, loud enough for all of Kauai to hear her, "Take a good look at Percy, Jiro. This will be last time on earth you're ever going to see this pest at the Coco Palms. I am about to fire this boy."

When Jiro heard Grace say that, he looked pleased as punch— almost as pleased as when he created his poi cocktail. I know he was pleased because his eyes crinkled. With me out of his kitchen, the inventory of the jars of mayonnaise would finally tally.

Standing at attention, I gave Grace my Scarlet Pimpernel rehearsed, sheepish, stupid, sissy, silly ass, contrite look. It didn't work because she continued talking to Jiro. Once again, I disappeared from her mind, speaking to Jiro about Lillie.

"The Lillie Russell party is puzzling, intriguing, and very mysterious. They will be out of the hotel the day after her birthday party is over. I want no slip-ups on your part on this dinner. Prepare food now for thirteen, even though I still count only ten people staying with her in the King's Cottages. No matter what, prepare a five-course dinner for thirteen. Charge Lillie Russell the full amount—add fifteen percent—no, make it a 25 percent surcharge for all the trouble that Miss Lillie Russell is causing Coco Palms and me. Oh God, I hope Gus and George Shipman don't hear about this. No matter if there be one or thirteen people sitting at the table, Lillie Russell gets charged for thirteen dinners including the tip. Jiro, thirteen is such an awful number. I am almost persuaded to set the table for fourteen. Thirteen . . . thirteen is such a bad luck number. It portends to be a bad omen. You mark my words, Jiro, there is trouble ahead for us."

Grace paused and once again remembered that I was standing at attention next to her. My mouth slung open as I listened to her astonishing words about Lillie's party.

"Percy, close your mouth. You look like you're going to swallow a goldfish. Jiro, what in heaven's name should I do with this boy?"

For the first and only time that I can remember, Jiro gave Grace advice: "Let me put him on the spit tonight. He has enough fat on him for two pigs."

They both laughed at my expense and while they laughed, very pleased with themselves, I shoved a small bottle of mayo into my pocket.

For whatever reason, I was forgiven once again. It must have been that Grace was pleased with my report from yesterday's activities - so pleased, she gave me another assignment. I was assigned to be an extra waiter at the Lillie Russell birthday party.

Wowee!

During the rest of the day, I did mental exercises to gear myself up for the evening. To sharpen my memory skills, I memorized the order of the presidents of the United States—I never got past John Adams.

Meanwhile, rumors had circulated around the hotel. Centipede Lady, dear Alice, recovered completely and was drinking gin slings in the bar, alone. Husband Eric had gone AWOL. Granny was showing off her newly-dyed flaming red hair and trolled the coconut grove twirling a Japanese parasol. One snide housemaid commented, "That broad is looking for action."

Tommy twinkled himself by the swimming pool, showing off his Ginger Rodgers tap routine. He dressed in a thong, hoping for a request for an autograph or a quickie with the local boy serving drinks behind the bar.

A housemaid reported that Lillie rushed out of Cottage 5 in full sail, wearing a purple caftan, with Gretchen the Swede mincing three paces behind her and gesturing frantically for Lillie to stop. Lillie stopped, turned around, and slapped Gretchen on the face. Stunned, holding her face, Gretchen still meekly followed five steps behind Lillie. Lillie, twirling like a twister, glided into Dockie's cottage, and slammed the door in Gretchen's face. The Swede fled back to Cottage 5 in hysterics, (I heard that information from Itsui) got on the telephone and called her husband, Sam Yamashita, the cameraman, and told him that after the birthday party she was flying home. Gretchen, Itsui feared, headed for a nervous breakdown.

Seconds later, Tony Pinto emerged from Dockie's cottage massaging his rump and skedaddled toward the Coco Palms zoo. He swore loudly that he preferred monkeys to humans. Anyone who witnessed Tony's exit felt he showed good horse sense.

Tilda ran out of the same cottage seconds after Tony and yelled back into the room, "Fuck you!"

Raul, a white towel wrapped snugly around his slim waist, opened the door to his cottage and saw Tilda pounding the ground with her fists. He ducked back inside and locked the door, and continued to lather up his abs in the shower.

Later that afternoon, Lillie, in full makeup, sequestered herself in the Flame Room and spent an hour preparing for the evening fete. Grace persuaded Lillie to have cocktails served at 6 p.m. with her dinner to commence at 6:30. With fingers crossed, Grace hoped that keeping to this schedule, there would not be another interruption like the evening before. I hid behind a potted plant in the Flame Room, and pretended to be the invisible Lamont Cranston, the Shadow (a character from the weekly radio show heard on Sunday nights). The Shadow clouded men's minds into thinking he was invisible, warned everyone, speaking like a mortician, "Who knows what evil lurks in the hearts of men . . . only the Shadow knows."

I performed as the invisible Shadow, looking for evil, and spied on Lillie circling the dining table in the Flame Room. Bemused at what she was doing, I watched her make strange preparations for the night's festivities.

I saw Lillie flit from chair to chair doing her thing. It flummoxed me. Not even the Shadow or Charlie Chan or the Scarlet Pimpernel could have had the slightest clue as to what Lillie was concocting in the Flame Room for her guests.

CHAPTER ELEVEN

August 19, 1960 – The Sputnik program: The Soviet Union launches Sputnik 5, with dogs Bella (Squirrel) and Estrella (Little Arrow), forty mice, two rats and a variety of plants. The spacecraft returns the next day and all animals were recovered safely.

On the dot, Lillie's supporting cast, without its star, walked into the Flame Room. They were arm in arm, giving kiss-kiss Hollywood pecks on rouged cheeks and were dressed to the nines. Fortified with straight shots of whiskey, they talked nonsensical gibberish as they walked into the room. Dockie broke wind after hearing a joke.

To prepare for the evening, they had rehearsed, in various keys, how to sing happy birthday and had mentally written, sticky-gooey monologues to express how much they adored their benefactress. The unwritten rules for the evening was to kiss her ass the moment she arrived at her party and to give her a standing ovation when she made her grand Joan Crawford, dramatic entrance. The most important rule: one never, ever upstaged Lillie. To upstage Lillie meant Siberia.

In spite of themselves and embarrassingly, her guests at one time in their lives could think back to when they turned a somersault or two for Lillie. Turned a somersault? At one time or another, they, at Lillie's insistence, had ruined a competitive actress's reputation, or spread an unkind rumor about a leading man she hated—all to remain in Lillie's orbit, keeping her at the top of the heap. But doing somersaults was getting harder as Lillie was no longer a bankable star, or young!

Why stick around?

Lillie was rich. If so inclined, she could set each of them financially up for life. That meant freshly squeezed orange juice served on a breakfast tray every morning of their lives. Times of desperation, out of a job, during those dark days, they prayed to the god Mammon. Since Lillie was childless and had no heirs, they asked, "Please god of material wealth have Lillie bequeath to me all her apartment buildings on Wilshire Boulevard."

As I wiped rat doodoo off a chair cushion, I observed with envy as Lillie's guests walked glamorously into the Flame Room. Watching them act so Hollywood, I, too, longed to be part of Lillie's world. I hummed under my breath, "Happy Birthday to you, happy birthday to you!" I planned to sing to Lille the loudest of anyone and on key!

After Hollywood entered the Flame Room, they stopped and looked around the room. All afternoon their minds had wondered what Lillie had been up to. Looking at the dinner table set before them, they were about to learn.

The dinner table had been set for thirteen. Grace had provided a long, white Irish linen table cloth that once belonged to the Russian Romanov family. At each place setting, leaned up against a crystal glass were purple bordered place cards. Lillie had handwritten in black ink on small pieces of velum, the names of the invited. Seeing the place cards, curious, the invitees sauntered casually around the dining table and searched for their names written in Lillie's unmistakably childish hieroglyphics.

From the odd expressions on their faces, I saw they had found their names on the place cards and discovered whom Lillie had seated next to whom, as well as the hideous things she had placed in chairs next to them. In that instant, they knew that Lillie was out to make her birthday party an event they would never forget.

Potty mouth Tilda spoke first, "Wouldn't you know it? The queen planted herself at the head of the table and put me nearest to her. She wants me within slapping distance because she hates me." I looked around the table for the guests reactions as she continued, "Think about it, kids, more to the point, that..." (Tilda was about to use the f-word, then changed her mind) "Lillie despises all of us."

After Tilda spoke, a frog croaked in agreement from the lagoon.

Tilda's voice cracked, "What in the hell is this?"

Tilda's hand had touched the head of a doll that sat upright in a chair between her and Lillie.

All of them stared at the doll and froze in their tracks. A wasp had stung them, and the wasp was named Lillie.

I made a mental snapshot of who sat next to whom and the macabre dolls that sat in the chairs next to them.

Lillie would be seated with her back to the lagoon, and on her right, a Charlie McCarthy dummy, then Tilda. Counter-clockwise around the table, Lillie had placed cowboy Tony next to Tilda. Then red-headed Granny; Raul, Lillie's husband with rash, followed next, at the opposite end of the table across from Lillie, sat Tommy Twinkle. Next to Tommy, Lillie had positioned a large doll with a painted face that featured large, ruby red lips and long eyelashes that were drawn with a black mascara pencil—representing to me, a lady of the night. The doll's head was covered with masses of blond curls pinned high on her head—a Marie Antoinette coif that the Queen wore before her head was chopped off. A blue ribbon held the mass of blond curls away from the doll's face. The marionette was gussied up in a red frilly evening gown—a gown that Marilyn Monroe might have worn singing, "Someone kissed my Fanny in Miami!"

On the left side of the table Lillie seated Dockie Wockie. Next to Dockie, Lillie had placed a hideous doll with a painted Salvador Dali thin, black mustache below its nose. What made the doll so gruesome was that Lillie had gouged out its eyes and lacquered the empty sockets with black nail-polish. Streaks of red nail polish (blood) streamed out of its eyes, giving the impression of two red rivers running down the side of each cheek. Added to its grotesqueness, Lillie penned an inky tongue that stuck sideways out of its mouth. The doll was dressed in a Roman toga.

The rest of the seating continued with Alice the Alligator, Gretchen the Swede and Eric the Hun. Eric was seated on Lillie's left—a place of honor. I thought that quite odd.

Gretchen, averted her eyes from the bloodied creature in a toga to her right and spoke softly to everyone, "I didn't know about any of this. Lillie didn't tell me anything! Everyone, Lillie is up to no good. Something is definitely rotten in Denmark tonight. I feel it."

Gretchen took a breath before she continued, "I want you all to know that Lillie has not been herself for a long time. No matter what happens tonight, please remember Lillie is under a great deal of strain."

Raul stood behind the Charlie McCarthy doll next to Tilda, stroked the puppet's head and said in his accented voice, "There is something familiar about this thing. I can't remember what it is, but

I vaguely remember Lillie's father saying something about this kind of foolishness a few days before he was murdered."

Tommy flipped the bird at Raul, and said, "Screw Lillie and her father."

Granny cackled once again and she spewed, "Watch it! Lillie is out to make sport of us tonight. It's her birthday and thinks she can do anything she likes. We ain't got much choice in the matter but to get drunk, keep out of her way, and don't say nothing to cause her to have a menopausal hysteric. And I know all about Lillie's hysterics, honey babies. I've seen 'em all, because I have been the cause of many of 'em, past and present, and them hysterics ain't pretty to be around. And, listen up, we have all been invited here to the Coco Palms for some diabolical scheme of hers!"

Granny played with "the lady of the night" curls as she spoke. Except for Dockie, not one person had looked at the blood-ied-eyed doll.

Lillie's guests who had gathered around the table were a nervous lot. Some fiddled with the silverware, some fretted that they were about to be boiled in oil. The real neurotics pressed their hands to their eyes and controlled the twitching.

Gretchen announced, "The Queen will arrive shortly. Her Majesty instructed me to tell you that you are to go ahead and order your cocktails. We are not to wait for her."

Buttercup, the bartender, heard Gretchen and raised high a bottle of Gilbey's Gin. Buttercup stood at a make sift bar, built that day just for Lillie's party – a flimsy wooden structure with woven coconut leaves covering it.

Granny and Tommy galloped towards Buttercup and screamed hysterically, demanding two Cary Grant martinis. Buttercup flexed his fingers and signaled to Granny and Tommy that he was ready to work his magic.

Granny and Tommy are certifiable lunatics. I must watch my back with those two clowns around.

Granny downed a Cary Grant in one swill and screeched, "Lillie has gone bonkers, Tommy, mark my word." She wiped her face with the back of her hand, and lowered her voice and cooed sweetly into Buttercup's ears, "Another of them Cary Grant's, cutie."

"Lillie has become a dangerous bitch," Tommy agreed. "I wouldn't be surprised if she has read all of Heidi's files."

"Who cares!"

Tommy addressed Buttercup twittering. "Another double Cary Granth, Mary. Heavy on the gin."

Buttercup hearing him being called "Mary," wanted to add arsenic to Tommy's gin. Loyal to Grace, he restrained himself and poured Tommy a straight martini. Martini in hand, Tommy noticed the bartender's tag, and sniffed, "Buttercup darling, is that really your name?"

If I was Buttercup, I would kick Tommy's little ass.

"Here brah, take your martini and go," growled, Buttercup.

"Hurry it up, you two dolts," thundered "Kaiser Wilhelm" Eric standing behind Tommy and Granny.

Buttercup barked to Granny and Tommy, "Come, on, let da others get drinks."

"Get the hell out of mit way," shouted Eric."

Tommy and Granny scampered to sit on a lava wall, near the rat hole, determined to get drunk.

Buttercup, taking charge, spoke in a gravelly voice and instructed the others, "Line up and I'll take your orders."

Lillie's guests dutifully lined up behind Eric now posturing as a Mussolini.

Eric was once a Nazi party member.

Dockie stood patiently at the end of the line. I thought it strange behavior so I gave him my Charlie Chan–Scarlet Pimpernel once-over.

I found the good doctor stone sober. Even more amazing, his white suit was ivory snow clean and pressed. More puzzling, he spoke quietly, not slurring his words, and using a gentle upper-class Brahmin Bostonian accent. When it was time for Dockie to order his drink, he made his request loud and clear, making sure that everyone in the room could hear him.

"My man, fill my glass almost to the brim with Johnny Walker Red." A wink at Buttercup, he added, "Add a splash of Coke for color, my good man."

Here's a piece of tittle-tattle from the studio steam rooms: When Dockie first began his practice in Hollywood, the Mecca of the Misplaced, he believed he was a gifted healer—a savior of lost souls. But Dockie made horrible mistakes with his patients—mistakes that prompted Dockie to drink whatever alcoholic beverage was available, one minute after the noon hour. To convince his staff, his patients, and the Medical Board of Inquiry that he was not an alcoholic, he disguised the alcoholic beverage by topping it off with Coca Cola. By his second year in Hollywood, he finally realized the truth about himself and that knowledge made him drink even more. The day he faced himself, he became an even more inept physician . . . if that makes any sense!

Every day, he went home, and reported to Heidi that he had healed the lepers of Hollywood, the men and women of lost dreams. He never fooled Heidi or the Medical Board of Ethics or his patients.

After he pressed his cool stethoscope to their chests, the actors who have come to him for help lost hope. They smelled either gin, bourbon or scotch on his breath. Even his nurse knew, if she wanted to keep her job, that Johnny Walker Red was his favorite drink of choice during his office hours.

Suddenly, I almost missed something important: Dockie had whispered to Buttercup that he wanted a Coke straight - without the Johnny Walker Red.

Lillie's evening had become even more twisted.

Do you remember that earlier I hid behind the coconut fronds of the makeshift bar to spy on Lillie? I had seen her set the place cards and dolls around the table. Lillie didn't hesitate one moment where she seated everyone or the dolls; except, where she wanted to place the mascaraed bloodied-eyed doll. The grotesque doll held the most important placement for her. I watched Lillie cradle the hideous puppet in her arms and then suddenly, with the fierceness of a Medea, gorged out the doll's eyes with her fingers. In seconds, she created two hideous caverns. For fifteen minutes she moved the doll from one chair to the other, but finally sat the offensive creature next to Dockie.

More digressions, please indulge me.

The Flame Room offered two things: Privacy.. The other thing, the Flame Room was, according to Grace, the only five-star restaurant on Kauai in1960. The broiled steaks, from Kipu Ranch, were the best on Kauai.

Trivia for the fashion-conscious: The Lizard Lady wore a slinky, black gown with a slit on the side of the dress that displayed for her entire universe of varicose veins. A purple bandage she plastered to the exposed leg. It was where the centipede had sunk its lethal prongs. Gretchen dressed in a fetching, blue-and-white polka dot gown—a suitable gown to waltz on a summer night on a Copenhagen water-front. Eric the Hun sported his old pith helmet, skewed so tight to his head—blood abandoned his brain He wore a khaki safari outfit, the same safari suit as when he directed one of his most unforgetta-ble films in Africa. That film was titled: *I Made Love to a Rhinoceros*. He dedicated the film to Alice. Dockie Wockie's pristine appearance didn't last a minute. After he bit into a caviar pupu, the hors d'oeuvre crash-landed onto his protruding belly.

Tommy twitted, "Oh no, Dockie! Can't you keep yourself clean for one goddamn minute?"

Tommy's costume came from the racks of a burlesque show. His skin-tight hot pink short pants prompted him to do a Ginger Rogers' tap dance. Tommy shuffled off to Buffalo around the dinner table, tapping his fingers on all the dolls' heads.

No applause. Tommy tapped dance around the table three more times. Still no applause. He bent over the stone wall, near the rat hole, and admired his reflection in the lagoon. He stood up, des-perate for attention, faced his audience, and loudly announced: "I am the flame of the Flame Room."

"You're frickin' right, fairy," Tilda answered, not amused.

Tilda looked splendid in a fitted pink and white *muumuu*. Her *muumuu* complemented the colors in Tony's Lone Ranger outfit.

Tony drawled, "Remember, to be a lady tonight, gal."

Granny dressed herself in an orange pantsuit. It was the most unfortunate color choice of the evening. The orange pantsuit was as repulsive as her makeup. She had spread the makeup on her face with a trowel. On her third Cary Grant, Granny lamented, "My legs were the showstoppers of America. These legs walked the streets of Washington D.C.and snagged a Kennedy for more than a handshake."

The classiest dressed person at the party was Raul Pasqual. He outfitted himself as Manolete, the Spanish matador. He gave the evening class.

Ole!

Back to Tilda. I kept waiting for her to spout a four-letter word, but she resisted the impulse. I discovered why: Tony Pinto had positioned his hand at her backside. Pinto had big hands and plenty of practice swatting behinds—ask his horse.

Tilda turned petulant. "Change places with me, please cowboy. I don't want to sit next to this mildewed Charlie McCarthy."

"Not on your tintype. I ain't about to change anything that Lillie put into her corral. I— . . ."

"Wait, that doll reminds me of something!" interrupted Dockie. He squeezed a slice of lemon into his Coke. I waited for Dockie to continue. But he didn't.

Tommy interrupted. He tapped his lacquered finger nail on the table and declared, "I can explain that doll to you, you old drunk."

Raul threatened quietly, "I would like to hear what Dockie has to say."

Dismissing Raul with the back of his hand, Tommy twittered on: "Never you mind, Raul dear. Dockie, dear heart, that doll sitting there is Charlie McCarthy. Charlie is a wooden dummy. He was created by Edgar Bergen. Bergen, a radio performer, is the best known ventriloquist in the United States. Everyone knows him. Charlie is heard making wisecracks on the radio every week. Is there anything else you want to know about that doll over there, my chums?"

"You little shit," Tilda snapped, "If you're so bloody smart, who is this bloody ass doll with his bloodied-ass eyes gouged out of its sockets?"

Alice suddenly raised her hand. "Oh, I know that one."

Pulling out a lace hankie from a beaded, black purse, she coughed into the hankie and intoned words speaking as a snotty Pasadena matron. I thought her voice sounded as if she was about to bid two hearts in a morning bridge game. "Darlings, I learned about that doll from attending my Greek Classics class at Vassar. My dears, that doll represents Oedipus Rex from Greek mythology. He gouged out his eyes, blinding himself, after he learned that he had killed his father and married his mother. My dearest darlings, if any of you had killed your father, the Beverly Hills Police would have locked you up in jail, and thrown away the key. If I added up all the nefarious things you have all done in Hollywood, all in the guise of making a film, gouging out your eyes would perhaps be the most appropriate thing for you to do. (Giggling.) Oh my, haven't we all traveled down a very slippery slope on Rodeo Drive."

Again, she delicately coughed into her handkerchief, and continued to intone, now stretching out her vowels, "I have the deepest feeling that Lillie put these dolls at this table to remind one of us of his or her past sins. Maybe for dessert, Lillie will ask one of you to gouge out your eyes. Wouldn't that be a hoot. Eric, dearest, please, why don't you go first?" Alice's eyes sparkled mischievously believing that she had become the brightest light in the room.

Eric, pushed Gretchen aside, and slapped Alice. Alice spun around and placed her beaded purse in front of her face to deflect a second hit from Eric.

The other guests froze like statues. Not one offered any assistance, not even Gretchen who stood beside her. In their silence, they telegraphed how much they loathed Alice. Slowly, Alice lowered the purse, stood tall, and defiantly smiled at them.

Why the venom against Alice? Is it because Alice is not one of them. Alice reeks of Pasadena. Her people have been persecuting Jews and gypsies since their recent arrival on Ellis Island. Movie folks, stand-ing around the table, may have become filthy rich but to Alice's people, they were to be kept in their place. Horrors, they were never to be mem-bers in their exclusive clubs or an invited guest at their dinner table.

Eric spat, forgetting his fake German accent, "Alice, you bitch. Implying that we are two Hollywood sleaze-bags. This is all Lillie's fault. She made us go crazy with her dolls. And as far as I am con-cerned, and I don't care if it's her birthday, Lillie deserves everything that has happened to her. We, I for one, have been at the mercy of Lillie's stardom for decades. I am not afraid of Lillie anymore because Lillie is finished as an A-list movie star. Kaput! And how dare you, Alice, imply, with your high and mighty airs, that any of us here at this table are not upright, honest citizens." Finished with his tirade, Eric wiped a thread of drool off his chin.

At the entrance, hidden in the shadows, two queens listened with mild amusement at the goings-on: One lady was the reign-ing queen of the Coco Palms Hotel; the other, the recently deposed queen of the motion pictures.

"Well, well, well." A theatrical voice boomed from the nearby shadows—it was a voice, that without the aid of a microphone had filled a three hundred-seat theater on Broadway. Lillie stepped in the room's light. She wore a shimmering gown, a singular piece of great art designed by MGM's creative genius, Adrian. Its silver threads cascaded down from a beaded bodice, and flowed to the floor like a thousand waterfalls. After Lillie's "wells," she emerged out from the dark shadows. One look at her, Lillie's guests yearned to either hide under the table or tinkle!

"Having fun at my expense, hmm? Aren't we all acting brave tonight? Especially you, Eric. The things you say about me when you think I am not listening."

Silence.

"Sit down," she ordered.

Scared as Peter Rabbits, they sat down with the sound of a gigantic "plunk."

Dockie broke wind. (What else!)*!*

Lillie had the foresight not to seat anyone human next to the "windbag". Laughter erupted when Dockie, blushing, pointed his needle nose at the Oedipus Rex doll.

Grace had remained in the background frowning.

Grace is not amused!

Lillie noticed Grace's displeasure and made a beeline for her place at the head of the table. She clinked a spoon on a wineglass and corralled her guests back into proper order.

Regal, playing Queen Elizabeth I, her second greatest film role, Lillie commanded her guests' attention: "Over there," she nodded at Grace, "is the wonderful lady who created this tropical ambiance. Oh, it so reminds me of Sound Stage Eight. Remember Gretchen -Paramount Studios, 1938? I suffered terribly in that awful humidity from the burning hot klieg lights that I had to endure week after week. And that smelly fake rain that showered on me eternally. I felt I was being buried alive under all that heat mixed with the smell of sex that exuded in that sound stage. But the worst thing was Bertoni's awful body odor. Still with all of that, I acted in one of my greatest role in *Rain*. I performed to a quintessential perfection without missing one sick day. It would have been a great film but for that old ham, Walter Bertoni playing Reverend Davidson. I wish to God Jesse Lasky hadn't put him in that movie. Never mind Bertoni. Tonight, I feel the same damn tingles as I did on that set."

Lillie paused and looked at Grace, "I was a far better Sadie Thompson than that poor, dear Rita Hayworth. I hear they filmed

Rita's *Miss Sadie Thompson* at your Coco Palms. Lucky, Rita, no Bertoni or smelly rain."

She rubbed her arms and continued, "Here I stand at the Coco Palms feeling the same tropical decadence. Thank you God that here tonight I don't have Walter Bertoni pinching my behind. The bruises he gave my perfect ass didn't clear up for six months. Oh, the wads of money I spent at Face Place to clear up my peaches-and-cream complexion. What an awful scene stealer that ham was. Sorry, I am digressing. Now, let me give you the real star of the evening, Miss Grace Buscher.

Grace walked majestically to Lillie as if she was playing Mary Queen of Scots to Lillie's Elizabeth I. The look on Grace's face, it was obvious that she was enjoying the moment. Positioned, next to Lillie, Grace coughed and prepared to speak. She gave a regal nod to Lillie indicating that she ready was bewitch the unbelievers.

. *Grace looked as beautiful as Rita Hayworth.*

Certain that she had their attention, Grace spoke in her practiced dramatic voice, "I weeeelcome you once again to Coco Paaaalms. This is your second night with us and I hope you are finding Coco Paaaalms a magical and spiritual place. Coco Paaaalms changes people and Coco Paaaalms will change all of you— that I promise. The change will be for your good. Coco Palms will bring roooomance back into your lives. And all of you who sleep next to this saaaacred coconut grove will even, perhaps, find your soul mates."

"Kauai is known as one of the four power spots on earth. Here, kahunas predict that on Kauai destiny will meet destiny, face to face. So, tonight feel the spirit of Coco Palms that surrounds you and, please, enjoy yourselves. When you hear the drums tonight, hear what your heart is telling you." Grace looked at Lillie as she said that. "Tonight is Lillie Russell's birthday. I consider Lillie Russell one of the greatest Hollywood stars of all time." Her arm touched Lillie as she continued, "So, Miss Lillie Russell from all of us at the Coco Palms Hotel, we wish you a veeeery happy birthday."

Tony drawled, "Miss Buscher ma'am, Coco Palms is magical. I'd bet my Pinto on that one." Tony looked at Tilda.

Tommy, seated across the table, drunkenly shouted, "Speak up, honey. I didn't catch one damn word you said! I bet some of it was a crock."

Grace abruptly left the table but not before she whispered into Lillie's ear.

Lillie nodded.

Coco Palms Hotel

CHAPTER TWELVE

1960 --- Popular TV Shows dominating America's prime-time viewing are The Price Is Right, Leave It to Beaver, The Donna Reed Show, Hawaiian Eye, and The Twilight Zone.

Big John stood next to the Flame Room exit. He looked as fierce as a Hawaiian warrior prepared to go into battle, especially, when he heard Tommy's twaddle.

Big John's Coco Palms regalia included a white shirt, white duck pants, and a bright, red sash tied around his waist. He wore a brown kukui nut lei around his neck. The lei made him appear like the king of the Coco Palms. His presence and velvet voice signaled two things: one, it was curtain time for Grace to begin her ceremony, and two, deck Tommy to the beat of a drum and string him up by his toes to the tallest coconut tree.

"Miss Buscher," Big John whispered.

Grace nodded, acknowledging him, but her eyes were turned back to the dining room. Alice had lifted both her legs off the floor and onto her chair. Grace caught Alice's eyes and gave her a reassuring smile. The smile promised Alice that there would be no centipedes heading her way.

Comforted, Alice lowered her legs, almost to the ground.

Seeing Alice, gingerly put her two feet back on the ground. Her words, after she was bitten by a centipede ringed in my head, "Someone wants to murder me."

The way the cuckoos had reacted to her Oedipus comments, dear Alice had more to worry about than centipedes. Her so-called Hollywood friends, including her husband, acted as if they were lining up to see who would get to murder her first.

I wished for another centipede attack but not on Alice. Eric was my target.

Grace read my thoughts. She turned to me and rayed her blue eyes into mine warning me not to mess up.

Then, graceful as an ice skater, she glided out of the Flame Room and into the Main Dining Room, where she posed in front of a standing microphone, and prepared to begin her magic.

When I was certain that I was out from under Grace's microscope, I circled the table, moving cautiously from chair to chair; and added cold salad forks on everyone's left side.

As I made my maneuvers, Lillie smoothed the silver threads that cascaded down from her dress, kicked the sparkling train behind her and in slow motion, settled like a falling zeppelin into her chair. It was a theatrical trick she had learned watching, Nijinsky, ballet star, do his squats.

And then, of all things, not speaking a word, Lillie made the sign of the cross and sprinkled wine from her glass onto the head of the Charlie McCarthy doll. She made another sign of the cross and confided to Tilda that she had just anointed the doll into a Mandarin, satanic cult.

Tilda became speechless, actually, catatonic. Charlie McCarthy, on the other hand, wore a bemused expression on his face.

Lillie was acting her favorite role, a mad woman. I read in **Screen Stories** *that Lillie had once been diagnosed as a borderline schizophrenic. Quoted by Hedda Hopper, "When Lillie forgets to take her pills, she changes moods as fast and, often faster as when Zsa Zsa Gabor shanghaied her lovers." That night, Lillie's behavior was bone chilling.*

Lillie madly jerked her eyes from guest to guest, stopping at Eric. She began to weave back and forth in her chair like a cobra threatening to strike. For protection, Eric had placed his pith helmet over his gentiles.

Electricity singed around the room when Lillie made her fingers into a gun and targeted each one of her guests telling them: "I want you dead."

My skin broke out in goosebumps in the most uncommon places on my body when I suddenly became Lillie's sole target. Her eyes began to burrow into mine.

I felt that Lillie was about to bury me alive in a cold Vincent Price mausoleum.

When a frog croaked in the lagoon concurring with my thoughts is when Lillie announced, "Fat boy, dinner may be served!"

The frog croaked again.

Whew! That frog had saved my life!

I nodded to the waiters, quivering in the wings, holding trays high in the air, and in an instant, the servers twirled into action.

"Bring on the dinner, boys!" Lillie giggled.

Scurrying around the table, the servers carefully placed in front of each guest a shrimp and avocado cocktail served in a delicate Venetian crystal glass.

The same people who had, moments before, stalled into neutral now shifted into third gear, skipping second. They began to chatter among themselves like frenzied, demented magpies

I circled the table, pouring water, and clandestinely observing the variety of facial tics. I could tell by the guests' tics, they were sitting on a keg of dynamite waiting for Lillie to light the fuse. The only thing that seemed to keep the evening from going nuttier, was the impeccable and professional service by the waiters.

I was a birthday present to Lillie from Grace. But what Lillie didn't know; I was a spy. I had explicit instructions from Grace to listen to all the goings-on, to pour nothing but wine or water. Only if the waiters asked for assistance was I to do anything more. It was through my own ingenuity and bravery that I had put the salad forks on the table.

Grace's last words to me had been, "After dessert, then and *only* then can you serve the after-dinner coffee. At that stage of the meal, you probably can't do much harm."

Grace might have remembered the previous night. When Alice, the Lizard Lady, screamed, I had accidentally poured a pitcher of water over Tilda's silicone tits, which I had named Twiddle-Dee and Twiddle-Dum. By my Charlie Chan deduction, Twiddle-Dee was a wee bit bigger than Twiddle-Dum. Finding her tits soaked in cold water, Tilda grabbed for my Gable and Valentino while spewing choice blasphemous oaths at me. I don't think, in all my sheltered life, that I have ever heard so many fuck yous. She further warned me that she'd cut off my movie stars if I ever did that to her again. I got away with the Tilda episode without Honey or Grace ever hearing about it because of the confusion of the evening—until I confessed to Grace.

Tilda didn't snitch on me to Grace or Honey and I gave all the credit to Tony the Pinto, since he was being a good influence on her. If Honey had known about the incident, she would have had Jiro cut off my Gable and Valentino and served them up as a delicacy on his buffet table for the Japanese tourists. Surprisingly, Grace found the incident humorous since she was not a big fan of Tilda's.

I had planned my strategy for the night: when I poured the wine into Tilda's goblet, I made sure that Tilda's hands were miles and miles away from my movie stars. I improvised a move to keep Tilda's grabbing fingers at bay. I was so creative that I swooned at the thought of my genius. It was to be a Herculean task. First, I maneuvered to get behind Tilda's chair and do a quick Balinese arm dance, squiggling my arms at many angles; then, with a free hand, I quickly poured Tilda's wine. All the while my other arm and torso had pushed my butt so far out that I could have served tea for ten on it. With that maneuver, I was sure to protect my Gable and Valentino from Tilda's grasping reach. Later, I planned to add to my resume: Coco Palms' Premier Contortionist.

As I danced my genius maneuver, I thought what sane person (Tony) would choose to have a girlfriend who cuts off Gables and Valentinos? Well, come to think if it, isn't that one of the jobs women perform when they get married?

As the dinner progressed, all eyes kept fixed on Lillie. One moment, she raged like a mad woman; seconds later, she was as sweet, sane and as gracious as Perle Mesta, Washington D.C.'s famous party giver. Not one person at the party had wished Lillie "Happy Birthday."

When dessert was served, out came Norma Desmond. Using the wild eyes as Gloria Swanson did when she descended the staircase during the last reel of Billy Wilder's *Sunset Boulevard*. Lillie dramatically rose from her chair, and demanded, "Put lights on me, my darlings. I'm ready for the cameras."

All eyes were glued on Lillie.

"There is an explanation to why you are all gathered here tonight, being my honored guests. I invited each one of you to Coco Palms for two reasons: First, to celebrate my birthday; second, to help me carry out a singular purpose of a very singular plan. Your hostess has been working on this plan for the past three weeks. The outcome of my plan, at present, is a foggy one, but I am determined to execute and finish my plan tonight. The fog will be lifted and truth will be revealed. Why the charade? That's the big question, isn't it, my darlings? And only one of you knows the answer."

Some of her guests looked dumbfounded; a few showed fear—the rest expressed hate.

"What in the hell is the old girl up to now?" Tony whispered to Tilda.

Lillie took a sip of wine before she continued, "We have all known each another for many years, some on more intimate terms than others. All of us have secrets and we hoped to keep our secrets from the world, especially from the press. Of course, Heidi Fleishacker was the evil rodent who knew all our secrets. She reveled at the thought of destroying us in the motion picture business and in our private lives. Her reason to live was to gather our dirty laundry, document our filth, and lock it up in a bank vault and when the time was right, blackmail us. Heidi had every one of us by our short hairs. I hope Heidi, the snake in the grass, is burning in hell, and is being roasted on a spit by the Devil, himself. Dockie, how could you have married such a monster?"

Dockie put his head slowly down on the table.

After taking a napkin to wipe her lips, Lillie took a sip of wine and continued, "Heidi left all her filth to Dockie. I happen to know that in her documents, she hid an awful secret which I am about to reveal; a secret that will expose a murderer sitting among us at this table. This murderer committed crimes so awful, so heinous, so devious . . . so evil, that in my judgment, he or she should join Heidi the Terrible in Hell roasting on a spit.

The only sound heard came frogs croaking in the lagoon.

"Oh God, I wish I hadn't given up cigarettes. What I wouldn't do for a drag on a Vicroy, for that matter any cigarette. After I expose the killer, we will put the murderer on trial here and all of you at this table will be his or her judge and jury. Your verdict and sentence will be a collective birthday present to me. I insist, and you don't know it, but all of you are involved in these killings in some fashion or other; otherwise, you wouldn't be sitting with me at this table. That is why I invited you.

The Flame Room lights flickered out. to darkness. The room felt as a cold a dungeon and the clocks stopped ticking. Time froze.

Waiters and waitresses stopped serving when a conch shell wailed announcing that Grace's torch-lighting ceremony was about to begin. But something was amiss tonight. The ceremony was a full half hour late.

Then, Grace's tremulous voice came from a loudspeaker, attached high in the rafters. Her voice was the only sound heard in the stillness of the Coco Palms night.

A frog croaked just before Grace spoke: "The nightly ceremony, recreating, recapturing for more than one hundred years . . ." For fifteen minutes, Grace kept us captive.

I moved stealthily to the entrance of the Flame Room, and prepared to abandon ship in case the killer got any fancy ideas. For protection, I brandished a glass pitcher of water in front of me thinking how a bucket of water protected Dorothy from the wicked witch in *The Wizard of Oz*.

I heard a chair scrape across the floor and felt a warm rush of air coming for me. I raised the pitcher high and threw the water in the pitcher into somebody's body.

The lights came back on, I expected to find a body flat out on the table, a face smashed in, or at least dear Alice, the Lizard Lady, drowned in her soup bowl with asparagus stalks sticking out of her ears. Contrary to my imagination, every cuckoo sat in place, except for cowboy Tony. He galloped past me retaking his seat between Tilda and Granny. I used my deduction that the cowboy had unzipped his Pinto at the trough to pee.

To my embarrassment, holding an empty water pitcher in hand, I had soaked Buttercup to the skin! Poor innocent Buttercup.

"Where is the Oedipus doll?" screeched, Alice.

"For God's sake, calm yourself, Alice." Lillie ordered. "Dockie, look under the table and see if you can find Oedipus."

On his hands and knees, Dockie scurried under the table looking for the bloodied-eyed doll. Down in the netherworld, without sending out a gas attack, Dockie soon emerged holding the body of the Oedipus doll in one hand and in the other, the Oedipus head.

"Somebody forcibly screwed the head off, viciously separating the Oedipus head from its body," Dockie informed Lillie.

"I knew it," screamed Tommy. "Something bad is going to happen to all of us."

The whole night, Tommy acted as drama queen.!

"Tommy, stop being a twit!" Lillie said. "Someone is playing an insidious game with us and I know who it is."

Alice, Granny, and Gretchen bolted for the door. Before they reached the exit of the Flame Room, Lillie commanded, "Come back here and sit down you three. My birthday party isn't over. There is more to come."

Dockie returned the broken doll back to its seat and meekly sat down. The ladies grudgingly followed Dockie, and all eyes again focused on Lillie.

Lillie surveyed her guests, "To continue, there is a ruthless and psychotic killer among us who will and I repeat, *will* be brought to justice and you, the jury will fit the punishment to the crime."

"When I first learned that there was a killer in our midst, I couldn't prove it and didn't know which one of you did it. But I kept digging because one of the victims was someone very dear to my heart. I am determined to avenge his murder. There isn't an ounce of forgiveness inside of my body as I stand here."

"Fortunately, for me. Dockie ran afoul financially and with the law. An under-aged patient nearly died from a prescription drug overdose. The under-aged damsel in distress, told her parents back in Iowa. Dockie came to me—no, ran to me—for assistance. I complied. A little money to the girl's parents, and a word here and a word to the Beverly Hills Police force, and Dockie was a free man—that is, if he can keep his long, lethal needles inside his medical bag and not go poking his needles into silly little twits who want to become movie stars. Shame on you, Dockie. Poor dear Darla was barely past puberty."

Dockie pounded his fists on the table, "That is a horrid lie, Lillie! I was framed and you know it!"

Lillie resumed, "I had my conditions, of course, to keep Dockie from going to jail. I made Dockie give me *all* of Heidi's files of filth. It took a little arm twisting, but when I reminded Dockie that one word from me, the Beverly Hills Police would come knocking on his front door, Heidi's files are mine."

Hearing that Lillie owned Heidi's files, the suspect's faces turned to the shade of puce, the same color of an underbelly of a flea. It dawned on them that Lillie knew all their intimate secrets. Torrents of blood gushed from their heads to their toes, remembering all the evil deeds they had done. Lillie owning Heidi's files, could mean a possible jail sentence in their future.

Lillie paused before she resumed speaking: "Within two weeks, I read all the files. I incinerated most of the filth—but not the smut on all of you. The dolls at the table have a purpose directly related to the smut I had read in the files. Think carefully, each one of you, and try to remember how each doll pertains to you, personally. The killer will know, as I do, which one of the dolls represents him or her."

"Nevertheless, you are all guilty of crimes that I never thought possible until I read Heidi's files. Whew! Not to be dramatic, I've been to the rodeo and back, but your crimes doing bedroom calisthenics really surprised me. They made Caligula look like a choirboy."

"You're no angel!" growled Granny.

"You're damn right, Granny. I am no angel. More to the point, I am an egotistical, selfish bitch. I am an over-the-top diva who has been a drama-queen on every Hollywood sound stage since the advent of, well, sound. But I have never, ever intentionally hurt anyone . . . except myself."

"Raul pointed an angry finger at her, "Oh, yes, you have."

"Yes, Raul, I may have caused you pain. Some of which, you must admit, you deserved."

"After reading Heidi's filth, I faced myself and realized what a dismal bunch of parasites some of us film folk can be. Many of us shouldn't be taking up space on this planet—myself included. But I am about to remedy that tonight, Raul."

Raul interrupted, "Where do you get off being the judge of any of us?"

"I want justice, Raul. And don't pretend you don't judge me. Just moments ago, I overheard Eric saying things about me behind my back that he would never have said to my face. And not one of you defended me, probably because he was right. Here you sit, all of you eating at my table, and putting up with that awful, horrid performance of mine, all because I am picking up the tab—tip included. Come on folks, you have been riding on my coattails for years and still hope to get more out of this old dame. You've been getting something for nothing for a long time from me, but tonight, it's time to pay the piper."

"Extra, Extra! Hot off the press! Von Bismark, sitting next to me, wants me to star in his next picture. What a laugh! I know how he screwed me over on his last film. And also I know I am not right for the part. Look at me, by no stretch of the imagination can I play a thirty-year-old . But Eric is desperate. He also hoped that if I took the part, it will hammer the final nail into my career's coffin."

Eric began to rise from the table. "I vill hear no more of this sheet. I leaf now."

"Sit down, Eric and behave yourself. And cut out that phony accent."

Eric was a coward. He obeyed Lillie meekly, acting as a little boy being punished by his mother.

"Here's the real truth, Lillie continued. "Eric is short of funds and needs Prudential Mutual Trust Company to finance his next picture. He needs a star, however old and tarnished. But no real star would ever work for him. He has become a real has-been, too! I am saying it in public tonight and I told him months ago that I will never be in one of his pictures again even if he offered me a million dollars. He's in a jam and he really hates me."

"Dat is lie!"

Ignoring Eric, Lillie ticked off more names, "Gretchen, Tony, Tilda, Granny, and Raul, I have kept you on my payroll for many years, and, I might add, for too many years and for too many reasons, all of which you each know clearly and most uncomfortably. My financial well has dried up for all of you, my darlings. Don't squirm. I know that all of you hate me, too. Wasn't it Socrates who said, 'Keep friends close, but enemies closer?'

Lillie said with feeling, as her eyes moistened, "Which one of you for all these many years that we've known each other has really been my friend? All I can see, at this moment, is fear and loathing. I believe I don't have one friend sitting at this table."

Tommy twittered, "I really like you, Lillie. I really do,"

"Oh, Tommy, now that Heidi is gone, you need another a person to suck up to. Oh, I do know my Tommy Twinkle well. If you and I shared a leaky rowboat, and the rowboat was sinking and could hold only one person, you'd throw me overboard to the sharks."

"I would not," whined Tommy. "I promise."

Lillie turned to Dockie again, "I could have sent you to prison, Dockie, no matter how much you protest your innocence. Enough said on that matter."

Looking into the grove, Lillie said unhappily, "Each of you would be happy . . . thrilled, actually, if . . . I disappeared into that lagoon . . . gone forever. But my darlings, I don't plan to disappear because I can swim better than Esther Williams—that MGM star who can't act her way out of a swimming pool, and that bitch knows it."

"Why are you doing this to us?" Tilda asked. She held out her empty wine glass for me to refill.

I cautiously approached Tilda, looking at her Tweedle-Dum and Tweedle-Dee, feeling my Valentino and Gable were cruising for trouble.

On reaching Tilda, Lillie reflected: "I am so tired. I'm so tired of looking at your faces. I'm so tired of looking at my face. I have a very old face that I don't recognize anymore. We are all puppets like Charlie here . . . so many unseen forces keep pulling our strings. Tonight, it is time for me to cut the strings."

As Lillie spoke: I had successfully poured wine into Tilda's glass, even though the wine bottle and my legs jiggled like Jell-O.

Also, while pouring Tilda's wine, Lillie pinched me. One pinch wasn't enough for her. The second time her fingers electrocuted my ass and caused me to spill red wine all over Tilda's Tweedle-Dum. Tilda, traumatized by Lillie, didn't even notice my spill and my Gable and Valentino hung peacefully to my body for the rest of the night, swinging gracefully like Christmas bells. I slipped silently away from Tilda, ecstatic, and thanked God, who was vacationing on Maui, that Tilda didn't castrate me.

I danced a little jig.

Unexpectedly, Lillie's voice rang out and addressed me, "Boy, is everyone's wine glass filled?"

I nodded yes.

Lillie raised her glass and once again addressed her audience, "A toast!"

"Stand by the bar, boy," Lillie commanded. I marched to the bar and stood straight as a guerrilla fighter in a John Wayne Second World War film and awaited further orders from General Lillie.

Lillie cleared her throat, "Tonight, since I am not a trusting soul, would anyone care to exchange my glass of wine with theirs? It is a custom Emperor Nero did with his family and closest friends. Any takers?"

"I will, Lillie." Tony sprang from his seat to exchange his wine glass for hers.

"Let's play musical glasses!" Alice shrieked, speaking out in a daring spurt of courage. Alice earned another three minutes of attention.

"Delightful idea, dear Alice." Lillie said sincerely. "Dear Alice, you are a very good person and I want you to remember that

Alice blushed showing off the scales on her face.

I thought that all of us have a similar Alice lizard look. Take a good look in the mirror, it will reveal that we all have a slight resemblance to Alice and to the sleepy-eyed serpents that crawled out of prehistoric swamps and became us.

Thinking back, that thought made me want to throw up.

Lillie continued, "To make this toast more exciting, I will have fat boy over there sing 'Happy Birthday' as we pass our glasses around. When my darling little Oliver Hardy stops singing, the glass in your hand will be your glass of wine to consume for the toast. Hmm. Quite a good idea, Alice."

Alice's Pasadena dysfunctional family game sounded very Republican.

"Alice, for adding pleasure to my evening, as a reward I am going to send you to Raul's dermatologist. We've got to do something about that skin of yours. Inside that body, you are really a grand girl, not to mention a saint to put up with the likes of Eric the Slug."

"Sing for us, Dough Boy, sing 'Happy Birthday' for me."

"How very grand of you to ask," I said, as I imitated Lillie's voice.

"I agree, very grand," Lillie said, imitating me imitating her.

I cleared my throat. I thought I was about to become a great-mega Hollywood star!

"Wait . . ." Lillie commanded, fingering her wine glass. "Before we begin this silliness, a word to the killer, and you know who you are: it is almost time to pay the piper."

"Now, sing out, boy!"

I sang, but I kept my eyes on Lillie's glass as it passed from hand to hand. I stopped singing on the second pass and made sure that Lillie's wine glass landed into my arch enemy's hand—Tilda.

Tilda, without thinking, gulped down the wine.

"Stop, Tilda. I haven't made the toast yet!" Lillie cried out.

Tilda stared at the wine glass, dropped it, grabbed for her throat, gasped for air and fell to the floor.

Tony yelled, "Tilda, darling!"

"I'm dying," Tilda rasped, "I've been poisoned."

Lillie reached out for Tilda and screamed, "No, no . . . no . . . no!"

Tilda's hand grasped the Charlie McCarthy doll and pulled it down on her chest. And then she laughed, "I'm not dying, you morons. It's just a joke."

Tony picked Tilda up off the floor, turned her upside down on his lap, and slapped her fanny—hard. He was furious. I prayed that big welts formed like huge red balloons on both her superbly shapely melons.

Tony was furious as he said, "Tilda, never ever do anything as lowdown as you have done to all of us just now. Apologize, girl, to everyone in this room, especially to Lillie. NOW!"

The Pinto had spoken. Tilda was stunned by the force of Tony's voice".

By the force of Tony's voice, Tilda stood up without saying a filthy word that was on the tip of her tongue and whispered, "I'm sorry."

Tony advised, "Keep your mouth shut for the rest of the evening. Any questions, Tilda darling?"

A frog answered for Tilda and croaked, "No."

"Say it so I can hear you, Tilda."

"NO!" Her eyes slanted at Tony, mad as a hatter. Her face had become bright red, holding back buckets of tears that wanted to stream down her cheeks like two raging rivers.

"Thank you, Tony!" said Lillie. "Fat Boy, pick up Tilda's glass and fill it up again and let's get back to my toast. And then on with the trial. Please, no more interruptions. Not from anyone. Must I remind you, Tilda, I don't like to be upstaged? There is only one star sitting at this table."

I scurried over to Tilda, picked up her wine glass, and filled it.

Now Tony raised his wine glass and spoke again, "Lillie, for luck of the Irish, which we both have a wee drop of, let's you and I exchange our wine glasses again."

Lillie nodded and exchanged wine glasses with Tony. She raised her glass and, as sweetly as she had done when she portrayed Queen Guinevere sitting at King Arthur's round table, and cheered, "To life!"

Chalices were lifted and Lillie's knights drained every drop of wine in their long-stemmed glasses. When the vessels emptied of their ruby color, and the light in the room shined through the Venetian crystal, each beholder discovered words etched on their chalice . . .

Made in Japan.

CHAPTER THIRTEEN

1960--Notable women who die this year include Edwina Mountbatten, Countess Mountbatten of Burma and last Vicereine of India; American actresses Margaret Sullavan, Diana Barrymore; and Grace Duchess Olga, sister of Russia's Tsar Nicolas II.

After the toast, a strong breeze wafted into the room. Lillie's guests stared mindlessly into an empty wine glass, waiting for her next revelation.

Lillie looked at all of them, smiled, and swooned to the floor. The applause was deafening, Raul and Tony gave her a standing ovation and cheered the loudest.

"Bravo!" Dockie shouted approvingly.

And then Gretchen added, "No one does it better or more graceful than you, Miss Lillie Russell. I remember the way you fell down the staircase in *Mad Cow Steps Over the Moon. You* got the best review of your life from *The New Yorker.* You've done it again. Lillie. You were truly magnificent."

"Right good, Lillie honey!" Tony said.

"Get the hell up off the floor, Lillie! You're gonna ruin that dress," advised Granny.

"She always upstages us!" groaned, Tommy.

Eric sneered, "A pain-in-the-ass.!"

Speaking louder, Tony sounded concerned, "Get your butt off the floor."

My eyes never left Lillie's lifeless body. Her baby finger hadn't moved.

Prodded by Alice, Dockie rose from his chair, and reluctantly sauntered over, saying, "I'll play her game."

"Maybe she hurt herself." Said Alice, worried.

Then Granny spoke, "Hurt, never. Lillie is tough as nails but she ain't as young as she think she is. Pulling a childish stunt like that at her age. Remember, darlings, that awful act she performed on location when Eric directed her in *Torrents on the Plains of Tarzana.*

Dockie bent down to touch Lillie's body.

"Having murder trials tonight at the Coco Palms, my Aunt Fanny," stood Twinkle. He tried to see what Dockie was doing.

"Lillie has gone too far this time . . . A murderer among us—that is ridiculous." Raul also stood by Twinkle, folded his arms and waited for Dockie's pronouncement.

Dockie, wobbly on his hands and knees, examined Lillie. He pressed his finger to Lillie's neck, lifted her eyelid, shook his head, braced himself on the table, and slowly rose. He spoke in heavy weariness, "Party is over. Lillie is dead."

Dockie's pronouncement told Lillie's crew that the curtain had come down and they were about to sail into an unknown future.

Bartender Buttercup, wet all over, whispered to me, "I never look at one dead body."

With no one in charge, a voice spoke to me—it was an unfamiliar voice. The voice told me that Lillie had been murdered. My penis quivered. A quivering penis meant for me to go into action.

Stepping away from the bar, I spread my legs out, gave Lillie's guests a fierce look, and announced, "I'm going to find Miss Buscher. Don't leave this room under any circumstances! Stay in your seats. Don't move an eyelash and don't mess with Buttercup. He may look like a soggy paper bag, but he's a fifty-belt Judo expert and with one karate chop, he could send you flying to Wilcox Hospital. Au revoir, mes petits."

On dangerous ground, I added the French showing these Hollywood types that I was someone to be reckoned with. Worse yet, there wasn't even the remotest degree of a Judo belt inside of Buttercup. Standing next to me, was a skinny, wide-eyed, red-headed local boy who hadn't dried off.

When I spoke next, I crossed my fingers, "Buttercup, stand at the entrance and let no one in or out of this room, even if they say they have go to the bathroom. Let them pee in their pants."

Cowboy Tony crossed his legs.

"Now, I am off to find Miss Buscher. Remember, we don't want anybody to leave this room because we don't want the killer to escape into the coconut grove, do we? Do we?"

Spiel finished, I sped for Grace and Big John. I looked left, then right, and then spied them walking briskly to the Palace in the Palms. I could see them clearly as their bodies were silhouetted in the dark by the flaming torches. The other telltale sign: Grace's identifiable white wicker basket glowed in the dark, carried by Big John.

I ran down the path and called hysterically, "Miss Buscher and Big John, come quick!"

Grace turned towards me. Her eyes warned me that she had consumed two scotches at the cocktail party. "Now what?" she growled.

"Lillie!"

She pressed her fingers on my lips and hissed, "Quiet, Percy. You're causing a scene."

I pushed her fingers away and stammered: "Lillie-Lillie . . . M-miss Russell b-bit . . . bit the dust in the Flame Room."

"Bit the dust? Explain yourself, young man. I can't understand you."

Miss Buscher's policy was: First, if anyone dies at the Coco Palms, never utter out loud the word death or let on in any manner that a death had occurred at the hotel. Her theory: the death word ruins vacations. Second, send for the hearse to retrieve the body only after midnight. Grace reasoned that after midnight, the guests were fast asleep in their rooms and weren't likely to see a shiny, black Cadillac hearse driven into the hotel driven by Mr. Souza. Her main objective was to keep her guests sleeping peacefully in their beds and keep them from thinking they could be next on the Grim Reaper's list. Third, call Charlie Fern, the editor of the Garden Island. Offer him three free dinners to keep the dead person's name out of his obituary column. A guest dying on holiday at the Coco Palms was not to be acknowledged, ever. In Grace's world, no one could die at the Coco Palms. In her book, a death could cause a massive checkout and the Coco Palms was not about to earn the reputation as a bad luck hotel. To make sure that only good luck surrounded the hotel, Grace planted red ti leaves all over the place and obliterated thirteen as a room number. That's why I stammered obliquely to her, "bit the dust."

Frustrated, to make myself clearer to Grace, I slashed a finger across my neck and rat-tat-tatted, "Lillie expired; passed away; went the way of all flesh; went to her glory; croaked; kicked the bucket; and was MURDERED! Get it, now, Miss Buscher?"

Big John reached out his big brown, muscled hands and was prepared to squash an ant—me. The red in his eyes indicated that he was going to pick up the ant and throw it bodily into the lagoon. I had a momentary cosmic revelation,: I was going to join Lillie in heaven or wherever the hell she went to.

Miss Buscher intervened, "No, Big John!" The sound of Grace's voice had the power to stop a charging tiger, a raging, stomping elephant, an avalanche cascading down a mountainside, and now blessedly, my death.

I still forgot myself and added a sassy codicil: "Miss Buscher, if Big John had killed me, you would have had two murders at the hotel and it would have been hard for you to disguise two murders as the black hearse can only fit one body in it at a time—especially since I am so fat. Anyway, you can't kill me. I know too much. Nah, nah, nah."

Miss Buscher grabbed the basket out of Big John's hand and was ready to fly me to the moon. This time, thankfully, Big John intervened, and took the basket away from Grace and gritted his teeth, and said, "Show us the body, Percy."

Up to my ankles in a puddle of sweat, I proudly announced: "I've kept all the suspects in the Flame Room and one of them has to be the murderer."

In seconds, I gave my report of Lillie's death to Grace. She soaked up all the details quickly up to the time when Lillie collapsed on the floor. Reaching the entrance to the Flame Room, Grace patted my tushy; it was her sign that I was forgiven.

I wished people would keep from touching/pinching my big, fat, moon-shaped buttocks. Some do it for luck; I am their rabbit's foot. Most want to know if my two man-size cream puffs are for real not silicone implants. For Grace, patting my tush meant that I was now part of her team. She learned that ritual watching football players walk off the playing-field.

Miss Buscher strode into the Flame Room, peered down at Lillie's body and swatted with her basket a squadron of mosquitoes circling the corpse. I told her she had earned the Silver Star for downing, in one swat, ten mosquitoes that headed for Lillie's body diving in a kamikaze attack.

Grace ordered, "Big John, carry Miss Russell's body over to Cottage 5. RIGHT NOW! Carry her upright in your arms - make it look as if she's had one too many. I don't want the island or the press to know what has just occurred in this room. Then, quickly, come right back here. I'll wait for you."

"The rest of you," Grace eyed the suspects, "gather up your belongings and be ready to follow me. Percy, go to the front desk and get the key to the Blue Hawaii Coconut suite. Open it up before we get there." After I left, she turned back to the suspects, "No words, no questions from anyone in this room. And when I say move: YOU MOVE!"

"You can't do dis to me . . ." spoke Eric as if he was about to jump out of his skin.

"I can and will do *dis to you,* that is, if you don't want to spend the next month or two behind bars inside Montgomery's Hotel— that's our name for our quaint county jail."

"But—" Gretchen butted in.

Eric whimpered, "Zhut up, Gretchen. I read bad things about ze cement jail with commode in the middle of cell. I make study of dat jail ven I vant to make, *Down the Drain behind the Bars.* But Miss Buscher, I vill pro—"

"Enough!"

Hearing Grace speak "enough," Eric panicked and squeezed his sphincter. General George S. Patton was alive and well living at the Coco Palms Hotel.

Out of breath, Big John joined us again and told Grace he had a difficult time stuffing Lillie into one of the closets.

Big John standing beside her, Grace ordered, "No more questions or comments from you Mr. von Bismark. Everyone follow me! MOVE! Walk calmly out of the room. Big John will be behind all of you just in case you want to pull any monkey business. Heads up, put a smile on your faces, and pretend that nothing has happened in here. Come here, Big John."

Grace whispered something into Big John's ear, "Elvis Presley, Rice, and you know who to call."

Minutes later, after I ran to the front desk, keys in my hand, I opened the door to the Blue Hawaii Coconut suite. Grace had this suite especially made for the Elvis Presley's *Blue Hawaii* movie production company. The suite was another one of Grace's fabulous hotel creations come true. She had decorated the room with blue palm fronds, blue toilet water, blue bedspreads, gold-flecked blue mirrors on the ceiling, on the walls, and gold coconut lights that hung from the ceiling that rained blue crystal teardrops. This suite was especially decorated for Paramount producer Hal B. Wallis. Grace designated the suite to be Wallis' *Blue Hawaii* production office.

Grace prodded the suspects into the room using her white basket. She wielded her basket as adeptly as Roy Rogers did in *The Arizona Kid* when he cracked a bull whip to round up frisky heifers into a corral.

"Sit down!" General Buscher spoke.

Obedient as French Foreign Legion recruit, marooned in the middle of the Sahara Desert, the younger recruits stretched out on the beds, and the over-sixties headed for the stuffed chairs. They all kept their eyes glued on Grace. Kiss-ass Twinkle-toes Tommy sat on the floor smack in front of Grace and crossed his legs lady-like. Wanting her approval, Tommy showed Grace all his capped, white teeth.

Big John, briefly gone, came back, bulldozed himself to the center of the room holding room keys and announced, "Woke up Sheriff Rice. He grumble plenty at me. Tell me to tell you he make drive from Lihue but only for you. He stay plenty hot under the collar. But when I say Lillie Russell, he put on pants."

"Good, Big John. Call Jiro at home and tell him to—"

"He gets mad at me if I wake him."

"I know he's sleeping, not to worry, tell him to fix a dozen assorted tuna salad, ham, turkey, and egg salad sandwiches and deliver them to this Suite 555. Have Mouse set up a portable bar in this room. Check on Buttercup. I think he fell into the lagoon. Have Donald leave his desk chores and bartend in here instead of Buttercup."

Grace, her eyes fixed on the weary suspects, predicted to Big John, correctly, "This is going to be a long night."

"Phone Marlene, Big John, and tell her you won't be home tonight. We don't want your wife to wait up for you thinking all sorts of things. But don't tell her why. We have to keep the murder of Lillie Russell our secret. Remember, I don't want the whole island knowing about this."

CHAPTER FOURTEEN

August 25, 1960 – The 1960 Olympics opens in Rome.

When the shock of Lillie's murder had worn off, each suspect tried to make sense of what had happened to them only an hour ago in the Flame Room.

Eric and the Lizard Lady argued tooth and nail about how and why Lillie died. Eric shouted at Alice that Lillie would be alive if Alice had kept her mouth shut. In the excitement of the fight, Eric dropped his accent.

"The wine poisoned her without a doubt, Eric darling."

"You stupid bitch, Lillie had a heart attack."

"I know who did it," said Alice, looking menacingly at Eric.

"Keep your mouth shut and keep your opinions to yourself if you know what's good for you, or you could be next!"

As the fight between Alice and Eric continued, Raul and Tony circled the suite, showing off their dorsal fins. It was as if two white sharks were imprisoned in a fish tank, looking for a way out.

"It sure doesn't make dang sense, Raul."

"If we don't get out of this damned place, out of Kauai, we could be stuck on this island for years, even decades, unless someone finds the killer," reasoned Raul.

Raul looked sideways at Big John standing at the door, and whispered, "As long as Big John is around, we don't stand a Mexican rat's ass chance to head for the border."

Dockie had collapsed in a heap on the bed and fell into a deep stupor, snoring, but not before he confided to Grace that he was certain from the color of her face, Lillie had been poisoned. Between his snores, musical toots, and train whistles, not to be discussed in polite company, dead to the world, everyone in the room dismissed Dockie and what he said to Grace.

The whining began.

"I demand you let me out of here!" demanded Raul to Grace. He next tried to sound as convincing as Pancho Villa sitting on a john in a Tijuana jail, facing a sheriff at gun point. "You have no right to keep me cooped up in here like a prisoner."

Tony lowered his voice, acting the role of the deputy-sheriff he played so well in his only screen hit, *Cactus Thorns on the Pecos.* "I didn't kill Lillie, ma'am. None of us did."

"What a preposterous thought that any of us in this room would have killed Lillie," sniffed Gretchen, looking out the window at the torches flickering in the coconut grove.

Alice, the Lizard Lady, stood and screeched hysterically, "I know who killed Lillie. I know exactly what Lillie was talking about and who she was talking about!"

Eric yanked Alice back into the chair and struck her on the head with his pith helmet, shouting, "SHUT UP! YOU VANT TO GET US THROWN INTO JAIL? SHUT UP, YOU STUPID VOMAN!"

Alice shoved Eric away from her, held her head, and burst into a flood of crocodile tears. It was the first time since she arrived at the hotel that I felt sorry for Alice. Although she didn't speak another word but I knew from the way she kept looking at Grace that Alice was onto something BIG.

After that outburst, I was certain that the Lizard Lady was a marked woman. I was sure that she was next on the killer's list.

"Mr. von Bismark," Grace growled, stalking the Hun like a tigress going in for the kill.

Standing in front of him, Grace said slowly, so he would not miss a word she said, and threatened, "If . . . if you ever hit a defenseless woman or anyone else in this room, in my presence, I will personally see to it that you be sent somewhere on this island where you will never, ever, see the light of day again. Do you understand me, sir?"

Eric became speechless. Hiding behind the pith helmet, Eric knew that, without a doubt, the woman standing in front of him would and send him to jail..

Grace menaced further, "Did you hear me? I do not and will not tolerate bullies in my hotel!"

Eric nodded.

Grace looked at Alice and taking her hand into hers, she asked, "Can I help you, Mrs. von Bismark? Are you all right?"

"No," Alice sobbed.

Grace gently stroked her stringy hair and asked, "Do you need medical attention?"

Gently nudging Grace's hand away from her hair, she whimpered, "No. Please, please leave me alone."

"Alice, if you have information that can help us solve this mystery, please tell me or Sheriff Rice when he arrives."

Hearing the words "Sheriff Rice," everyone in the room pressed on their red alert buttons, except Dockie, who continued to snore having a nightmare—sex with Heidi in her vault room.

Loud staccato knocks shook the carved wooden palms on the suite's door. Grace's Pandora's Box opened up and the Blue Hawaii room turned into a three-ring circus.

Mouse, the clown of the kitchen, looking more like Mickey Mouse than Mickey Mouse, weaved into the room balancing three stacks of trays piled with sandwiches oozing Best Foods Mayonnaise (guess who added that to the order). Behind the pantry boy, Mutt lumbered into the room looking as a weary as Dumbo the Elephant. He dragged the collapsible makeshift bar behind him and, with a muscular free arm carried a basket of bottles of hard liquor, mixes, and a bucket filled with ice. Leftover peanuts and crackers from Lillie's party were added to the mix. Following Mutt, Big John stormed into the room with Sheriff Rice in tow. At first look, Sheriff Rice had the look of a lion tamer in a circus or a brassy master of ceremonies in a Las Vegas girly strip show. The Sheriff immediately took center stage.

Rice, wearing a crooked badge on his right shirt pocket, boomed out, "Gracie, honey, I came as soon as I could put on my pants. I drove in record time down by the golf course and passed blood alley without any naughty night marchers doing their ghostly deeds on me.

"If you'd behave yourself, Sherriff, you wouldn't have to worry about those floating spirits," chided Grace.

"Clementine broke a record getting me from Lihue to Coco Palms."

"Clementine?"

"My vintage model T, not my horse, Gracie."

Standing in the middle of the room, Sheriff Rice spread out his bowlegs so wide that a sugar train could have billowed black smoke up his crotch. Taking a deep breath, he circled the room and gave each suspect the once--over. Immediately, the suspects sat up, except for Dockie, he was still snoring and poop-poop-a-pooping.

Feeling the fierce gaze of the sheriff on their faces, and by the looks of his enormous stomach, the suspects anticipated that the sheriff was about to rip out his six-shooter and plug 'em.

With Sheriff Rice in the room, the suspects'fears had come true—they were never going to leave Kauai; or at the very least, would be locked up for life in the Kauai jail.

The Montgomery Hotel jail had earned the reputation similar to the rusty ones found in Tijuana, Mexico. The Kauai jail was comparable to the one in Mexico, where captured Pancho Villa had the trots after drinking too many bad Tequilas. That Mexican jail received five stars for its fleas. The Montgomery Hotel rated a Michelin one star for its creamed tuna, two stars for its toilets, and five stars for its ocean view.

Since he was familiar to me, I can accurately describe Sheriff Rice as a man of large girth, fat—immense. He had a big head, popping eyes, bushy eyebrows, walrus mustache, florid complexion, and a Cuban cigar stuck out of the right side of his mouth. His red flannel nightshirt stuck out the backside of his pants, making him appear, to me, a Falstaff among sheriffs.

"I'm Sheriff George Harry Rice. So that there is no misunderstanding among any of you, on Kauai, my word is law."

He gave them a long, lingering, menacing look before he turned to Grace, "Gracie, what's going on here at the Coco Palms that's so important you had to wake me out of a Technicolor Marilyn Monroe dream."

"There's been a murder, Sheriff."

"Murder?"

"Lillie Russell, the movie star."

"Oh baby. Sorry to hear that, gal. She was my all-time favorite movie star."

After Grace got him up to speed on the details of the murder, he again scanned the suspects. He wanted to see this time if he could find a guilty look in any of their eyes.

Finding that they all looked guilty, he growled, "When I discover the maverick who killed my favorite movie star, that varmint can be sure our punishment on Kauai is quick, sure, and swift. Without a please have mercy on me, out you go in the ocean with the sharks with no fuss, no muss. We save money on Kauai by not having hangings or electrocutions in our paradise. Gracie, what evidence have we got?"

Pointing to Dockie, Grace offered, "The doctor lying on the bed, snoring, thinks Lillie was poisoned. I had her body removed by Big John to Cottage 5 to wait for the hearse to pick her up. You might want to order an autopsy."

Looking down at Tommy, flashing his white teeth at the sheriff, Rice asked, "What's your name, boy? "Tommy Twinkle."

"Really?"

"Really."

"Well, Twinkie Toes get off your twinkly arse and wake up that old fool I want to ask him a few questions; in fact, I want to ask all of you a few questions. If any of you need to go to the bathroom, use that door over there, or if you get thirsty or hungry, or need to get a drink or grab some of them sandwiches over there, now is the time to do it. You aren't moving from this room until I've interviewed all of you. Get off your arses and get a move on."

About to meet their doom, the suspects lined up to tinkle. Inside the bathroom, locking the door, some tinkled in the toilet, but most threw up their shrimp cocktail into the seventy-pound giant clam shell basin, with the exception of Tony the Cowboy. Tony peed the Yangtze River into the blue water making the toilet water become the color of the Amazon River.

While the suspects attended to their necessities, the sheriff questioned Grace, "Any other evidence?"

I piped up, "The dolls."

"Oh my God, I forgot about the dolls. Percy, take my key and run back to the Flame Room. Get the dolls and show them to the sheriff. George, I locked them up inside the Flame Room just in case you needed fingerprints."

I grabbed a soggy egg salad sandwich, drenched in Best Foods Mayonnaise—for strength you know—and ran to retrieve the dolls.

My thought as I left for the Flame Room and the dolls was: If you happen to get into a crisis like I was in, mayonnaise gives you courage, makes you happy, makes you brave, makes you handsome, and clears up zits. But, most of all, and I know this for certain, it makes you own the most beautiful, the biggest, the fattest arse in the whole world.

As I squiggled my fat ass out the door, I dripped mayo on my shirt. Behind me, Grace, looked at the mess I made, and warned, "Not one word to anyone about what is going on in this room or what happened to Lillie Russell. If I hear that you have opened your mouth, you will spend the last of your productive days cleaning out the toilets in the Montgomery Hotel without a bottle of mayonnaise in sight. Listen to what I am saying, Percy. If you don't obey me, as further punishment, I will send you to the Kauai Surf Hotel with my compliments."

I found it difficult to skirt a path to the Flame Room without running into the pestering night staff who badgered me with a thousand questions.

Nora the Nosy was the most persistent and kept asking me, "What's happening in the Blue Hawaii Palms suite?"

Wiping mayo off my mouth, I whispered, "I am sworn to secrecy but I can tell you this,: without my help, Miss Buscher would be in the soup. As to what happened in the Flame Room, it's mum's the word!"

I added mysteriously, now rubbing mayo off my pants, and, as I stabbed my heart dramatically, I said, "Draw your own conclusions. If you tell anyone what I just said, Miss Buscher will have you making beds at the Kauai Surf until the day you die and that's worse than going to hell."

Feeling righteous that I had followed Miss Buscher's instructions to the letter and not given anything away, I sashayed into the Flame Room.

Opening up the Flame Room door, I was jolted out of my smugness. Under the table the Lady of the Night and the Charlie McCarthy doll, like the Oedipus Rex doll, had their heads yanked forcibly away from their bodies.

When I reentered the Palm suite carrying the maimed dolls, Dockie was awake. Sheriff Rice had made the rounds of all the suspects, except for the Lizard Lady and Dockie. Alice sat in her chair and had clammed up. Her once flapping trap was shut so tight that not even a Gestapo agent could have pried her lips apart with a crowbar.

Since Sheriff Rice had discovered only a gist of what had happened, he walked to Grace and contemplated his next move. Putting his burly arm around the Coco Palms manager's waist, giving her a big bear-hug, he suggested, "Gracie, honey, if you don't mind, I'd like to interview these varmits alone or in twos or threes; I'll get more out of them that way. I have given orders to my men that none of these Hollywood types are to leave this hotel, or for that matter, this wing until I solve this case."

Fiddling with the keys in his pocket, he asked, "What's the possibility, Golden Girl, of helping me out?"

Gus had coined the name for Grace as The Golden Girl.

Hearing the sheriff call her Golden Girl, Grace flinched, thinking that if Gus knew what was going on at the Coco Palms at this very moment, he would surely fire her. But being more resolved than ever to solve this case on her own and to keep Gus from knowing anything about her madness, Grace was even more determined to get to the bottom of this mess before Elvis Presley arrived on Kauai.

Clapping her hands like a schoolmarm—a way to get children's attention, Grace explained to her "prisoners," "Here is what I am going to do. Some of this I have already put into place even before the sheriff arrived. And to be clear, there will be no comments from any of you about my plan. You will follow my instructions to the T. If not, those of you who wish to make a foolish detour from my plan will be housed at the Montgomery Hotel with the sheriff's blessing and mine."

Grace stopped her train of thought, looked at Alice, and mused out loud, "Here is what you have to look forward to if housed at the Montgomery Hotel—other than having centipedes as your roommates. If you plan to spend time in our jail, I redecorated the Montgomery prison cells during the filming of *South Pacific*. We had a slew of overbooked guests and I had nowhere else to put them. Alice, some of them were from your hometown of Pasadena and I thought the Montgomery Hotel would be an ideal alternate place for them to stay—so authentic Kauai. Alice, you will be pleased to know that, since the toilet was in the middle of the cell, I hid the ugly, old, brown toilet under a large, colorful, flowered tea cozy. Very cheerful. The salted corroded bars on the windows—I antiqued them gold. I pushed the sagging beds against the cell walls and made room for a little, white plastic table to handle room service from the prison cafeteria. As for the cots, I covered the paper thin mattresses with the most adorable quilted bedspreads designed with balls and chains, manufactured in Des Moines. Wouldn't it have been divine for a Pasadena lady of quality to tell her friends that she had stayed in jail while visiting Kauai? Gus, the spoilsport, wouldn't allow that to happen and, to make matters almost untenable to me, the local government kept all my decorations, and the county chairman, a Democrat, spread a rumor around Kauai that the interior decorator of the jail cell was the cross-eyed, illegitimate son of our Republican mayor."

Out of her reverie, the occupants in the room, aghast, looked at one another in disbelief. Each understood that anything could happen to them at the Coco Palms with a crazy woman in charge, so they had better mind their Ps and Qs.

Stupefied by conjuring up another Coco Palms legend, Grace watched to see if the masses would rise up and storm the Bastille. Finding them sitting quietly and nonplussed, Grace knew she had the prisoners in the palm of her hands and continued on course.

"I have selfish reasons for my plan: in two days, Paramount Studios arrives here to film, *Blue Hawaii*. I will not have Paramount Studios cancel out because of Lillie's murder. Lillie has a guaranteed occupancy in the King's Cottages until tomorrow afternoon.

Three o'clock being our checkout time. The day after tomorrow all the King's Cottages belong to Mr. Elvis Presley, Mr. Hal Wallis, and Paramount Studios. The Elvis Presley reservations were confirmed six months ago. On my orders, my staff has packed up your belongings and moved your things into rooms on this floor. You may not, and I stress *you may not* return to the King's Cottages for any reason. Remember what the sheriff told you. We are looking for evidence to convict the guilty party, and I will not give any of you the opportunity to vamoose out of Kauai; and most importantly, I am doing this for your own safety. I do not want another murder to occur at my Coco Palms. That being said, housing all of you on this floor will make it easier for the sheriff in his interviews. Your room assignments will be different from what you had in the King's Cottages. I hope, for your sake and mine, this will be only a two-night experience and, unfortunately, at my expense. Needless-to-say, I am going to have a hard time explaining this loss of room revenue to Mr. Guslander, my boss, and Treasurer George Shipman, in Honolulu. But that is my problem, not yours. I have less than two days to solve this murder and if I am unsuccessful, I will have no choice but to turn you over to the sheriff and then it will be up to him to do what he wants to do with all of you. I just can't imagine any of you sitting on my tea cozy in the middle of a cell."

The same old frog croaked in the lagoon.

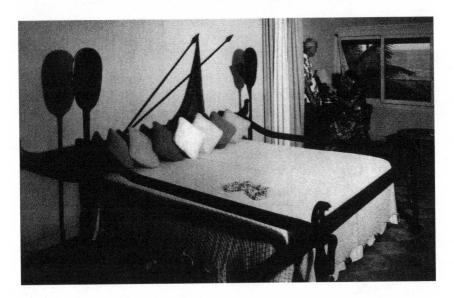

Wailua Kai Room

CHAPTER FIFTEEN

August 25, 1960 – The USS Seadragon (SSN-584) surfaces at the North Pole, where the crew plays softball.

"We will use the Blue Hawaii Suite as our meeting room. Call it our *ohana* room, our family room. Alice von Bismark, I assigned you to 2a by yourself for reasons that are so apparent to me that I am appalled that I have to do it.; room 2b—Dr. Hubert Nutt Trescutt also a single. Eric von Bismark—2c—a single; Mr. Pinto and Miss Francis 2d; Ms. Granny Myers and Mr. Tommy in 2e; Mr. Pasquale and Mrs. Yamashita in 2f. You are all adults and I don't see any reason whatsoever for my mix-matching people in my room assignments. All the rooms are located down the hallway. For your information, no other guests are housed on this floor or in this building. There is one elevator that leads to the lobby and from there it's a short walking distance to the Lagoon Dining Room. Next to the elevator is a fire stairwell that leads directly to the bar and swimming pool. Both exits will be guarded by the sheriff's men. During these two days, none of you are allowed to leave your rooms without an escort and all your meals will be served in your rooms. Since you are my guests, the food and drinks will be limited in choice and amount. If you wish anything above and beyond what I am offering you, you are to pay cash for the extras. I am not about to be stiffed by any of you, though it appears to me that I am going to be at the losing end of this entire affair. That's it. No more questions. A Hawaiian policeman, carrying a pistol, will be posted outside each of your doors. The pistol is to prevent the killer, or any of you, from getting an itch in your hitch. These men will insure all of us a good night's sleep."

Von Bismark, holding his pith helmet in front him, spat, "I vill sue you for every dime you own and destroy your career, and this filthy Coco Palms vill become nothing more than a home for cockroaches, rats, and centipedes. What do you say to that?"

Grace did not respond and performed as cool as Susan Hayward (an Academy Award winning actress) walked stoically to the gas chamber in *I Want to Liv.,* instead, Grace crooked her middle finger and signaled for the suspects to follow her single file down the hall to their rooms.

As they entered the hallway, Grace took Eric aside and answered him, "From what I have observed and experienced about you, Mr. von Bismark, I will personally see to it that my friends in the motion picture business know exactly how you have behaved here at the Coco Palms; that is, if you have not been found guilty of Lillie's murder. Then, that's another story entirely. Isn't it? When I have finished telling my tales about you to all my friends in Hollywood, Mr. Eric von Bismark. you will be most fortunate to have been hired to clean toilets at the Hollywood Studio Club."

Before von Bismark could reply, Grace faced him squarely in the face and commanded, "No more nonsense out of you, Mr. von Bismark. Big John, take Mr. von Bismark to his room. Your suitcases and personal belongings are in your rooms already and, I might add, all in good order."

"Where in the hell is that famous aloha spirit I've read about?" Tony spoke as he signaled to Tilda that he had to go badly.

"Cut the noise, Cowboy, just mosey your cute, little ass into our room. Forget the aloha spirit; that died with Lillie a couple of hours ago." Tilda shoved Tony into their room.

"Just one more question, Miss Buscher," the Mexican white knight asked before he entered his room. "Why change roommates?"

"For your protection, Mr. Raul. I wanted to break up any unhealthy alliances that may have been formed and further, I have cut all phone calls on this floor. For all intents and purposes, to the outside world, Lillie Russell is alive and well and you are still her guests attending her birthday party. As far as the Hollywood press is concerned, I have made sure that nothing untoward has happened at the Coco Palms Hotel. I repeat: I am doing all of this for your health and protection, because I know for certain that someone staying on this floor is Lillie's killer. Let's leave it at that. It's been a long night. It will be good for all of us to have a good night's sleep. Mr. Raul, for your information, the aloha spirit remains alive and well at the Coco Palms. If this had happened at any other hotel in Hawaii, or at any resort on the Mainland, or for that matter anywhere in the world, all of you would have been photographed, fingerprinted, and sent directly to the hoosegow. What would the authorities have done with you in Mexico, señor?"

"There are too many unfair laws in the United States to suit me," groused Raul.

"Someone said that to me only a few days ago after I kicked him off the grounds. He called me 'a fascist pig' for doing it and would have killed me on the spot if given the chance. The man was drunk or on drugs and he and his pit bull had terrorized our guests on private property. I called the police. They took care of him swiftly, but always staying within the law on Kauai. So, we are in need of laws for protection. If given the chance, knowing for certain that a person will not be caught, people will steal ashtrays, cheat on bills, and lie when looking you straight in the eye. Tonight, if it suits and the murderer has the opportunity, the killer will kill again. I read last night in a psychiatric journal, left behind by a guest, that amoral people justify their actions blaming the world and say with sincere conviction that their parents are the cause in their lapse in morality. Therefore, señor, within the laws of the County of Kauai, I am holding you all on a tight leash. All of you have shown to me by your actions that not one of you is to be trusted. I repeat not one of you is to be trusted. *Buenas noches, mi amigo.*"

A sulky Raul entered his room and slammed the door.

Sherriff Rice, standing behind Grace, observed, "Gracie, they all look like guilty varmints to me. But for the life of me, I can't figure out which one of them did it."

Before Dockie entered his room, he looked at Grace and nodded his head.

At that moment, looking back, there was something about Dockie that was not right. He knew something about Lillie's killing and that I was sure of.

Alice stopped in front of 2a and cried out, "I KNOW WHO DID IT AND THAT PERSON IS GOING TO FRY." Coiled at the door like a rattlesnake, fangs out ready to strike, and after spitting out her venom, the Lizard Lady stumbled into her room and shut the door quietly.

Somebody whispered in the darkened hallway: "That was a very foolish thing to do, Alice. You're going to be next."

The hall had emptied out and the policemen began to stand in front of the doors of suspects. The policemen looked at stalwart and as formidable as the Royal Household Guards of England. The same who stood at attention in front of Buckingham Palace wearing bearskin hats. Our guards' eyes signaled, "No fool around with me!"

I cradled the dolls in my hands and announced to the sheriff, "All the dolls' heads have been decapitated."

Sheriff Rice took the dolls out of my hands, inspected each head, then the bodies, looked back at me in disgust and raged, "You dunderhead, you botched the case. With your greasy mayonnaise hands all over the dolls, I'll have no fingerprints worth checking on."

I was an addle-brained fool. Doggone it, I hadn't thought about the fingerprints. But in murder mysteries, as in Shakespearean plays, the fool will turn out to be the wiseass one.

The sheriff shoved the dolls back into my arms and ordered, "Look at me, Percy. Quit daydreaming." Once my attention was back on him, the sheriff babbled on, "We are dealing with a psychopathic killer, so keep your wits about you - you could be next on his or her list." When I heard him say "next," the sheriff poked his fat finger into my fat belly to make his point.

It hurt. In retaliation, I poked my fat finger back in his fat belly. I made him hiccup. He made his point and I made mine.

Miss Buscher, out in the hallway, spoke loud enough to make sure that anyone listening behind closed doors could hear her—especially the killer. "Lillie's body has been removed from the hotel for the coroner to do a complete autopsy on her. Dr. Wallis suspects that Lillie, by the green color of her skin, was poisoned by a lethal dose of taxin—a rare poison extracted from the leaves of the yew tree."

Bong! Bong!

The blue clock in the Blue Hawaii suite struck twice. It reminded us that it was two in the morning and pitch black outside.

Back from Maui to get His swim trunks, God spilled black ink all over the hotel. Returned to Maui to sun Himself, ride the waves, eat a chicken salad sandwich at the Wailuku Hotel. With Him gone, new mischief occurred at the Coco Palms.

As I turned out the lights in the Blue Hawaii suite, standing alone in God's inky darkness, I had only one thought in my mind: this morning, all was not well at the Coco Palms Hotel. Thinking that thought, goosebumps attacked my body.

In my hearts of hearts, I knew that no matter how well each of the guests was protected sleeping in their canoe beds, the murderer would find a way into any of the rooms, break off a wooden piece from the canoe bed, and bludgeon someone senseless with it. I was right— the killer did strike and it was just before the clock bonged the hour of three.

CHAPTER SIXTEEN

September 5, 1960 – 1960 Summer Olympics take place in Rome: Cassius Clay wins the gold medal in boxing.

Six, the next morning, volcanic hysteria erupted in all the nooks and crannies of the hotel. Grace's employees scurried all over the hotel grounds going bonkers because, not knowing, about what really happened to Lillie, made the Coco Palms employees go nuts.

Living on a small island, everybody on Kauai felt they had the right to know everything about everybody. Because we live on a small island, we are all cooked up in the same pot. We, the people on Kauai, just can't help ourselves. We must know what's cooking in our stew— especially, when somebody added a pinch of hot chili peppers into the pot. Jolljamit, we demand to know who the hell put the spice in and WHY! Working for Miss Buscher kept me on my toes. and the Lillie Russell murder was frosting on the cake.

That morning, from the hotel corridors to the hinterlands of the coconut grove, the staff had spread the most outlandish rumors about Lillie Russell. All the gossip, added up to one thing —not one person knew the real scoop.

What made it even more maddeningly crazy for me was Miss Buscher had bolted her office door since 6 a.m. She made sure that all us nosy Parkers couldn't hear the shenanigans being plotted in her war room.

Before the sun rose, Grace's musketeers—Big John, Elsie, and Mrs. Nakai —had circled their wagons inside her office. Miss Buscher made each of them take blood oaths and swear on their virginity to keep her secret plans under wraps.

Damn. Damn. Damn. I guess I was considered a part of her second string team, because I wasn't included in Grace's present goings-on. Upset at being left out of the Buscher loop, though I knew a lot, I was determined to find out all the skinny of what was now going on in Miss Buscher's war room.

First: I interviewed the hardcore Coco Palms' blabber mouths—staff members who wore invisible stethoscopes around their necks. These stethoscopes let them overhear things that were not to be repeated, but after hearing the tittle-tattle, the tittle-tattle was never kept under their coconut hats. Spreading gossip, true or not, was these blabbermouths' reason to live.

All I got from one of them was, "I know nothing. Go to Mrs. Nakai's room."

Squaring back my shoulders, pretending I was a soldier on the front lines with bullets whizzing all about me, I walked to Mrs. Nakai's room. As I hungered to be on the front line, the I-knew-it-first team, my strategy was to hide behind a garbage can outside Mrs. Nakai's basement sewing room. As soon as I lifted the garbage lid, smelled the fragrance of rotten, fermented pig's feet, I did penance as I overheard Mrs. Nakai gossiping to Grace on the telephone. The smell of rotten garbage now wafting into my nostrils, I was inspired to make up a slogan: "Loose Lips will help Percy catch the killer."

Wasn't I dumb!

Not so dumb. I knew that amid the whirring sound of her sewing machine, Mrs. Nakai wheedled juicy morsels of information out from any housemaid, the yardman, bartender, and especially the bellmen who had unpacked the guests' suitcases. Mrs. Nakai's sewing room was located under the lobby, it was sound proof. Coco Palms informants shared confidences freely to Mrs. Nakai, knowing that no one could hear them and it was all in accordance with the gospel of Grace Buscher's Coco Palms Bible and Mrs. Nakai's doctrine of Zen Buddhist teachings. Mrs. Nakai's phone was busy all-day long from her war room to Grace's war room with the latest news of who did to what to whom and where.

Beginning to smell like a rotten cabbage, I heard Mrs. Nakai whisper into the phone that one of the housemaids had spilled the beans about Lillie Russell's disappearance to two major gossip snoops in Hollywood.

"Miss Buscher," whispered Mrs. Nakai. "I stay hear Bitsy after she clean King's Cottage, I don't know where she get the smarts, phone Hollywood gossip columnists, Louella Parsons, and Hedda Hopper. Bitsy tell Lillie Russell dead or near dead, because she no sleep in room. Bitsy tell the maids, Rhonda and Harriet who tell me that Hollywood gossip ladies tell Bitsy that Paramount Studios going to cancel Elvis Presley *Blue Hawaii* movie."

A waft of rotten meat hit my nose, and that smell—and this is a real don't-tell—reminded me of Bitsy.

From a good source—my old, wet bartender friend, Buttercup—I heard that Bitsy was a raging alcoholic. She was delusional about her importance on the housekeeping staff. Once a week, like clockwork, Bitsy passed out and slept her hangover off behind a potted palm near the ladies' bathroom in the lobby. She never made a bed in the allotted ten-minute time, but continued to think that she was the number one housekeeper. Sometimes, Bitsy's gossip was close to the truth, but most times it never hit the mark. Bitsy's ace in the hole and the reason she kept her job at the Coco Palms: she was the mother-in-law of the mayor—and that was a big ace in the hole, especially if you lived on Kauai.

Mrs. Nakai, squeaking, continued to talk about Bitsy to Grace. "She stay criticize you behind your back. She tell everyone in the hotel that she can run Coco Palms more better than you even with her five little fingers tied up with a string. Bitsy tells everyone she is the queen of the Coco Palms, not you. Everybody knows she is terrible bed-maker, no take out the brown stains in the toilet bowls, and has the biggest toilet gossip mouth in Coco Palms. But Miss Buscher, everyone in the hotel stay away from her now, cause Bitsy has bad breath. Too much drink."

Bitsy's breath was known to wilt orchids, change people complexions, and tarnish silver.

"Moreover, Miss Buscher, no one in hotel can prove that the Bitsy's rumor no true, but as far as calling Hollywood, that's one big lie."

What was true, Mrs. Nakai informed Miss Buscher that Bitsy was nursing a big hangover, and had wilted a hundred-dollar floral orchid arrangement she carried to Room 234. She was in a mood and outright mean.

There are people in this world who just want to be mean for no other reason than just wanting to be mean. Bitsy was one of them.

I offered Miss Buscher a cure for Bitsy meanness: chew two tablets of Ex-Lax. It promises to clear up complexions and bad behavior.

Dishwasher Herman, my great source of titillating gossip, confided out of hearing, recovered from a bad breath attack from

Bitsy, squealed, "Eh, brah, Bitsy no have the *kala* to call Hollywood, California. Where she get the moolah? No worry about Bitsy. She one big fat, ugly ass, dragon breath, rat fink!"

In Grace's and the Coco Palms' favor, spreading rumors in 1960 was difficult as Kauai was in the middle of the Pacific, and news from the Mainland arrived on Kauai on a slow boat to China." When news from Kauai reached Beverly Hills, the information was a week old and oft times not reliable and more times than not "Gone with the Wind."

After hearing the Bitsy story, Grace became cautious: Not taking any chances, she ordered Itsui, the hotel telephone operator, to respond to any phone calls from the Mainland from reporters to deny any rumor about Lillie's death and to add that Miss Russell ate a half a papaya and drank her coffee that morning in her cottage and I she is very much alive. If that piece of information won't squash the reporter's curiosity, confide to the caller that Lillie had been afflicted with the Coco Palms curse— too many gin and coconut milks the night before. The movie star extraordinaire is sitting on the pot— too occupied to answer the phone even if her life depended on it. Translated, Lillie Russell is cursed with the legendary Kauai trots.

The most reliable rumor of the morning arrived from Sleepy, the chubby bellhop, who wandered everyday aimlessly around the hotel with half-mast eyes. That morning, he won the coin toss and delivered the breakfast trays to the suspects on the second floor.

Sleepy reported to the other bellmen: "When I reach Lizard Lady's room, she no answer knock. Calvin, the policeman, handsome guy like one Clark Gable, use pass key open up door. I drop breakfast tray when Calvin say, 'no look.' He tell me nude body on floor with centipedes crawling all over it. I run for my No Doze."

Calvin slammed the door shut and locked it. Following instructions, he searched for Miss Buscher and advised her to come to Room 2a pronto. That's all Sleepy knew about the Lizard Lady Alice drama, but he was dang sure something deadly happened inside of Room 2a.

For me, the word *centipede* was the zinger in his story, but the second time Sleepy repeated his story, he embellished it and made it more dangerous. He embellished his story with a dozen scorpions—so typical of Coco Palms gossip.

Later in the morning—this isn't a rumor, because I actually overheard Elsie on the phone talking to the local police department—as she jotted down the message, she said out loud, "Sheriff Rice has left for Hilo. Brother dying. Gracie, you are in charge of the Russell case."

Oh, baby, I remember telling myself: Grace was going to have her wish come true and become a Miss Marple. She was to become the Agatha Christie crime solver detective of the Coco Palms . . . of Kauai . . . of the whole world. I asked God, please don't come back from Maui and please, please, please, have Grace make me be her number one son, Charlie Chan."

After Elsie took the message into Grace's inner 'sanctum, not a second passed when I heard Grace scream. It was a scream that would have sent Attila the Hun running for his mother.

After the scream, Grace shouted to Elsie, "Find Percy! I'm sure that sneaky scamp is somewhere outside my office and probably has his ear glued to my door."

Prying my ear away from the door, Elsie dragged me into Grace's office. Thoughts came into my head that I was to be sentenced to the guillotine or burned at the stake for spying, I walked into her office Grace, hanging my head, and wanted to ask for mercy.

I stood awaiting my death sentence and nothing happened. I found Grace was distracted. She was observing a small, wide-eyed intruder, a gecko, make its way across the ceiling.

My jaw hung to the floor as Grace spoke slowly still watching as the lizard as head out her office door. the floor, "I am sure you heard everything that Elsie told me, that Sheriff Rice has put me in charge of the Russell case. I want you to listen carefully: first, it is unfair of him to do that. Second, I am a hotel manager, not a law enforcement officer; third, I wish he'd have left me alone to run my hotel and put someone, other than me, in charge.of the Russell case"

I thought that Grace's words didn't ring altogether true.

The gecko looked for a way to exit the office as Grace took a cigarette out of her basket, lit it, and inhaled. After blowing smoke out of her mouth, she spoke, "I will to do anything in my power to make sure *Blue Hawaii* will be filmed here even if it means playing detective for Sheriff Rice. I am so worried that if *Blue Hawaii* does not happen at the Coco Palms, the hotel will lose millions of dollars in revenue and in publicity. The hotel could be foreclosed within a week and, you and I, and everyone else working here at the hotel, will be banished from the premises. We could spend the rest of our days picking up shells. And it could happen, my boy. So, what I am about to tell you is privy for your ears only. If you spill the beans, I promise you there will be another unsolved murder at this hotel. And against my better judgment, I am about to confide to you a grave secret. From past experiences, I do not tell sensitive hotel business to anyone because there are certain things that occur at the Coco Palms that are only my business. I have not told Gus including my best friends, Myrtle Lee and George Shipman about Lillie Russell and now, Alice. Why I am about to trust you with Coco Palms' future and mine, I find it hard to explain. Either, I am crazy or desperate. But you have been in this mess since the beginning and now it is time for you to grow up and become a man. Are you ready to grow up, Percy? Ready to leave your childish *Photoplay*—movie star fantasies behind? Because we are dealing with a real killer who is on the loose at my hotel and who could murder any one of us at any moment, at any time." Grace paused and whispered with great conviction, "if this person so chooses."

I tinkled a little as I watched the gecko trying to leave the office.

"GET THAT GECKO, PERCY!" yelled Grace. "TAKE THAT BROOM IN THE CORNER AND SWEEP THAT UGLY CREATURE OUT OF MY OFFICE."

I got the broom, opened the office door, and swept away and flew offending gecko for Elsie's desk.

As I closed the door and put the broom away, Grace drew in a breath and continued. "Calvin, the policeman, came for me and Big John this morning because something dreadful happened to Alice, speaking of unfortunate geckos. Immediately, I ran to Room 2a. The Lizard Lady—that's your expression, I believe—was laid flat out in the middle of the room, nude and dead. Her face had turned a purple color. What made Alice look so ghastly was that her eyes were wide open and from the look in her eyes, her stare, I had the impression that Alice, Mrs. von Bismark, had met the devil. Her lizard mouth had been silenced with masking tape. The unspeakable horror of the scene was the slithering centipedes, by the dozens, crawling all over her nude body."

Hearing from Grace, thinking of purple Alice, I needed a big jolt of Gone with the Wind's Aunt Pittypat's smelling salts to keep me from fainting

Crack! Grace slapped her hand hard on that desk. It kept me from falling down in a dead heap before her. When the color on my face returned, she continued, "Big John used Calvin's nightstick to sweep the centipedes off her body. He gathered up all those awful creatures into the corner of the room and...," Grace stamped her foot on the floor when she said, "killed all of them with his boots. Three things I hate at my hotel: rats being number one, centipedes a close second, and third a nosy employee. Now I have a fourth hate: a murderer."

At least I came after the rats.

"It is clear to me and to Big John that Mrs. Alice Downes von Bismark was murdered by the same person who killed Lillie Russell."

She paused to let me digest the last sentence.

Picking up the thread of her story, Grace continued, "Now, my lad, since we have little time to clear up the murders, I am counting on you and Big John's assistance. Big John covered Alice's body with a sheet, stuffed her body in a laundry cart, and pushed it down into Mrs. Nakai's sewing room. He hid the laundry cart in the back of the room, behind a rusty old sewing machine, where Mrs. Nakai keeps her cleaning rags. Tonight, after all the guests have retired, Mr. Souza's hearse will pick up Alice at the back entrance of the kitchen. I told the mortuary to paint the hearse yellow to make it look like one of Mr. Otsuka's honey pot wagons. But before that, Dr. Wallis will do a preliminary autopsy on her body, at noon, behind a screen, of course, in the sewing room. Mrs. Nakai will burn a ton of incense while Dr. Wallis is doing his procedure. Alice smells of turnips. The smell of turnips, from my study of poisons, indicates that Alice was not killed by the centipedes but by something more lethal. Dr. Wallis will clear up my notion during his autopsy. I want to be sure that Alice died from poison not from the stings of the centipedes. If her turnip smell wafts from the sewing room into the dining room, I solved that one with Jiro. I am in luck because today' on Jiro's buffet luncheon menu for the bus loads of Japanese tourists from Osaka, he featured his special of the day: 'medium-rare liver, onions, garlic topped with a braised turnip sauce.'"

Grace glanced for my reaction.

I wanted to throw up.

"The braised turnips were my idea. Wasn't I the clever one? Now the questions remain: how did the centipedes get into the room and if she was poisoned—how? Now that I am in charge of the case, I have devised a plan. I am going to call a meeting with all the suspects, reveal to them Alice's death, and see if I can discover a guilty reaction on their faces."

Grace put out her Viceroy cigarette and lit a filtered Camel one. Exhaling a lazy stream of smoke into the air, she said, "Let's you and I watch their reactions. The guilty person is bound to give himself away----or maybe it's a her."

Making kiss-ass to Grace to keep in her good graces, I wooed her by saying: "You are a truly gifted detective, Miss Buscher—better than ten Sherlock Holmes. Please, please consider me to be your inscrutable Charlie Chan, your second-in-command."

Grace wooed back, "Sometimes, and only sometimes do I think you are worthy of your salt, Percy."

For the rest of my days at the Coco Palms, I tried to become the best kiss-asser in the hotel because I found out that "ogging people" worked!

Grace said: "Before lunch, I'll have the guards gather up all the suspects for a meeting in the Palm suite and that should keep all the nosy Parkers, inside or outside the hotel from learning about the murders. I've instructed Jiro to send two trays of food to Mrs. von Bismark's room. That ruse should keep all the press snoops quiet for the afternoon. You can also stop any rumors of Lillie's death by spreading it around the hotel that Lillie Russell and Alice von Bismark are now roommates and are very much alive. Bottom line, we want Elvis here at Coco Palms making *Blue Hawaii*. I keep repeating this, because it is so important for my survival. Alright? I am counting on you, Mr. Smarty Pants? Right? I repeat, I am counting on you, Mr. Smarty Pants. Right? Right? RIGHT?"

After her third "right," my lips puckered, and I just couldn't help myself smile, being that I was now the world's consummate kiss-ass. I, true to form, I gushed to Grace, "You're smarter than three Sherlock Holmess, four Miss Maples, and five Charlie Chans."

"Right you are, my number one son." Grace lobbed a ball of flattery back into my court and it hit my soft spot—my battered ego. Holding her ball in my hands, she made me feel like a big shot.

Oops!

I swaggered out of Grace's office, feeling I was "king of the mountain," I forgot about the banana peel that waited for me to slip on and crack my head open on the concrete walkway. Like a stupid Humpty Dumpty—one that I had been since the day I was born—I forgot that something bad always happens to me when I believed I had become someone special.

Slipping on banana peels was God's gift to me to keep me from feeding my big, fat ego. A crack on the head brought me back to reality and made me remember who I really was: a poor, stupid human being like everyone else. Now that I had become a professional kiss-ass, I had become lower than a dung beetle.

But my ego, that day, won the battle. I told myself to hell with the banana peel, the dung beetle, and old Humpty Dumpty. Life was all about ME! ME, CHARLIE CHAN, THE GREAT!

CHAPTER SEVENTEEN

1970--Rock band Jefferson Airplane co-founder Paul Kanter states, "If you can remember anything about the sixties, then you weren't really there."

I delivered handwritten notes to the suspects' rooms—notes that Grace had scrawled in haste. I was feeling on top of the mountain after receiving my blessing from Miss Buscher. So, it was a cocky, little, fat delivery boy who presented notes stuffed in green envelopes to the suspects. Hands on my hips, I smirked at the suspects as they tore open their envelopes. With glee, I waited for their reactions, tapping my foot on the floor.

The message inside the green envelope read: "Meet the hotel manager in the Blue Hawaii suite at 11 a.m." Without showing any appreciation for my personal service, without giving me a civil reply, they shoved me out of the door and snapped that if I didn't get out of their sight that very instant, they were going to bite my head off.

I made a hasty retreat and grumbled out loud for everyone to hear me, "I am only the messenger."

I felt unappreciated and performed a Pinocchio. I circled back to the suspects' rooms, knocked on every door, smiled, and said sweetly, "this is a don't tell" but, the meeting is an announcement that their immediate release from the hotel. I giggled riding down the elevator, because each and every one of the dummies believed me.

At eleven, the guards pummeled the suspects single file down the hallway and steered them into the Blue Hawaii suite—all expecting their freedom. Overhearing Raul talk about his release from the Coco Palms, on reaching the door of the suite, the guards informed him that they were not being released.

That disappointing news made each suspect tack into their brains a mental list of complaints. At the top of their complaint list was Me. The dirty trick I had played on them, each suspect thought that I was the worst little fat wise-ass kid they had ever encountered. A codicil to their list was a recommendation for my demise: fire met, boil me, and then drown me in the lagoon. Better yet—tar and feather me. For the first time since Lillie died, the suspects were in agreement about one thing: kill the messenger.

Without sleep, the guards had become grumpy. They were not about to take shit from these gaggling geese. They shoved the prisoners one by one into the suite and before they entered, each suspect was warned by the guards by demonstrating a finger slicing across their necks—to be polite to Miss Buscher . . . or else.

, The first thing they encountered, walking into the suite, was Grace, Big John, and me standing at the opposite end of the room. With the view of the coconut grove behind us, the suspects saw faces as forbidden as three Easter Island totem poles. My side, the thing I noticed after they entered the suite was that Dockie Wockie wasn't among them.

Once inside the suite, von Bismark took off his pith helmet, threw it on the bed, walked around the room, sized up the situation, and looked for a possible escape. With a Germanic look on his face and his rigid stance, Eric acted as if he was about to direct one of his major box-office failures: *I Caught Your Hand Under My Skirt.*

Eric, puffed up as if he was the director in charge, barked menacingly, "When I get released from this hell hole, and can get my hands on a telephone, I will sue this island, this hotel, that damned police chief, and, of course, you, Miss Buchwhack, for everything you own. You are at the top of my list to sue after that fat, little twerp standing over there."

ME!

Granny, leaned against a wall for support, and cackled: "Shut up, Eric. I want this done with . . . over with . . . as much as you do and to hell with Lillie. She's dead and she was a curse to me all my life. I want out of here because I have plans to get on with my life. I have things to do before I die." Her words spoken, the orange popsicle with red hair pushed me out of the way and plunked herself down in a chair. The force of her flaying arms, flew me into the wall, leaving me stunned.

This was one tough broad! She had the strength of a killer.

Slouched down in her chair, Granny, advised. "Get on with it, Gracie, and forget that dick," she gestured to Eric.

Grace ordered, "Everyone, sit like Granny. As soon as you are seated and quiet, I have announcements to make!" Sphincters tied in knots, suspects rushed to sit on a bed, on the floor or on any chair that was available.

Their attention captured, Grace began: "The good doctor is not with us presently. He is under the weather. I am having hot coffee poured down his throat, and, hopefully, he'll be sober enough to join us before the sun sets."

"When are we getting out of here?" Tilda interrupted, without once interjecting one of her favorite four-letter words.

"All in good time, Tilda. No more questions, please, or you will keep us here longer than either you or I care to imagine or want. Let me finish with my announcements. Sheriff Rice has left for Hilo. He deputized me to continue with this case. He is shorthanded. Two of his men are down with the flu, and felt that, I, and my Coco Palms staff, can solve this case without him being present. The Island of Kauai has much to lose if solving Lillie's mysterious death is delayed any further. Sheriff Rice feels confident that I can handle the situation. Strange, you think? This is Kauai. On Kauai, we do things differently. We are known to the other islanders, across the channel, as "the Separate Kingdom." We run our affairs according to our own likings, our own rules, and some say to our own whims. What we do is perfectly legal. So, that you know that I am quite legit, this morning, I was formally sworn in ,as a full-on deputy ,by the sheriff's brother, Judge Philip Rice."

Grace paused to let her announcement sink in. The only comment came from Eric. He mumbled into his pith-helmet, "Heil, Hitler."

Grace pretended not to hear his remark, and continued, "More disturbing news, Mr. Eric, your wife, Alice von Bismark is dead. Murdered. Her death is particularly gruesome because of the way she was killed."

Without an ounce of remorse in his voice, Eric, like his Nazi forbearers, opened up his black heart, and spewed, "She got what she deserved. I told her to shut her mouth. You should have kept me in the same room with her. I could have protected her. Now, I will sue you for even more big bucks. Let me out!"

Grace smiled at Eric and continued: "Alice's death was caused by not one centipede but by hundreds. But I have a feeling, by the smell of her body, that she was poisoned like Lillie, not killed by the centipedes. Either way, the manner in which she died is unspeakable. Her mouth was taped shut so she couldn't scream for help. The person who murdered her is one of you in this room. You, the killer, may be assured that her death was a painful one. I want the killer to know that there are strong karmic forces always working on this Island. What you give to Kauai, good or bad, this Island will return that gift to you a hundredfold."

I saw Tommy titter, Tilda cough uncontrollably, Tony dribble in his pants, Raul close his eyes, Granny scratch her arms, and Gretchen feel the scar on her face. Their movements, told me they were all guilty in Alice's death.

After Grace looked into their faces for signs of guilt and spoke again, "I plan to end this affair in a matter of hours. If any of you has the desire to leave Kauai, ever, you will cooperate and assist me in solving these two crimes."

With a look of steely determination, the hotel manager then ordered: "I need to learn the meaning of the dolls over there in the corner of the room and I want to know your relationship to Lillie and to Alice. Therefore, I am conducting interviews again!"

Grace looked at her watch. "Goodness, it's noon. I'll start the interviews right after this meeting. We'll eat a late lunch."

Grace took a loose cigarette out of her basket, lit it, and said, "To give you fair warning, Lillie Russell passed on certain pieces of information to me that I was not to reveal to anyone unless something out-of-the-ordinary happened to her during her stay. It was obvious to me that she feared for her life. I remain very much in the dark as to why she placed the dolls at the table and what each doll represented. I believe once I understand that, I can solve the crimes."

Gretchen called out to Grace: "Miss Buscher, Lillie had me buy the dolls before we left for Hawaii. She did not buy those awful things on a whim. They were part of a scheme of hers. Each doll had a story to tell, a story which Lillie planned to reveal at the party."

Gretchen laughed, "Lillie had a sordid sense of humor and seemed unnaturally gleeful whenever she talked about the dolls. But she always spoke to me about the dolls in a vague roundabout fashion. What I did comprehend was that the Oedipus doll had something to do with her father, the blond doll—her past, and the Charlie McCarthy doll—her showbiz career or someone else's showbiz career. How she placed the dolls at the table and who they sat next to was deliberate on her part. Lillie did nothing in her life without great forethought."

I interrupted Gretchen: "I watched Lillie put the dolls in the chairs. She changed her mind a couple of times about where to place them. But the one doll whose placement she was certain of was the Charlie McCarthy doll."

CHAPTER EIGHTEEN

November 27, 1960 – Lana Turner, movie star, marries her fifth husband, Fred May.

Grace gave me a withering look. I said something I shouldn't have because Gretchen stopped giving out more important information. Gretchen closed her eyes and clammed up.

Ouch! Big Joe's knuckle pressed hard into the crook of my back.

Raul, the white knight, broke in, "Señorita Buscher, the Oedipus doll had to represent her father. She never knew where he was until . . . maybe . . . three years ago. One day, a man showed up at her front door claiming to be her father. And oddly enough . . . he was the real McCoy. Being reunited with her father, Lillie forgave him for deserting her when she was a little girl. After he reappeared, Lillie provided her father, Arthur, with his own home on Hilldale Avenue in West Hollywood. Lillie was very happy reliving her childhood days with Arthur—days she thought she had lost forever. A big gap in her life had now been filled. So content with her life, Lillie stopped drinking and, for a time, turned into a lovely human being—the Lillie I once knew and loved."

Raul crossed his legs and smoothed out his pants before he continued: "I can attest to what I am saying, because I have been in and out of Lillie's life for years. I was someone she could lean on when the going got rough. We were married but not married—good friends— more like brother and sister. We lived our own separate lives. I have a ranch in the valley, which she bought me—it was payment, I believe, for making her socially acceptable in Hollywood. While her father was around, I saw a lot of her. I call that period in her life the real Lillie, because she was kindness itself. When her newly-found dad, Arthur, was murdered, the unattractive Lillie reemerged. This trip to Coco Palms has been the longest time I've been around Lillie since Arthur died. Actually, I was surprised to receive the birthday invitation. Bringing us all together, I can only conclude, was a sick joke on her part. Since our arrival at the Coco Palms, I have been waiting for her punch line and last night I got it. I am now sorry from the bottom of my soul that I accepted her invitation."

After Raul spoke, he looked sad. He became an older man.

Granny broke in, "The doll with all that lipstick on it, the cheap looking floozy doll reminded me of our good old days in San Francisco—my whoring days. Lillie was a young kid when I picked her out of the gutter after she was abandoned by her father. Lillie caught on to my business right away. From the beginning, she had class. She was born with class, and could easily mingle with the crème de la crème of San Francisco; men who wore Brooks Brother suits; drank martinis at the Bohemian Club; and acted as if their stink rarefied the air. All these big shots saw something special in Lillie and took her under their wings. There was something real genuine about Lillie—even the rogues from the Barbary Coast saw it . . . men who had raised themselves up from the ranks of thieves, cutthroats, and married sluts from my whorehouse. My men clients protected my Lillie."

"In my day, I knew all the power brokers of San Francisco real well. I can name all of them and once upon a time, all of them sat at my table eating my food."

"San Francisco changed when the older generation died and new power brokers rose from the ranks. The new power brokers pretended that their kind came from grand dukes and duchesses from some country that they made up in their minds. It proved the adage that money buys you anything you want in this world and can turn the dregs of humanity into counterfeit lords and ladies. Being stupid, I reminded them of their scurrilous backgrounds as cheats and cutthroats and made many enemies in the City by the Bay. I left Frisco taking Lillie with me."

Granny stretched out her legs before she continued her tale: "I like Los Angeles. Them scalawags in Hollywood are more down-to-earth folks. They never lied about where they came from—only in the movies do they act like dukes and duchesses. Movie folk are proud to tell you from whence they came, except for them highfalutin folks serving tea in Hancock Park and Pasadena. Real down-to-earth Hollywood folks never forgot where they came from—mostly are the Jews who fled Europe and began working in this country as rag merchants or worse, low occupations that they owned and operated down in the bowels of the American cities. These folks are rough around the edges but they are real as hell. The reason I stuck by Lillie is she never forgot from whence she came from and never forgot her old friends. She kept me close to her and when she became the biggest star in Hollywood, she kept me closer. And I say this as a fact that without her, I'd be living in the gutter. And I thank God that Lillie was a forgiving person, because I crossed her more than once.

I bet everyone in this room has stabbed her in the back. If she were still alive, I'd hate to be the poor bastard who killed her father. Now that I think of it, maybe one of them big shots in San Francisco killed her father as a revenge on me. And another thought comes to mind Gracie, her father had as many enemies in San Francisco as I did."

Granny pushed on, not before she looked around the room for reactions, "One of them reasons Lillie brought us here to the Coco Palms was to remind us how we all disappointed her. The Charlie McCarthy doll has me wondering, though. There is real meaning behind that doll and who she placed the Charlie doll next to and that's you, Tilda."

"Shut up, you old, ugly buzzard."

Ignoring Tilda's outburst, Granny carried on speaking merrily that she got a reaction, "And why come to Hawaii? Why come to this godforsaken island to spend her birthday? If she wanted the tropics, she could have stayed in Beverly Hills and given her birthday party at Trader Vic's. Pardon me, Miss Buscher, who in the hell has ever heard of the Coconut Pissy Palms outside of some dinky, little travel agency in Kalamazoo. I can tell you this, you make me spend one more day in that room with Twinkle Toes over there, I'll end up in the loony bin scratching my nails on walls. Last night, I locked myself in the bathroom and knocked myself out taking two aspirins. Need my beauty sleep," she paused. "Actually, that's a lie—a bottle of brandy kept me company. And for your information, Miss Buscher, any of us can get out of those rooms easily. The bathroom windows are a cinch—just shimming down one of your coconut trees is a piece of cake." Granny finished talking, sighed and looked longingly out at the coconut grove as if she were in love.

Granny's eyes flickered telling her story—I felt the old lady had fibbed . . . a bit of it, anyway.

Tommy skipped to Granny, pinched her cheeks and smirked, "Granny keeps the water running in the bathroom all night and even though the water is running, She snores like a drunken sailor. I bet this old broad slept through the San Francisco earthquake. My problem with Granny: she locks the bathroom door and makes me pee out the window."

Poking her bony finger into Tommy's ribs, Granny snarled: "Take your hands off me, buster, before I give you one punch in a place you won't forget. I ain't as sleepy as I act. Remember that, kid!"

"Lighten up, Granny," Tommy twittered as he kissed her rouged cheek. Turning to Grace, Tommy offered his opinion. "About those crazy little dollies, though I wasn't a close friend of Lillie's, I bet my bottom dollar that they were a joke on us all . . . to keep us from getting bored at her party . . . that's all. I gotta admit those dolls have caused a little commotion around here. I am still wondering how she was going to fit those little munchkins into her perverted charade. Putting on a trial—my foot. But I guess we'll never know."

The Cowboy sounding like his horse, weighed in, "Here's what Tilda and I think! Those dolls do have a definite purpose and I'll bet my Pinto on that one. What her purpose was . . . remains a mystery to us. Tilda and I can't rightly figure that one out, we've tried. God knows, we have tried. Only Miss Lillie, it seems, could tell us that one. Here's what I'd do, Miss Buscher, see if you can find out if Lillie had a grudge against any of us and, find out what Alice knew about Lillie's past . . . and here's a question for you—Dockie Wockie. He is from one of the grand influential Trescutt's in Boston. Is he alive or did he get killed, too? If anyone knows the dirt on all of us, that would be Dockie Wockie. Remember, Dockie inherited Heidi's files after she died. He must have read the files and because of the horse manure he found in those files, maybe he's dead, too. Look, Lillie purchased Heidi's files, and after reading them, she died mysteriously."

Grace answered Tony directly, "Dr. Trescutt, by my last check, is very much alive. He is sleeping it off. Don't you worry, the good doctor is at the very top of my list of suspects. With a little coercion and black coffee, I plan to gather a great deal of information from him. Now to the business at hand: you'll all be escorted back to your rooms except for Tony and Tilda. You two, please stay behind with me."

After I heard Grace, Eric scrunched his pith helmet back on his head, and for no reason that I could find, he gave me the finger. Big John grabbed his finger, and personally escorted him out of the room, screaming. Tommy, Granny, Gretchen, and Raul followed behind a yowling Eric.

About to enter their rooms, Grace warned the suspects not to try to jump out the second story bathroom windows. "No matter what Granny said, you'll be sure to break a leg and be caught immediately and driven to the Montgomery Hotel and jailed without parole."

Before I closed the door to the Blue Hawaii suite, I watched Big John shove Eric into his room, but not before I made sure that Eric saw me give him the finger.

Blue Hawaii Suite door closed, Tilda and Tony, sat on the bed, watched Grace settle in a chair facing them. They held their breaths waiting for Grace to speak. It became a time-out for Grace, Tilda and Tony to gather their thoughts.

In the timeout. Tilda stretched out on the bed, laid her head down on a pillow, and let out a slow sigh of relief. Tony galloped to the bathroom and took a tinkle. After washing his hands three times, he sat down on the bed, next to Tilda, and held her hand.

Tilda, broke the silence said, cautiously, "You are a very perceptive woman, Miss Buscher."

The door opened, interrupting the moment, letting Big John join us in the room.

"Tilda honey, you don't have to say anything to nobody. We don't owe this lady anything. Honest, Miss Buscher, we didn't kill the old girl."

"We did, Tony. We weren't being fair. We knifed Lillie in the back by what we were doing. She didn't deserve what we did to her. We should have played fair."

Tony nodded and spoke: "Yea. Yea, I know. Look here, Miss Buscher, we've been carrying on an affair behind Lillie's back for a year and a half. I couldn't help it. Tilda is as pretty as a picture and the most upfront gal I know. She has a terrible toilet mouth—which is improving, if you haven't noticed. I love Tilda from the bottom of my heart."

"Let me go further, Tony. I have been Lillie's confidante and stand-in since I was an extra in *Ashes in the Pit*. She picked me out of the crowd and set me up for life—on one condition—that Lillie always came first. Lillie was good to me, always. When Tony came into the picture, temptation was too much for me to turn down and I began seeing Tony on the sly. I felt rotten about doing it, but we couldn't help ourselves."

Tony drawled: "We couldn't, Miss Buscher, really, we couldn't help ourselves. In all fairness ma'am, Lillie kept me around to make her feel young and desirable. She was never in love with me and sex was never an important part of our relationship. What was important and what she wanted from me was for everyone in Hollywood to think that she had a stud, a toy boy, in her stable, and for Hollywood, the studio, and her fans to see that she still had IT. In the back of our

180

minds, Tilda and I knew that if Lillie had found out about us, she would have felt betrayed and very embarrassed. I didn't want to do that to her. And we didn't murder her. We had no reason to kill her. Did we darling?"

Grace stood up, looked out the window and watched the coconut leaves rustle in the wind. She turned to Tony and Tilda and raised her hand as if to stop traffic, manure had begun to pile up in the room.

Grace proclaimed: "First of all, I know what you two were doing. The maids told me you were going through the secret doors in the King's Cottages; second, you haven't told me everything. Tony, you didn't mention that Lillie had you removed from a film for no reason at all and a film where you were to co-star with Gary Cooper. You were cast as the villain—a part that you do so well. Starring in that movie with megastar Cooper would have been a huge break in your career. Tilda, what about your beauty shop? Rumor has it that Lillie pulled all of her money out of your beauty shop and was going to finance a much younger, very talented, male hairdresser with his own shop, placed square inside the lobby of the Beverly Wilshire Hotel."

"Where the fuck did you hear that crap?"

"No reason to swear, Tilda. You promised me, honey."

Looking into Miss Buscher's eyes, the cowboy sputtered, "Where'd you hear that horseshit?"

Grace winked at me. A cat had caught two lying, yappy myna birds napping and wallowing in their petard.

I was the one who told Grace those rumors.

Grace purred: "You two are very much at the top of my list of suspects. You knew that if Lillie found out what you two were up to she would have had her pound of flesh. And you must have had an inkling that she did know about your treachery by the way she had been treating you both, lately. Give Lillie Russell credit that she wasn't born yesterday. Being on the outs with Lillie and the loss of her generosity—meaning her money—I find that to be a very strong motive for murder."

Tilda spat: "If you are so damned smart with all your deductions, what about Alice? Where does Alice fit in this? Why would we want to kill Alice?"

"She was blackmailing you!"

"For what?"

Tony stood up indignantly at the same time Grace flung herself out of her chair and confronted Tony wearing two-inch high heels. Even in her heels, Tony, wearing his cowboy boots, overpowered Grace's slight body by more than a foot and half. Not to be intimidated, Grace squared her body next to his, and announced: "The interview is over. Big John, escort Tilda and Tony back to their room and bring me Eric von Bismark."

Tony looked at Grace before he ambled out the room and spoke quietly: "Ma'am, I'd watch myself! You're heading into dangerous territory."

"Is that a threat, Tony Pinto?"

"No Ma'am, but I'd take it as a strong warning. Be careful. You could be stepping on a nest of rattlesnakes and I wouldn't want anything bad to happen to a pretty, little lady like you."

"I'll be careful, Tony Pinto. Don't you worry your handsome face about me; I'd worry about Tilda's pretty little face. Do enjoy the rest of your stay at the Coco Palms. I'll send two Mai Tais to your room with my compliments."

Grace smiled at them and warned, "Sip them carefully. You never know what's in them."

As the door to the suite closed, a wave of fear clouded over Miss Buscher's face. Watching Grace deep in thought, thinking about Tilda and Tony, I stood at the window quiet as a possum, sipping a Coke. I, too, was filled with unanswered questions—questions that danced in my head like naughty sugar plum fairies.

Ten minutes passed while we waited and waited for Eric von Bismark to make his grand entrance. The long delay signaled that we were about to witness the last scene from *Macbeth* and we weren't to be disappointed.

The suite door opened with a bang. Big John held the protesting movie director by the scruff of his neck and tossed him into the middle of the room. With Big John's other massive paw, he forced Eric to sit in a chair opposite Grace.

To keep him seated in his chair, Big John pressed down with his two hands on von Bismark's pith helmet.

Feeling the pressure from Big John, Eric screamed: "Take your heathen hands off my helmet. Remember who I am? I can sue you for . . ."

Eric stopped screaming when Miss Buscher glared at him in such a way that could have stopped a charging rhinoceros. With Big John's hands pressing harder on his head, Eric was foolish but not dumb, self-preservation utmost in his mind, Eric switched his screams to whines.

A signal from Grace, Big John took his hands off the human flotsam and apologized, "I had to do it Miss Buscher. He didn't want to come."

"You sadist pig," Eric mumbled under his breath. He used the same voice as his character actor, Carlo Bineri, spoke playing Mussolini in Eric's whimsical musical, *Waltzing with Hitler on Bastille Day.*

Called a sadist pig, Big John tightened his hands slowly around Eric's neck and said quietly, "Sir, one more word out of you and I'll squeeze harder."

It was fact that bullies puddle when they are confronted directly; von Bismark was no exception.

Eric stood in defiance and played in front of Grace two of his favorite victim charade roles: Napoleon brooding on the Isle of Elba and Hitler hunkered down in his cement bunker, hours before he committed suicide.

Hearing no applause or seeing any noticeable reaction from Grace, defeated Eric sat down and the Blue Hawaii Palm suite quieted down into a morgue. Grace rose, closed the curtains, and turned off the chandelier lights, darkening the room. The only light in the room came from a table lamp. The light from the lamp reflected on Eric's pith helmet and face. Grace Buscher in charge, the room turned into an FBI interrogation room.

At that moment, I mused that if Grace's interrogation failed its purpose, I planned to jam slivered pieces of bamboo under his fingernails.

Sweat percolating on Eric's upper lip , Eric intuited the thoughts in the room and without warning, raised up his hands, made a sign of surrender, and pleaded: "Please, please, don't hurt me. I confess— my infected hemorrhoids made me act the way I do."

Eric, once again, tried to divert Grace's interrogation by telling her he was going to perform different male and female roles from his movies. He began by gyrating his body and flailing his hands in the air and explained to Grace that he was Tokyo Rose falling into a vat of quicksand.

Grace giggled, in spite of herself, watching him writhe on the floor and said in a determined voice, "Eric, enough of this nonsense. Big John pick him up, put him back in the chair, and stand behind him."

"Yes, Miss Buscher," Big John saluted."

Eric back in his chair, Big John crossed his arms and stood guard once again. Eric, still not listening to Grace, began performing again like a full-fledged crazy man foaming in the mouth. Feeling the pressure of Big John's hands again on his pith helmet, von Bismark stopped foaming and for some crazy reason that I couldn't comprehend, he suddenly began to concentrate on the flora-patterns on the carpet.

Grace lowered her voice and spoke: "Now sir, you didn't like your wife very much, did you? In fact, you hated her."

Eric jerked up his head and screamed: "How dare you talk to me in thiz manner. You forget yourself, madam. If I were not a gentleman, I would get out of diz chair and slap you silly."

Big John's finger ring tapped on his pith helmet. Eric reasoned correctly that if he carried out his threat, Big John would twist his head off in as neat a manner as the mangled dolls' heads lying in the corner of the room. Only Grace's arm waving at Big John kept Eric's head attached to his body.

Grace continued on, steadying her voice: "I am sure your wife would know all about that. Hitting women seems to be your most manly trait. Let me pose the question to you again,: did you hate your wife?"

He yelled out to no one in particular. "Yes, I hated her! But I didn't kill Alice and I didn't

kill Lillie! But I would have liked to have killed them both. I married Alice for her money and that's no secret. All her fancy Pasadena friends knew it, all of Hollywood knew it. But now Alice's money belongs to me. Me! I made sure of that when we made out our joint wills. Did you really look at Alice? Did you ever really look at Alice? Alice was the ugliest creature God ever created." He paused to wipe with his hand spittle that had spewed out of his mouth.

He wiped his mouth once again before he continued with his tirade: "As for Lillie, I . . . I, alone, destroyed Lillie's career. I didn't have to kill her. I murdered her without lifting a finger on her last movie. I, like Louis B. Mayer, destroyed any actor's career with the help of a film editor. My film editor was Morris Kazinki. Morris owed me his job. Film editing is the all in motion pictures. It wasn't the first time I killed an actor's career in the editing room. I was thrilled when Jack Warner assigned me to direct Lillie's last picture, even though she had a secondary part at best. I insisted in my contract that I had the final cut. and I made sure that, in each frame of the film that Lillie appeared she looked ten years older than she appeared off screen. Hell, she was on the skids and Lillie couldn't harm me anymore. I retaliated for all the years Lillie made me jump through hoops when she was the biggest cheese that walked down Hollywood Boulevard. From the beginning, she had treated me like dog shit . . . Since the first day we met, I was crap to her. In her prime, behind her back, I spread through my dear friend Heidi, that she was the biggest disappointment in the sack in Hollywood history. I made sure that piece of dirt got into print and she never found out who did it—in the beginning, that is. I am sure, after she got a hold of Heidi's files, she knew who the Judas was. That rumor really hurt her pride, that fucking conceited bitch. Probably, Lillie not only found out that the sack rumor came from me but she also found out that I had been a member of the American Nazi party before the Second World War broke out. I did have reasons to kill Lillie, but she had many more reasons to kill me. Obviously, she didn't kill me and I didn't murder her. But I am thrilled in every bone in my body that both Alice and Lillie are dead. I repeat myself: I didn't murder either one of them, but, now, with both of them on the other side, out of my way, my career remains intact and my finances are so secure that for the rest of my life. I am sitting pretty. Better than sitting pretty, I am now worth millions. Know that I think if it, I don't have to direct that crappy picture that Lillie alluded to. That conceited bitch wasn't the only name I used for getting financing, I threw in other names: Marjorie Main, Judy Canova, Binnie Barnes, and Vera Vague. They were my collateral backups. Let Lillie and Alice roast in hell for all I care. I am untouchable now and what a fortunate man I have become. I have always been lucky, Miss Buscher and I will deny everything I have said in this room. Neither you nor anyone else on this island of Kauai or anywhere else in this world is going to put me behind bars because there is not one shred of evidence to convict me. I have, as I said, become rich and untouchable!"

Finished with his tirade, Eric stood, raised his right arm, and gave us the Nazi salute. Eric had spewed his entire harangue without using his accent. What he didn't notice was that I wrote down word for word everything he had said.

Exhausted, out of breath, red in the face, Eric crumbled into his chair and hiccupped. His body replaced the toxic oxygen he had spewed out on us. Hiccups back in control, Eric bent over and traced with his finger the purple hibiscus pattern woven on the carpet.

With an exclamation mark, I spoke out loud to Miss Buscher, "Eric is certifiable!"

Grace nodded, "Mr. Eric I got what I needed. No matter how much you protest, Mr. von Bismark, you are at the very top of my suspect list. Big John, take him back to his room. This I can promise you *Mein Kampf* director, justice will be all yours."

Eric rose and marched to the door as Big John followed closely behind him. The director turned and lashed once more at Grace: "I will remember this day, this hour, this minute and what you have done to me for the rest of my life. Every minute you have kept me prisoner, I will repay you in kind and seek revenge—an eye for an eye. It will be your eye, madam! And I will personally conduct a vendetta against you as I did on Lillie and spew as much venom on you as I did on that hated Alice. When I am through with you, Miss Grace Buscher, you will be lucky to be cleaning the guests' shit in this hotel. You will be finished working in the hotel business forever. As for Heidi's files, with Lillie dead, so are the files dead. So don't worry about me, Miss Hotel Manager. I would frankly worry about what is going to happen to you and YOU." He said that pointing at me and continued speaking to me, "I will remember your remark for the rest of my life. Certifiable! Death by poisonous centipedes is far too good for you, fat boy. Good afternoon."

The smile of a Cheshire cat suddenly appeared on Grace's face as she replied sweetly to Eric, "And a very good afternoon to you, Mr. Sylvan Seltzer from Toledo, Ohio."

At that moment, I saw if looks could kill, Eric, the wannabe Nazi, would have gassed us all at Auschwitz.

I waved goodbye to Eric as he left and parodied a popular song, singing to him, "I Would Like to Set this Nazi on Fire."

Grace instructed Big John, speaking slowly, making sure Eric heard every word she said, "Big John, do not touch even one hair or harm any part of Mr. von Bismark's body, not even his ridiculous pith helmet. I want to keep this man very much alive and very well. I want him Mr. von Bismark to remain all in one piece."

Big John pushed Eric, dragging his heels down the hall, into his room.

From the fierce look in Big John's eyes, I saw the Hawaiian giant wanted to throw the bugger head first down into Kauai's ten-mile-long, -mile-wide, three thousand-feet deep Waimea Canyon.

Opening up the curtains to let the light back in the room, Grace called to Big John, "Bring me Raul Pasqual."

In a flash, Raul arrived, dressed immaculately in black. Standing in the doorway, he glowed like Sir Lancelot—the Sir Lancelot I read about in *King Arthur's Knights of the Round Table.* The sun shone down on Coco Palms that afternoon because Raul stood in the doorway.

Grace said softly: "Please come in Mr. Pasqual. You take my breath away; you look so handsome."

Raul blushed and then spoke to Grace as if he was speaking to a queen, "Miss Buscher, please call me Raul."

"Raul, please call me Grace. Please, sit over there. Would you like coffee?"

"Thank you. I can help myself." I handed the knight a freshly brewed cup of Kona coffee.

"Cream and sugar?" I asked.

"No thank you, young man. I take my coffee as we do in Mexico . . . strong and black."

Grace spoke, "If you don't mind, I'd like to keep Percy and Big John with us in this room. Because of the sensitivity of what has happened, I believe in having second and third parties around to guarantee what is said between us will be accurate. Keeps the record clean—and straight, so to speak."

Seated in a chair opposite Grace, Raul crossed his slim legs and sipped his coffee. After a moment's hesitation, the Mexican murmured, "I have no objections to second and third parties. I have no secrets. I believe I have explained myself, and everyone in the world knows my situation with Lillie. Regarding Alice, I had no recent communication with Mrs. von Bismark, except I saw her on my last visit with Lillie on the set of her final film."

"Thank you for your honesty, Raul. A quick reminder to see if I have the information correct: you married Lillie early in her career but you hardly ever lived together. She bought you a ranch in Encino, next to the Clark Gable property. You never had children."

"Lillie couldn't have children. A botched abortion in San Francisco ruined any chance of Lillie having children."

"Did you love, Lillie?"

"I once did but we remained good friends. No sex. Recently, after her father was murdered, I found her difficult to be around."

"She gave you, what should I say . . . a hefty monthly allowance?"

"She did. How do you know all this?"

"It is common knowledge in Los Angeles. Hollywood is a small town and everyone seems to think it is their right to know everyone else's business, not unlike the busybodies who live here on Kauai. A small community is a small, noisy community no matter what part of the world one lives in. I have good friends in the Hollywood community and I have been busy on the telephone learning all I can about Lillie's guests. I am sorry for my abruptness, but I want this mess to be cleared by tomorrow morning."

"Good luck on that. I have told you everything I know. I didn't kill Lillie or Alice. I had no reason to."

"You had no reason to kill Lillie?"

"What do you mean?"

"Come on Raul, you haven't told me everything."

Boy, when Grace said that, the friendly air was suddenly sucked out of the room.

Grace said pointedly, "Raul, what about Conchita and your two children with her?"

Hearing Grace say "Conchita" and "children," my mind traveled into an underground subway, curved around a corner, and crashed dead into a brick wall of surprise.

I wondered where in the hell did Grace get that piece of information?

It was a long time before anyone spoke. It was Grace who broke the silence: "Isn't it true you have . . . a friend . . . a companion who has lived with you for years as a partner? You have two children by her—a boy and a girl. Isn't it also true that you asked Lillie for a divorce so you could marry Conchita? Isn't it also a fact that Lillie said she would give you the divorce, but you would have to give up the ranch and your allowance. There was a public fight on the set of her last von Bismark film and, you, in anger, were heard threatening to kill Lillie. This was corroborated by witnesses on the set. There hasn't been a divorce."

Raul's lips tightened when he replied: "It was important for Lillie to keep our sham marriage intact. It all boiled down to Lillie's out-sized ego and to keep up appearances among her friends, as well as her star image in Tinsel Town. For all of Lillie's bravado, she was a fragile, and insecure woman. I love Conchita and my children with all my heart, but I am too old and too impoverished to give up the ranch and my annuity."

Raul paused before he whispered: "Yes, I did threaten Lillie but I didn't kill her. I was angry and I said things in anger that I didn't mean to carry out. I would never harm Lillie. What happens to me now, to my ranch, to Conchita, my kids, I don't know. Lillie's death changes everything. I don't know what she put in her will about me. She may have left me a poor man . . . and without the ranch."

"Thank you for telling me the truth."

"May I still call you, Grace?"

"Of course, may I still call you, Raul?"

Raul stood, placed the coffee cup back on the table, put out his hand and shook Grace's. "I would feel it an honor if you would call me Raul. Since, I have nothing more to add, may I excuse myself?"

Grace nodded.

When Raul left the room, his armor was still shining; in fact, in my eyes, Raul glistened in the sun.

Grace looked at me and winked. "Now . . . for Granny Goose."

Granny had to be assisted into the room with Big John and Lance, the Clark Gable handsome policeman, holding her up, each with a hand under an arm.

Granny was "not steady on her pins," as my Aunt Daisy coined the phrase. It was a kind way of saying that those ladies of an age, sixty-five and beyond, who tippled secretly in their closets, were drunk. Wanting to make a good impression, Granny and those like her who tippled, gargled with Listerine before they met their public. Granny forgot the Listerine because my nose twitched when Big John and Lance glided her past me into the suite. Granny's breath reeked like a barroom floor soaked in bourbon. At the exact moment, Grace and I reached the same conclusion that the aged redhead needed a bath and a healthy application of French perfume spritzed into parts of her body that had not seen the light of day since the French revolution.

From Granny's bloodshot eyes, I deduced that she must have sneaked out the bathroom window and had been carousing in a downtown Kapaa bar.

"Granny, are you all right?" Grace asked sounded concerned.

"Yessth!"

Still concerned, Grace raised her voice and made hand signals as if she was conversing with a woman who had forgotten her hearing aids. "Can you understand me?"

"Yessth!"

"I have only one question for you. How did you stab Lillie in the back?"

Granny suddenly replied soberly, "You know about the abortion?"

"Yes."

"So, you- . . . know about the abortion. Hmm. The botched abortion. Well, it was my fault. I got a doc on the cheap. Lillie didn't want to have a child. Lillie wanted to be a movie star. Once, early on, I tried to stop her from becoming a movie star, because she was my biggest moneymaker. But this guy, Howard, need I give you his last name, came along one rainy night in San Francisco and promised to make her a movie star. I told Howard that Lillie was a drug-addict and a marked woman because she was blackmailing on all the big shots in San Francisco. The truth was, Lillie did have a few important clients, but she wasn't blackmailing anyone. Howard went away, and no movie star contract came Lillie's way. Lillie wanted revenge. She told a bigwig friend of hers to close me down. They did. I went flat broke. We both ended up in the same soup because none of the big wigs in Frisco trusted Lillie or me anymore. We left Frisco under a cloud, fleeing for our lives. We made up by time we got to L.A. But there were still times, during those years, when I could have killed Lillie, or she me, even best friends get jealous of each other—especially if one of them becomes the big somebody that the other person had always wanted to be. Friendships can be complicated. But I never harbored bad feelings against Lillie, because she always took care of me. Lillie kept me close and made me dependent on her purse strings. It was her sweet revenge."

She burped. Then, she continued still sounding sober: "I didn't kill Lillie. Hard for me to believe that Lille is dead because she was a hard girl. She was born hard. Her father's murder didn't help her one bit. I think I know something about her murder but I can't prove it. My head is fuzzy all the time now. I'm not thinking clearly. I am having long nights with lots to drink."

Throwing her head back, she exclaimed, "Damn bad luck this life gives some of us. This world is either a piece of damn good luck or a piece of shit, but 'it's mostly damn piece of shit. The lucky ones are the ones that can just sail through life, couldn't you just kill them? And you know Gracie, honey, I just may turn out to be one of them. I'm alive, ain't I? That says something."

"Granny, there are two other stories told about you and Lillie. The other story is that you shanghaied Lillie to Los Angeles, getting her out of town after she was raped by one of your notorious clients. You saved her life. Which is the true story?"

Slurring her words again, "Take yoursh pick, honey. Whish story do you like best? What in the hell is truth anyway?"

"You were lucky to have a friend like Lillie."

"I am one hellava lucky old broad, believe you me." Shaking her head, trying to make sense out of her nonsense talk, Granny thought a bit and repeated: "I guesh I was lucky. Wasn't I? Can I have some of that coffee? I might think straighter."

I handed her a cup of coffee and Granny drank it down in one swallow.

Licking her lips, she purred looking at Big John and Lance, "I like my coffee strong and black, just like my men." She laughed so hard at what she had said, she spilled the coffee on the carpet.

Wiping up the mess up with a napkin, Granny asked: "May I go now? You didn't ask me if I killed Lillie?"

"I didn't, did I, Granny? I've had my tabs on you, so don't you worry. The men will take you back to your room and I'll send you a pot of coffee. You need to keep your wits about you. If I were you, Granny, for your own safety, I'd stay put in your bathroom."

"Don't you worry about me, honey, I have my wits about me all the time. I mish nothing."

"I don't believe you do. But, right now, keep a tight rein on yourself. Listen carefully to me, Granny, hold on, because we are almost at the end of the story. Big John and Lance, take Granny back to her room."

When Big John and Lance went to pick up Granny, she slumped into their arms like a rag doll. They lifted her off her feet and dragged the Raggedy Ann doll back to her room. When she reached the door of her room, she swayed back and forth into the boys, feeling their biceps.

She chortled: "Just like I like 'em: strong, brown, handsome, and big. Come on inside, boys, and let me show you a good time."

"Sorry Miss Myers, we're working men." Big John said that as he blushed.

"Too bad, boys. I was about to give you both the experience of a lifetime, because it was I who taught Miss Mae West everything she knows."

I believed that from that moment onward, when these two Hawaiian lads became old men, they would sit around drinking beers and wonder what the hell Granny had in her candy store.

Grace called out from the suite, "Big John, send me Tommy Twinkle."

In minutes, Tommy tap danced down the hallway and performed an Ann Miller routine just for the boys.

"Hi, Miss Buscher." He stood in the doorway and before Grace could say "don't do it," he belted out his own rendition of, "I'm A Grand Old Fag."

For Grace, Tommy wore his last years' Fourth of July costume: a red, white, and blue star-spangled ensemble, glittery short pants, and a fringed shirt slit to his navel. A black top hat completed his Busby Berkeley musical ensemble.

"Come in, Tommy."

Tommy tapped into the room, grabbed the coffee cup out of my hand, sat down, crossed his legs lady-like, chattered to Grace without taking in a breath: "Gracie, may I call you Gracie? Of course, I shall call you Gracie. Gracie, Gracie, Gracie. Now Gracie darling, how can I be of service to you? You know, I don't think anyone murdered little old Lillie. Lillie was much too butch for that. I think the old girl did herself in . . . after all, she was past her prime and her last movie was a pure disaster, pure trash. As for that beastly Alice, the gnome, she just ran into some damn bad luck. To clear up any misunderstanding, I was not, and never have been, one of Lillie's intimates. I was only invited to join her party . . . to keep Dockie off the sauce. After all, I was his wife's best friend, and in the memory of Heidi, I agreed to join this little farce. I guess I let Heidi, Lillie, and Dockie down. I was surprised you moved me in with cranky old Granny, but I am not one to complain, ever, especially, to those who are in power. But Gracie, Granny is driving me crazy with her madcap antics. Rumor has it that Dockie is zonked out of his mind. Must have taken Lillie's death to heart . . . truth be told, he probably has too many scotch bottles stashed in his suitcase. I can't tell you how many so called accidents he's had in his practice. Now, my darling, how can I be of help to you?"

Thrusting his coffee cup out to me for a refill, he twittered, "More coffee, Mary."

Grabbing the cup out of his hand, I filled it to the brim, hoping some of it would spill over on his spangled shirt.

Tommy reminded me of a grownup Kewpie doll. I didn't like him.

Grace placed her chair close to his, sat down, and faced him. "You say you didn't know Lillie or, for that matter, Alice well."

"No," he hesitated, giving Grace a questioning look before he answered further. "No, I didn't, but I did read Heidi's files about all their scandalous doings. Thursdays were our day, Heidi's and mine. We reserved a back booth at the Brown Derby for our wet lunches so no one could overhear us. While we ate our Cobb salads, she'd amuse me by reading from some of her most scandalous files. My God, she had the real dirt on everyone. The only file she would not let me read was mine. What a tease, she was. Oh, how I miss our Thursday noonday lunches."

"Weren't you ever curious what she had in your file?"

"Never! Darling, there is nothing in my life that would of any degree be of interest to anyone outside of Paducah. My slate is a complete blank—clean as a fucking whistle."

"You must have been surprised when Dockie sold Heidi's files to Lillie."

"Appalled, actually."

"Why?"

"Heidi would never have wanted anyone as morally corrupt as she was to have those files—especially not Lillie."

"Morally corrupt? That's an odd thing for you to say. I would have thought that since you were Heidi's best friend, you would have been heir to the files."

"Yes, you would have thought so, but it wasn't in the cards for me. But then Heidi always dealt from the bottom of the deck. Human beings are generally known to never write wills that are fair. What people say and what they actually do are two precisely different things. Most people, especially in Hollywood, talk in hollow words."

He tittered nervously when he confessed further, "Actually, between us girls, I would have liked to have seen what was in my file . . . only for my amusement, of course."

Grace paused and looked at Tommy. "Rumor has it that when Dockie sold the files to Lillie, not all of them were accounted for. As you say, the bequests and human beings are not always reliable."

"We are digressing, aren't we, Gracie? I can't help you on the murders, really I can't. And I value my life in Hollywood too much to be a snitch. Gracie, the only secret kept is the one not told. But somehow Heidi learned all our secrets, even the ones not told, and wrote them down in her files."

"Wouldn't it have been amusing if Heidi had a file on herself? Now, that would have been really interesting. Her files do interest me. I do have more questions on the files, but that will have to wait until I sober up the good doctor. You have been most helpful. I plan to solve these murders by tonight. I have to—Elvis and Paramount Studios are arriving on schedule and in less than twenty-four hours, they will take over the Coco Palms. By the way, I love your outfit. You are quite the entertainer. I, too, would have loved to see what was in your file."

"Boring stuff, really, my darling. My parents were in the entertainment business. I suppose you would say I owe my talent to them.

Gracie, my family played the same vaudeville circuits as Mickey Rooney's and Judy Garland's families—the Yules and the Gumms. Those folks were typical driven theatrical parents, but, off the record, as far as the Yules and Gumms go, as parents, I thought they were sadists to their children. They turned their children into . . . into people not fit to live in the real world. Poor talented Judy and Mickey were true geniuses. Mickey came out the better because he finally married a good girl."

Grace smiled as she said, "I want you to know, Mr. Twinkle, you, like the rest of Lillie's guests, are high on my list of suspects."

Rising from his chair, Tommy sighed: "Whatever is your pleasure, Gracie dear, but you're barking up the wrong tree with me. I did not kill Lillie or Alice." Placing his cup of coffee carefully back on the table, he stared into Grace's eyes, "Gracie, I would be careful who you accuse."

"I am always careful, so don't worry about me. I am going to have a surprise for all of you this evening. And, Mr. Tommy Twinkle, I shall know all the answers to these murders before the night is over."

His face lit up like a jack-o-lantern as he said, "I can hardly wait for that Gracie, darling. Well, *ta-ta!*" That said, Tommy Twinkle tap danced out into the hall.

When he left, I gagged. Twinkle's toxic vibes lingered in the room. If there had been time before the next interview, I could have sprayed the entire room with Clorox and Lysol, I would have.

Gretchen was next—the Swedish lady with the Japanese last name and the crooked smile. Gretchen walked into the room in a puff of fairy dust.

"Sit down, Mrs. Yamashita," Grace said, offering her a cup of coffee she served her personally in a pretty little cup and saucer.

Placing the coffee cup and saucer very lady-like on her lap, Gretchen began the conversation without prompting from Grace—something I believed she would have done drinking tea with the Queen in Buckingham Palace.

"Miss Buscher, I have been close friend to Lillie for many years. She trusted me, not only with her personal affairs but with her makeup and hair. Makeup and hair are of prime importance to a star. I concocted the secret combination for her hair color. The color I concocted made Lillie look like a natural blond. Her real hair color was a mousy brown."

"In Hollywood," Gretchen confessed, "hair color and hair-style are two of the most important aspects of an actor's appearance—male or female. I created special wigs for Debbie Reynolds, Jimmy Stewart, Burt Reynolds, Sean Connery, Ida Lupino, and Betty Grable."

Grace smiled, touching her hair, "It is true for me because Gretchen, my hair turned snow white before my eighteenth birthday. I have been coloring my hair ever since. Some darn old gene went south in my family. Any suggestions about the color of my hair would be most appreciated."

"Your hair color is most attractive. Keep it the champagne color . . . it suits your face." Gretchen sipped her coffee and continued. "Let me cut to the chase: Something went wrong with Lillie. It had to do with her father's murder. Just before he died, Lillie said her father had acted strangely . . . too jubilant from his normal self. He'd make remarks like, 'I've caught that son-of-a-bitch red-handed and that person better not pull a fast one on me this time.' Two days later, his house on Hilldale caught fire and burned to the ground. The firemen were able to pull his body out just before the house collapsed. The autopsy found that he had been strangled with a scarf. The

Hollywood Police Department labeled it murder. The killer has yet to be found."

"Did Lillie have any suspicion about who the killer might be?"

"I think she did. That is why she came to Coco Palms to celebrate her birthday. She looked for a place as far away from Hollywood as she could find. She wanted to have all the people she suspected in a contained area, all under one roof—trapped on an island."

"Can I consider you a suspect?"

"Yes. For the past few months, Lillie and I have been estranged."

"Your face lift?"

"My face lift! Look at me. Lillie wanted me to replace Tilda as her stand-in. She was suspicious that Tilda was not being loyal to her by fooling around with Tony, and Lillie persuaded me that I could make more money being not only her stylist but also her stand-in. There was a big but! The big but was to have a face lift so I would look more like her. A darker look . . . a lighter look—a Lillie look. So I did it. I don't know why. Sam and I have enough money, goodness knows. The face lift was a botched job as you can see. I did not only not look like Lillie—I came out of the operation theater appearing like the Phantom of the Opera's sister. I blamed Lillie for my disfigurement and could have killed her on the spot. I didn't but my husband Sam got his revenge. He was the cinematographer on her last film directed by the well-hung Eric the Nazi. In cahoots with Eric, Sam shot Lillie from all the worst angles he could think of with nary a filter, and he made sure that every age line was not only clearly visible but appeared as deep as the Grand Canyon. With his camera and Eric's direction, they ruined Lillie's career. Lillie was oblivious to all of this because she was so distracted by her father's death. If you find the person who killed her father, you will find Lillie's killer."

Gretchen paused. She rose from her chair, handed me the cup and saucer with one hand and with the other hand she touched her face. Her unconscious gesture reminded Gretchen of the horror she saw every day in the mirror.

Gretchen patted Grace's hands, looked out the window that overlooked the coconut grove and said wistfully: "I did not kill Lillie and I am also not proud of my feelings toward her. I am not proud of what Sam did to her, but he loves me very much and he is presently looking for a doctor who will reverse what I did to myself. Please make note of this: it was my decision, not Lillie's, to have this face lift and I take full responsibility for what happened to my face." Overcome with emotion, she sighed, "May I be excused? This has not been easy for me to tell."

Grace took Gretchen's hands and held them tight. "Thank you for your candor. I shan't need anything more from you this afternoon. I will be seeing you at dinner. I promise you, Gretchen, this will be your last supper at the Coco Palms. You will be returning to your husband soon. I have all the information I need. Take a nap. You're going to need it."

Gretchen closed her eyes and nodded. "I will be glad to be home again with Sam."

After Gretchen left the room, I asked, "What about the doctor?"

"I will interview him before dinner."

CHAPTER NINETEEN

October 14, 1960 – John F. Kennedy first suggests the idea of the Peace Corps.

"What dinner?" I asked.

"I am going to recreate Lillie's birthday party . . . the same meal, same seating, and then proceed with the evening as it was from the beginning to the moment when Lillie died. I plan to smoke out the killer tonight because the killer is going to make a mistake." Grace, for the first time, took the elevator down to her office.

Grace flummoxed me.

The elevator was installed in this building within the month, without permits, as requested by Hal Wallis, and paid for by Paramount Studios. Hal Wallis was arthritic and had a hard time climbing steps. Grace agreed to the elevator, on the strict condition, that it would be dismantled and taken out on the day the director yelled, for the last time, "That's a wrap!"

Grace was adamant. "Elevators do not belong at the Coco Palms Hotel." It took years of friendly persuasion by Gus to have TV's placed in the hotel rooms.

Not an hour passed before I was summoned into Grace's inner sanctum. When I entered, Grace stood up behind her desk holding a clipboard in her hand. A yellow-lined legal pad was attached to the clipboard.

"Percy, you observed Lillie's dinner."

"Yes."

"Did you pay attention?"

"I did."

"Go over the seating arrangements with me."

I visualized where each guest sat going around the table starting with Lillie.

"Here is the seating as I remember it. Lillie was at the head of the table with her back to the lagoon . . . no, she faced the lagoon . . . no, her back was to the lagoon; on her right was the Charlie McCarthy doll, then Tilda, Tony, the fancy lady doll . . . no . . . Tommy Twinkle, then the fancy lady doll, Granny, the Oedipus Rex doll, Alice, Gretchen . . . then Eric . . . I think."

"You haven't got it right—you're missing the doctor and Raul."

"Let me try again . . . Lillie . . . Charlie McCarthy, Tilda, Tony, Raul, Granny, Tommy, painted lady doll, Dockie, Oedipus Rex doll, Alice, Gretchen, and von Bismark—that makes thirteen. And may I add my two cents— I know who the killer is."

"Hmm," said Grace as she ignored me. "I believe that's correct, but I'm still not sure. Tonight there will be fourteen for dinner. I will never have another dinner party for thirteen in my hotel *ever* again. I wasn't thinking straight when Lillie Russell talked me into it. I have sent out the invitations to all the suspects still living . . . And because tonight is my Mahjong night, I've asked my chums to join me in the Blue Hawaii suite. They'll be filling in for the missing people and the broken dolls. Gladys will play Lillie. Anna will play the floozy doll. Lou Habets will play Alice. Lou will love that and I'm having Kate Hulme portray the Oedipus Rex doll. Katie will do that part deliciously."

"Will the doctor be sober enough to attend the party?"

"He will. I am presently making sure of that. Big John is pouring gallons of coffee down his throat as we speak."

"What about the Charlie McCarthy doll?

"That is my role," answered, Grace.

After handing me four sealed envelopes, Grace instructed: "Take the hotel station wagon and deliver these personally and immediately to Gladys Brandt, Anna, Hulme and Habets. Inside these envelopes are my background notes about the characters so they can perform their roles during the dinner party. The dolls, I believe, have real significance in solving these crimes. Remind them to be at the Blue Hawaii Palm suite at 7:30 p.m. sharp—right after the torch-lighting ceremony. Not a minute sooner. I want to surprise our suspects. I've invited the suspects to come at 6:30 p.m. I want to get them a little high before the games begin . . . all except the good doctor. Right after torch lighting, I'll escort him into the dinner party myself

Holding the envelopes, I asked, "Who do you think the killer is?"

"It's so obvious, Percy. But since you already know, Charlie Chan, why should I tell you?" You think you're such a smarty pants.

"I'll bet my pith helmet on Eric. Yes? No?"

"I'm not going to tell you, but before this night is over, you will know everything. Tonight, everything will be revealed. But Percy, remember, what curiosity did to the cat. Be on tap to help at the bar and pour water and coffee and assist Big John in any way he asks you. No more questions. Tonight, remember, Big John speaks for me.

And, young man, after dinner, you are to report to me for one final last instruction.

The rest of the day passed at a snail's pace. But in a wink of time, I had delivered all the invitations to Grace's "inner circle."

All day, I longed for the sun to hunker down under the horizon so Grace's game could begin. I was fidgety all day; it was as if *ukus* (vermin) were jumping in my pants. Because of my edginess, the day went from bad to worse: I spilled gravy on my good shirt at lunch, I sent a guest to the wrong room, forgot my favorite aunt's birthday, and paid a big fat fine for speeding into Kapaa. To add insult to injury, I was fined ten dollars for not renewing my driver's license.

When the witching hour arrived and the night of reckoning was about to begin, my nerves had short-circuited.

At 6:30 sharp, the suspects arrived with their police escorts into the Blue Hawaii Palm Suite. Big John greeted them with a bone-crushing hand shake and told them that tonight they are the guests of Miss Buscher. Once entered into the suite, each gasped with surprise at what Grace had done. She had set a lavishly decorated table in the center of the room with their names written on place cards. Pink hibiscus and green ferns were carefully placed lengthwise down the center of the table, added with small lit pink and white candles placed in front of a dinner plate. The candles cast a flickering light on the knives and forks.

Stunned, the guests walked around the table and looked faint, noticing that the place settings were the very same as the night Lillie was murdered.

Grace was up to no good. The look in the suspect's eyes flashed back to the night Lillie Russell lay spread-eagle on the floor.

As they circled slowly around the table, they stumbled around like zombies. The suspects reminded me of the gruesome, bandaged actors in von Bismark's horror film, *Eating Eye Balls with the Living Dead.*

The moment, the suspects had entered the suite, not one of them had touched the other or had spoken a word, but, the look in their eyes, each wondered who in the room is the killer—except the killer.

Eric gave a sly glance out the window. He looked for a quick escape into the coconut grove.

Thwarted, below the window, stood a young, muscular Hawaiian wearing a red *malo* guarding the building. In his hand, he held a torch that lit up the grass below the suite making an escape into the coconut grove, even by Houdini, out of the question.

Seeing that there was no escape possible, frustrated, Eric addressed the bartender, breaking the silence, "Goddamn it, I need a drink! A double scotch on the rocks." Since his interview with Grace, except for a few vits here and a few vats there, he had dropped his atrocious German accent faster than he had dropped the Nazi party after the Japanese bombed Pearl Harbor.

Gulping down his scotch, he mumbled, "I wonder what Gracie has up her sleeve?" He spoke to no one in particular.

"I sure could have used that Gracie dame in my business," snickered Granny, grabbing for the gin bottle sitting on the bar counter. After pouring two inches of clear liquid into a tumbler, she swore, "Ah, the hell with it."

As Tony handed Tilda a gin and tonic, the cowboy said quietly, "Honey, what do you think happened to Dockie?"

Tilda took a sip from her drink before she replied, "Pulling up daisies with Lillie and Alice."

Eric spoke in a scared voice that he never used when he directed his thriller, *The Noose Hangs Higher Than the Empire State Building.*

"Pay attention, everyone.. Keep on the alert tonight. There are a couple of new things I've noticed: the outside hall, the guards have abandoned us.. Only Big John over there watches us. That means we are about to be killed or let go. I am reminded of Agatha Christie's, *Ten Little Indians*. In that movie, all the guests were mysteriously killed one by one." Eric gave out a hollow laugh. "And then there were none. Pretty soon, each and every one of us is going to disappear like Dockie." After he laughed, he took a big swig of his drink, and lapsed into his fake German accent and said to himself, "I don't sink dat so funny?"

Granny yipped while holding a gin bottle in one hand and a glass in the other hand, "Shut up, Nazi, before I crack you over the head with this bottle!"

With faces of a sphinx, Raul and Gretchen sat in their chairs, sipped their gin and tonics, and together watched with faint amusement the von Bismark's meltdown.

A conch shell blew, followed by a blackout! The lights in the hotel inked out as they did on the night Lillie was murdered. Graces nightly ceremony had commenced. Grace's voice could be heard in the distance narrating the ceremony. When she finished, signaled by drum beats, Hawaiian runners ran around the Coco Palms lighting the grove as they had done for the last decade. During the torch-lighting ceremony, not one person in the Blue Palms suite moved or spoke, frozen in place, as each remembered Eric's voice, "who was next?"

During the torch lighting, Big John had coughed a number of times to make sure everyone in the room knew that he was present and in charge.

His cough was a comforting interruption to me. I stood motionless next to the bartender, thinking that I was next to die.

When the lights flickered back on, everyone stood still as stone in their same positions. Surprisingly, Tony's bladder held tight. Not one person had moved even an inch.

Two raps on the door— Grace's signal. After Big John rapped twice from our side of the door, he opened it. Grace entered briskly wearing her white *muumuu* and a red carnation lei. Beside her, Dockie Wockie walked steadily in a pristine, white suit without any gravy spills on his tie. Dockie's face was shaved and there wasn't a smell of alcohol on his breath.

Seeing Dockie, Granny gasped as Tilda whispered to Tony, "He's alive."

Behind Dockie Wockie walked the regal Hawaiian person, Gladys Brandt, and the attractive third grade teacher, Anna Bishop. Entering the room arm in arm, they burst into laughter seeing Eric's pith helmet and the black patch over his eye. Both eye patch and pith helmet were askew.

Next, walked through the door was the author of *The Nun's Story* and Grace's celebrity on the island, Kate Hulme. Kate's formidable French nose twitched. It signaled she smelled trouble. Behind Kate followed Marie Louise Habets. Lou minced five steps behind the formidable Kate. Since the first day she met her friend, Kate, once a nun, Lou acquiesced all her worldly goods to Kate and referred to Kate, in jest, as her Mother Superior.

It was an evening that I never forgot!

CHAPTER TWENTY

November 8, 1960 – John F. Kennedy is elected as President of the United States, winning over Richard M. Nixon.

Grace glanced around the room, counted the bodies and made sure that all participants were present and accounted for.

After she had looked directly into their ashen faces, Grace announced: "Tonight I am about to recreate Lillie's birthday dinner. Perhaps by recreating the dinner, we will finish what Lillie had planned to do—discover her father's killer. As a result of the interviews I have conducted with all of you, I have an inkling why Lillie was murdered and who did it. I have asked friends of mine, who live on Kauai to assist me in tonight's charade. They will play Lillie, Alice, and the dolls. May I introduce Gladys Brandt—she will be Lillie Russell. Miss Lou Habets will portray Alice; Kathryn Hulme, the Oedipus Rex doll; Anna Bishop, the floozy doll; and I will sit at the head of the table with Mrs. Brandt and kibitz. The word *kibitz* means I am running the show and I will also represent the Charlie McCarthy doll. Take the same seats you had on the night of Lillie's birthday. There are place cards on the table that will help you to remember your seating."

Silently, the suspects moved in slow motion toward the table. The way they moved, it became apparent that each felt they were about to be hung up by their heels or shot by a firing squad. Fearing that this was their last supper, each suspect looked as morose as the men and women painted on an El Greco canvas. Each stood muted at their places and waited for Grace to speak.

In the back of the room, Grace's actors looked over their scripts as she began to direct the suspects. "So that I can concentrate on the purpose of the evening, dinner will be served in courses—taking time between each course to let the actors act out the script that I have written. Since I was not present at the dinner party, if I have not been accurate with any of the events as they occurred that evening, you have my permission to correct me. Gladys, Anna, Kate, and Lou, please now join us at the table. Sit where you find the name of the character you are portraying."

"Everyone, now, please, be seated," Grace commanded.

Everyone seated at the table, Gladys (Lillie) rang the dinner bell on the table, and began the night's festivities. The suite door opened and Big John entered with the waiters holding their trays of food high in the air. Waiters, moving with the agility of dancers in a Jerome Robbins ballet, placed the soup (kimchee bisque) and a small dinner salad (a Gus concoction of mixed local greens and caramelized almonds) in front of everyone in a matter of seconds.

"While you are enjoying your salad and soup, Gladys—or Lillie—here, will bid us welcome."

Gladys stood tall and regal, cleared her throat, and cut to the chase. Gladys must have read that great actresses always cleared their throats before playing Lady Macbeth.

After a little cough, rounding out her vowels, Gladys proclaimed, "I believe, by your actions before and after we arrived on

Kauai, that each one of you for your own and very personal reasons would have liked to have murdered me in my bed or at my birthday party. The truth is I don't like you and you don't like me."

Von Bismark jumped up indigently from his chair and protested: "I will not sit here and listen to your drivel. Woman, whoever you are, you are not Lillie and how dare you imply that ve all vanted Lillie dead. We lufted Lillie."

Everyone at the table nodded their heads in assent to von Bismark's assertion.

That snapped their girdles.

Grace interrupted and looked at Big John standing by the doorway and nodded her head. Big John motioned with his hands for the director to sit down and shut his mouth. Eric panicked because he remembered that it was only a short while ago when he felt Big John's humongous paws squeezing his neck. Feeling his bruised neck, Eric sat down and mumbled under his breath that one day he'd have his revenge on Grace and Big John.

Always, Eric wanted to have the last word and gave his best last shot to Gladys, seated next to him. Von Bismark gave her his very much practiced Yul Brynner Mongolian look—a look that he telegraphed to Gladys that he wanted to kill her. Gladys, not impressed with his Mongolian act, picked up a dessert spoon and thumped his pith helmet twice, warning him to behave himself.

I giggle, in spite, of trying to act serious Eric had as big a fat ass as mine. Fat asses, according to Freud and Jung, indicate a fat ego.

After Eric's outburst, the guests glued their eyes on Grace as she explained: "I wrote this script after hearing your interviews and as a result of many long-distance phone calls I made to Hollywood," Grace paused. "Gladys—pardon me—Lillie, please continue on."

Gladys, enjoyed herself immensely, and continued: "Let me repeat, each one of you would like to see me dead, but this evening is not about me. This evening is about the murder of my father. One of you sitting at this table killed my father and it is my intention to find out who it is!"

Gladys took her eyes off the script, into the role of Lillie, improvised and glared at all the suspects; then, without speaking another word, sat down.

In her seat, Grace repeated, "When we find out who killed Lillie's father, we will discover Lillie's murderer."

Grace's words made Dockie choke on a lettuce leaf, Gretchen drop her spoon in the soup bowl, and the others waited for Grace to drop the other shoe.

"Well, I'll be hogtied. If this ain't the most far-out piece of crap that makes sense since I have been kept a prisoner is this insane cuckoo's nest," guffawed Granny. After she spoke, chugged down a Primo beer in one swallow.

"I'll be fu—"

"Tilda, honey!" Tony warned.

"I'll be . . . fudged! Lillie's old man's death is behind all of this."

Tommy squeaked: "Oh, come on. None of us knew the old man. You're off your rocker, Gracie. If I did meet him, he sure didn't make much of an impression on me."

"We all met him," Gretchen said as she reached for her glass of white wine. "We met him last year at Lillie's Christmas party. We were all there. Every one of us sitting at this table was there. I remember that distinctly! I was living with Lillie at the time recovering from my plastic surgery. After the party, Lillie said her dad had a high old time, but something funny happened at the party that he didn't anticipate. Someone he met at the party tickled the hell out of him."

"Nah, I think you got it all wrong, Gretchen. Daddy Dear had too many Jack Daniels. But you're right on the money on one thing, Daddy Dear had a high old time." Tony offered his opinion as he put his arm around Tilda.

Dockie, who hadn't said a word since he entered the room, spoke up: "He was having a high old time, I agree with Gretchen and Tony on that, but Daddy wasn't drunk. Believe me, I know all about drunks. Funny, strange actually, that was the last party that Heidi and I attended. Heidi died not long after that, too. The two deaths are connected; of that I am certain."

Dockie was stone-cold sober.

Raul added his two cents: "Remember, I knew my father-in-law better than anyone in this room. Lillie's dad lived on the edge. He died because, he skated on thin ice. He knew something that he shouldn't have known."

"How did he die?" the Oedipus doll (Kate) asked Dockie.

"Arthur died in a fire. His home caught on fire and by the time the firemen got to him, he was dead . . . but not from smoke inhalation. He had been strangled with a ladies' scarf. Whoever killed him set his house on fire, hoping that by the time the firemen found him, all that would remain of Arthur would be a pile of ashes."

Grace once again took control of her narrative, "Let's stop the charade for a while and enjoy our entrée. You received a call from my secretary inquiring whether you wanted fish or beef. Tilda, I believe you wanted a vegetarian meal. Correct?"

"I am cleaning up my act, Miss Buscher."

Grace cooed to Tilda, "You are so like Coco Palms. See, we do change people who stay here. Someday, I will do the same for myself, that is, become a vegetarian. Everyone drink up. Percy, see that everyone's glasses are full of wine. Tonight, we are serving a house white and red. Your choice. In the next few moments, let us relax, digest what you have heard, and enjoy the meal. After we finish eating our meals, the dolls will begin their narrative. So, bon a petite. If you have to excuse yourself for any reason, Big John or I will escort you to the bathroom. I don't want anyone to run out on us—now that we are at the finish line."

"Fat chance that we can get out of here. Jack-the-Ripper had more compassion than this dame ever gave us," Eric muffled that comment to Lou Habets holding a napkin in front of his face.

Not fond of Germans, because of the war, Lou turned her back on Eric and engaged Gretchen in conversation. Lou and Gretchen became friends immediately and talked about the inconsequential things, which is so often the norm at large dinner parties.

The expressions on everyone's faces told me that Eric had become the leper of the night.

Eric felt the negativity in the room and fiddled with his pith helmet.

Eric was stupid. His big, fat ego didn't understand that acting as an arrogant son-of-a-bitch had made him the killer.

I tapped on Eric's helmet to hear if there was anything inside his head and heard nothing. That figured! I explained to Big John, "The blood in Eric's head has gone south. Since the day he wore long pants, the blood in his head has headed south and left him brainless. Think about this Big John, there is something to be said for some men inheriting from God a small Vienna sausage. I bet Einstein had the smallest dick in history."

Eric kicked me.

"Ouch!"

Too many clues pointed the finger to Eric, the Hun. Surprise endings are only found in the movies.

During the dinner, there hadn't been much conversation. Everyone kept their traps shut.. Each feared that one careless word could point to them out as the killer. The exception was Gretchen and Lou. They threw caution to the winds, taking a great liking to one another, chattered as two magpies.

As preplanned by Grace, everyone had become loopy from the alcohol intake they had consumed before dinner and during dinner. Caffeine kicked in when their Kona coffee arrived. Caffeine combined with their alcohol intake, each fought the impulse to scream and yell, yet, couldn't control their eyes fluttering around the table trying to hold onto their sanity.

As soon as the dinner plates were cleared off the table, jittery fingers drummed musically on the table, a sign that each suspect yearned to be back to a time when they turned somersaults in a sandbox. They longed to be a child again when life was simpler. One plus point, they breathed a sigh of relief when Grace didn't choose in her charade to play musical glasses. If forced to relive that game—the game that killed Lillie—they would have all stabbed themselves with their dessert forks.

Time stood still for them because Grace held their futures tight in her hands. The combination of alcohol, caffeine, and Grace staring at them—three potent intoxicants… the suspects' eyes quit fluttering and turned cartwheels. Inside their heads screamed that if they didn't get out of the Coco Palms soon, they'd all go mad in Grace's *pupule* (crazy) house. It seemed hours to them before Grace raised her spoon, clinked her wine glass, and, once again, gained their attention/.

"We'll continue our charade as dessert is being served. Anna, you begin."

Anna, playing a young Lillie, read from a script in the cheerful voice of a little girl. "It was my twelfth birthday. Even though my mother had died tragically the year before, Arthur, my father, and I lived happily in a flat on Sutter Street in San Francisco. I was happy until the day he took me to see Greta Garbo in MGM's *Anna Karenina*. After the movie, he treated me to a hot dog and a chocolate ice cream soda. That day, my life as I once knew it, was never the same again. Daddy told me to wait for him out on the sidewalk while he drank a beer in his favorite theatrical bar, The Lillian Russell. My father never returned for me. I sat down next to the entrance of the bar and waited and waited for him. I searched for my father's face among the sea of men going in and out of the bar. All day long, I waited and waited, huddling by the door to keep warm. Night came and no Daddy. Before that awful day, my name was Agnes Baxter. My daddy's name was Arthur Baxter. Then Granny appeared out of nowhere."

Granny stood up in a trance and spoke in a voice from long ago. It was as if the twelve-year-old girl was right in front of her. "Honey, your daddy told me to come get you. He had to go away . . . sudden like."

Looking at Grace, Granny broke from her trance. "Miss Buscher, that little girl looked at me with big, wide eyes—still, sad eyes; as if she had suddenly died when I told her that."

Anna broke in and continued to read from her cue card: "Granny took my hand, forced me to get up and asked, 'What's your name?' I told her, 'My name is Lillian Russell.'"

Granny looked at Anna as if she was speaking to Lillie when she was a little girl, "Well, Miss Lillie, that's as fine a name as I ever heard. Lillian Russell was a great Broadway star. Your daddy said your name is Agnes."

217

"My name is Lillian Russell. You see, the name Lillian Russell will help my daddy to remember where he left me. It will help him to find me."

"Now this is the truth, Miss Buscher," Granny spouted in an angry voice as she remembered the past and looked at Grace. "Arthur had some trouble with some theatrical folks. They took a contract out on him. Damn that Arthur; he could never keep his mouth shut and he always looked for a quick buck. I took his child back to her home on Sutter Street. The flat had been completely trashed by these nameless folks. Arthur never told me the circumstance or the names of these fiends. He said I was to protect his child. As you all know, I ran a fancy house and Arthur was one of my clients. He had put aside some money for Lillie and gave it to me. I had some thoughts of using this child in my business, to be one of my girls, because she was more than beautiful and looked more than her twelve years. But I protected her. I sent her to a Catholic school in Belmont, California for three years, but by the time she turned fifteen, she had blossomed into one of the most damned beautiful woman God ever created. I have told many stories about Lillie's beginnings, but this is God's truth. One of my clients, while I was out, raped Lillie. I made two decisions that day: one to get even with that bastard; the other to get the hell out of Frisco before another similar incident could happen to her. I did both. By the time I left San Francisco with Lillie, this creep related to the wealthy Fisk family, had mysteriously disappeared and he has never been found. I sold my business to one of my girls, packed up our duds and took the train to Hollywood with Lillie to try our luck in the movies. From the moment Lillie walked down on Hollywood and Vine, her life has been grist for the movie magazines. I don't know how Heidi found out about Lillie's San Francisco beginnings, but that bitch Heidi didn't know all of it—although she thought she did—and threatened to write about it in her trashy newspaper column that Lillie had once been a prostitute. When Lillie bought Heidi's files, Lillie told me that there were paragraphs of lies about her underlined in red ink. Lillie also told me before we came to Hawaii—not to Heidi's credit—that just before she died, Heidi had changed her mind and had promised Lillie she would never use that information or make any attempt to blackmail her. Heidi knew that she was on rocky ground and could be sued by Lillie. When Arthur reappeared and found his Lillian Russell, all was forgiven by Lillie. Having her dad back in her life, Lillie believed she was living in heaven. I also believe down in my nasty, little heart that something happened at Lillie's Christmas party that caused Arthur to be murdered. Arthur's death turned Lillie's life back into a living hell. To keep it straight, Lillie was never one of my girls, but she did have a botched abortion because of the man who raped her. That's the truth. Even though I saw Arthur at the Christmas party, we never spoke to one another. I hated him and thought he was a bastard for what he did to my Lillie."

Anna sighed as she and Granny sat down together. Anna put her cue card on the table and concluded, "That ends my tale."

"Kate, Oedipus Rex," Grace commanded, "continue the story."

Kate, ever wanting to be a dramatic actress, stood and spoke as if she was orating to a Greek audience in Epidaurus (the amphitheater in the Peloponnese.)

About to read from her cue card, Kate did a dramatic breaststroke with her right arm. To gesture with an arm while one acted was something Kate read that Sarah Bernhardt did in all her performances in Paris. Moving her arm as if she were doing a backstroke, Kate spoke in her lower register as Lillie's father: "When Oedipus Rex learned the secret that he had married his mother and killed his father, he paid a price for the truth and gouged out his eyes. I, Arthur, Lillie's father, learned a secret that killed me. I paid the ultimate price for threatening to expose the secret. Only three people knew this secret: the killer, Heidi, and me. For the record, Heidi had a file on me, too. When Lillie bought Heidi's files, mysteriously, my file was missing . . . removed by the killer."

"But!" Kate spoke up beyond a whisper, which made her voice sound even more dramatic. ". . . that secret is about to be revealed!" Kate stopped speaking whence came a deathly silence in the room. Just the wind rustling the coconut leaves out in the grove was heard.

"Well, goddammit, what is the frickin' secret?" spoke an exasperated Tilda. This time Tony didn't scold her; instead, trying to comfort her, he gently held her hand.

Grace reached down and picked up the head and body of the Charlie McCarthy doll. "It all has to do with this doll!"

"I know what that is. I remember now," Gretchen interrupted.

Holding up the body of the doll, Grace insisted, "Tell us Gretchen."

"This is what Lillie told me before we left for Kauai. The day after the Christmas party, Arthur came to Lillie's house and gave her this doll. This doll I didn't buy. He acted very disturbed and very crypt and spoke to Lillie in only riddles. Riddles about when he was in show business and the acts that he performed in. He rambled on, not making any sense to either Lillie or me. As I told Miss Buscher, Lillie passed off Arthur's visit believing her father had one too many drinks. Not hearing from her father, Lillie assumed, wrongly, that Arthur was sleeping off a bad hangover—but the night of Arthur's visit to Lillie, he was murdered. After the murder of her father, is when Lillie began to investigate the years before she was born and the missing years after Arthur left her sitting at the bar door waiting for him to return. It was the only reason Lillie bought Heidi's files. As you might remember, Miss Buscher, when we first arrived, Lillie on the phone shared with us that she was waiting for a telegram from her lawyer. I found the telegram in my room when you had our belongings moved over to this wing. Reading the telegram, it confirmed that Arthur had a safe deposit box at Bank of America - the Westwood branch. Lillie gave instructions to Mr. Hargrove, her lawyer, who had Arthur's power of attorney, to retrieve the contents of her father's safe deposit box and send them to her at the Coco Palms. She never lived to see what was inside that safe deposit box because the it and its contents hadn't arrived at the Coco Palms. The contents should have arrived by now at the hotel."

Cherries jubilee was flambéed next to Grace as Gretchen spoke. The light of the flames on the grill flickered on Grace's face as she informed her guests: "The mail plane will arrive from Honolulu after midnight. I have been assured that the contents of the safe deposit box will be on that plane. I had hoped they would be here sooner and hoped to share them with you at my dinner party. I feel that all the answers we need to clear up this mystery are on that plane. Sworn in as a deputy, I have the authority to unseal the box as soon as it arrives, read the contents, and then, I promise you, justice will be served. I also have good news for you,: this is your last night at the Coco Palms. As of tomorrow morning, I no longer have any jurisdiction to hold you here as my guests."

"You mean prisoners. I knew it!" screamed Eric. "You vil be sued by me and everyone else sitting at this table. You had no right to keep us here in the first place." After von Bismark spoke his mind, he thrashed about in his chair like a madman trying to get out of a straitjacket. (Acting a role from one of his bio-movies, *I Was Bit in*

My Left Testicle by a Singing Cobra/.) Ever vigilant, he kept his good testicle and good eye on Big John.

Lou smiled in delight because Grace told her that it was her turn to play her role as Alice.

Sitting next to Eric, Lou stood, looked down at the director, and spoke to him directly while she read in her quiet religious way from the card she held in her hand. "I am playing Alice, your wife, Mr. Director. I would be careful what you say to me, because I wrote down all the things you did to me and to the others at the studio during all the years of our marriage. I kept a journal containing a complete record of all your misdeeds. I wrote down all the despicable things that you did to me and Lillie. This journal is now in Miss Buscher's possession. After I died, she found it among my things in my room. So, I would be careful who you would be suing, Eric."

Eric snarled at Lou, "If you weren't a lady, I'd . . ."

Johnny-on-the-spot, Big John stood behind Eric's chair and, without any direction from Grace, took off Eric's helmet, and mashed Eric's head into the plate of cherries jubilee as he said, in a gentlemanly way, "Sir, I wouldn't do anything . . . or say anything more if I were you. Can you hear me, sir?"

Eric gurgled in the cherry juice and said, "I do!"

"Let him up, Big John."

Eric raised his head with a squashed cherry stuck to his eye patch and two cherries smashed on his left cheek looking two big, angry, red boils.

Grace laughed at Eric and said: "Well, we'll just have to wait and see who's suing whom, won't we, Mr. Eric? Breakfast will be served in this suite at eight tomorrow morning. This is our last meeting and I did promise that I would have all the final answers by tonight, but we will have to wait for the midnight plane to land and learn them. The solving of the two murders will be announced tomorrow at breakfast with someone under arrest."

Grace picked a cherry off of Eric's face and continued, "Now, everyone—that includes you Mr. von Bismark. Please, Eric, wipe the rest of the cherries off your face; you look very foolish. Please do so now, so the rest of us can enjoy ourselves eating Mr. Guslander's famous dessert. We will conclude our dinner with a Pick Me Up Charlie, my favorite after-dinner drink."

Eric took his napkin and wiped his face, and wanting to curse Grace, instead said, "Damn it, what is dis 'Pick Me Up Charlie?'"

"It's Coco Palms' favorite brandy drink. One drink and you'll have to excuse yourselves and return to your rooms. Last instruction: you are all to remain on this floor and in your rooms until tomorrow morning. Guards, though not seen, are still on the property and kept around only for your protection. Have a good evening."

"Heil Hitler," Eric saluted Grace with the juice of one remaining cherry trickling down his face.

Ignoring Eric's boorishness, Grace waved her hand for Gladys, Kate, Lou, and Anna to rise from their seats and follow her out of the room.

After Grace and her party left, Tilda spoke very much annoyed: "This evening was a bust. We didn't learn one damn thing. Why didn't Oedipus finish his speech? Why didn't Charlie McCarthy speak? This has all been madness."

"Let's get the hell out of here and to hell with the cherries jubilee and Pick Me Up—who cares?" Raul spoke wanting to have the last word.

CHAPTER TWENTY-ONE

1960 – The world population is 3,021,475,000.

As Grace left for a final drink with her gang, she had pulled me aside and whispered: "Follow what I say closely and do not deviate one iota from what I am about to tell you to do. It could mean life or death for both you and me."

I did a little Tony Pinto in my pants when Grace gave me her instructions, especially when she told me to follow the instructions to the letter or it could mean death for the both of us..

The suspects, feeling out-of-sorts, abandoned the Blue Hawaii suite in dribs and drabs. Their last supper had not solved one "damn thing"—it only left more questions and a bitter taste in their mouths. Most importantly, the killer had not been named.

Grace wasn't very smart having all the suspects leave the Blue Palms suite with all the strings untied. What sacred me, the killer was alive and well and at large. When Eric gave the Nazi salute, I felt Grace should have hogtied von Bismark then and there and sent him to prison to be done with it.

To hell with Mr. von Bismark, I thought bravely, I had more important things on my mind—trying to remember word for word what Miss Buscher had instructed to me to do. Damn it, I wish Grace wouldn't whisper so.

At 11:30 p.m., prior to Miss Buscher's return from having drinks with Kate, Lou, Gladys, and Anna, I was to sneak into her bedroom, squeeze myself under her bed, and wait. Wait for what?

At 11;30 p.m., I did as I was instructed, I squeezed my fat body under her bed, and propped my head up against a stack of Agatha Christie's murder mysteries and waited

Minutes later, I felt another presence in the room. The nervous type, I chalked it up to my

imagination, but . . . It couldn't be but I was, I just heard slow, deep breathing somewhere in the bedroom.

After midnight, the doorknob rattled.

I should have gone to the bathroom before I took on this adventure.

In walked Miss Buscher. I watched her white shoes walk to the dressing table and heard her sit down on the stool at her vanity table. I peeped out from under the bed, saw Grace look into the mirror, and twist open one of the jars of Elizabeth Arden "vanishing" creams.

As instructed, I resumed my position under the bed and listened for every noise or sound made in the room. Tonight, I was so on the alert, I heard a pin drop.

What I heard next was Grace's fingernails opening an envelope.

A frog croaked.

Then I heard papers rustle in her hands as Grace said quite loudly to herself: "I knew it had to be something like this. This will make for a most interesting breakfast."

Without rhyme or reason, her next sentence was not to herself, or to me, for I was not to speak until she called out my name.

Grace said, "You can come out now."

Instinctively, I wanted to come out from under the bed, but I continued to follow Grace's instructions.

Once again, Grace said, "You can come out now. I know you are in this room."

A rustling sound came out from behind one of the Japanese screens—the screen that stood in the right corner of the bedroom.

A voice said, "How did you know I'd be here?"

"You had to come so your secret would be kept."

"You are too smart for your britches, Miss Bushwhack. You know what I do to all smarty pants."

"Yes, I do. You kill them like you killed Arthur and Heidi."

Tommy Twinkle spoke to Grace in a man's voice—a voice that I had never heard him use before.

He repeated, "Like I killed Arthur and Heidi . . . because they knew too much."

"They knew?"

"They knew that I killed my parents and the police had been looking for me for years. The case is now cold, closed, and, as far as I know, no one is looking for me. Those two snoops got in my way. They would have gone to the police and opened up the case against me."

Grace spoke back in a calm voice, "Before you do away with me, just the hell of it, actor to actress, professional to professional, tell me in your words what was this all about."

"I'll humor you, Gracie, for a minute," Tommy said, standing behind Grace at her vanity table.

Meanwhile, I remained as quiet as a possum under the bed, carrying out Grace's instructions to the letter.

"My parents were vaudevillians. Their act was Ben and Mabel—a singing and dancing duo. They weren't very good—mediocre at best

. . . until Ben came up with a brilliant idea when I turned three. I was a precocious little brat who could never shut up and mimicked all the movie stars, so Ben brought me into the act: Ben and Donny— the greatest ventriloquist act in America. Ben made me up to look like a doll . . . and it worked. Because I was supposed to be a dummy, my parents kept me hidden away. In my early childhood, they suffocated me daily. Whenever they brought me to the theater, I was made to lie in a custom-made wooden box. On stage and off, they treated me like a dummy, the only difference was, they had to feed me. One thing they didn't figure on— I grew taller. They refused to see that. Neither Ben nor my mother, Mabel, ever treated me like a human being and they wouldn't let me out of the act. They kept me a prisoner night and day until, one day, in my frustration, I killed them. After I shot them, I burned them up in the house where we were living. Their only friend was a singer playing on our bill: Arthur, the blue-eyed baritone—mediocre at best—Lillie's father. He knew all about me. He told the police about me after they found my parents' bodies and there was a warrant out for my arrest. I disappeared and became Tommy Twinkle. It was easy to do because no one, except Arthur, had ever seen me without my dummy's makeup on. He once walked into my parent's dressing room unannounced and saw me. Arthur recognized me at that Christmas party at Lillie's, because I had had too many drinks and performed one of the routines that my mother and father did in our dummy act . . . and bingo! My cover was blown. The only other person who knew about me was Heidi. Again, after too many drinks at the Brown Derby, I confessed my secret to her thinking she was my best friend. I was too valuable to her, I thought, and she promised me that she would never give me away. Unfortunately for her, she figured out that I had killed Arthur. What I did to my parents didn't matter to her, but she was afraid that what I did to Arthur, I would do to her. When Arthur reappeared, because of me, she created a file on him and me for her protection. I was now not to be trusted anymore. Arthur's murder upset our once precious applecart. I didn't trust her and she didn't trust me. Taking no chances, I pleaded with Heidi to burn my file and Arthur's file. She wouldn't. I gave her a lethal injection from Dockie's bag and I stole my file. I would have gotten away with it—because Dockie is such a drunk—but what I didn't imagine was that Heidi copied my file and kept it in a separate safe deposit box among other secrets that included Lillie's and Arthur's files . . . all for her perverse protection. Dockie hadn't a clue what he had inherited. The old fool had messed up with an under-aged actress and sold Heidi's poisonous files to Lillie to keep him out of jail. Lillie had her suspicions after her father died, especially after she found out that some of the files were missing. Her suspicions created the birthday party at the Coco Palms. My dear, with Lillie dead, I thought I was home free. But you know too much for your britches. I am going to take this pretty, little pink scarf put it around your neck and it will be all over in a twinkle."

"You'll never get away with this . . . Per—" Tommy clamped his hand over Grace's mouth.

"This is Tilda's scarf; she dropped it in the hallway. They'll think Tilda killed you . . . or Eric. But I didn't kill Lillie. I was going to, but never had the chance. Someone else did it for me. I'd point my finger at Eric for that murder. Alice wasn't my doing either." His eyes bulged as he kept his hand tight over Grace's mouth, and with the other hand, he twisted the scarf around her neck and whispered into Grace's ear, "It won't be long now, honey."

From under the bed, it sounded as though Grace was trying to call out my name while she was gagging, so—not taking any chances—I peered out from under the bed and saw Grace's face had turned the color of a pretty hydrangea blue. Being the inscrutable Charlie Chan that I am, I deduced that she might need my assistance, even if she wasn't calling out my name clearly.

I scrambled out from under the bed and yelled as per her instructions, "Help! Miss Buscher needs help! And Tommy—stop what you are doing!" I proudly added, "Tommy, stop what are you doing!" Then, I added my own coup de grace, "You are a fiend, Tommy Twinkle!"

Tommy dropped the scarf and ran for the open window. Too late! A large, brown hand reached up from outside the window and Big John jumped through the screen into Grace's bedroom. He grasped Tommy by the scruff of his neck and held him high in the air. Tommy Twinkle wiggled and screamed, sounding like a chicken going off to the chopping block.

With both hands, Miss Buscher massaged her throat and gasped: "Percy, why didn't you come out sooner? I could have been killed."

"I couldn't make out your words clearly and I didn't know how dramatic you wanted to make it," I spoke to her, defending myself.

When Grace's face turned back to a hazy pink and before she could slap my head, the bedroom door opened and to my surprise, more to any surprise that I could think of . . . in fact, I could have fainted . . . Lillie, Alice, and Dockie appeared.

Upon seeing the three of them, Tommy Twinkle fainted.

I, on the other hand, dazed, wanting to speak in a brave John Wayne voice but sounded more like a depraved Joan Crawford, yammered: "Well, blow my britches and snap my garters. God must not have wanted you three in heaven. Ain't you three a sight for sore eyes. How in the hell are you? Let's have a drink!"

Whatever prompted me to say such stupid things in a time of a crisis, when in reality I wanted to vomit and scream—well—only Freud and God could explain.

Grace slapped my head as Big John laid the prostrate, unconscious Tommy Twinkle down on Grace's bed. When Tommy opened his eyes, Grace, Lillie, Alice, and Dockie had surrounded the bed. Conscious once again, Tommy remained motionless, afraid to move, and looked unbelieving at the two people he thought had died. I stood in the back and observed because I had disgraced myself in Grace's eyes.

It wasn't my fault that Grace almost got it in the neck. Grace needed elocution lessons.

Lillie looked at Tommy, his eyes fixed on hers, and then she spoke: "Tommy, we heard everything you said and you were tape recorded. There is no question about your killing your parents, my father, and Heidi. I had no real proof and so we, all of us here, created this theatrical drama to catch you red-handed. Dockie and I were certain of your guilt and Alice wanted to get the goods on Eric. We were all in cahoots with each other since the beginning of this trip. I am afraid the telegram from my lawyer and the safe deposit box were only a ruse. I have to thank Miss Buscher for being our impresario extraordinaire—Florenz Ziegfeld. We have had time to think how we are going to punish you. Big John and Miss Buscher let us read about some of the old Hawaiian customs, and since we are here on Kauai at the Coco Palms, we have decided by consensus to deliver your punishment by our own hands—not in the hands of the police. We feel we are more just than any of our lawmakers."

Alice smiled, looking quite pleased as she said to Grace, "Remember Grace, Mr. Eric's punishment remains in my hands."

Dockie, without the slightest smell of alcohol on his breath, spoke in a low voice, "Tommy, you can have your choice of how you want your punishment is to be served." Taking a breath, rapping his knuckles on the wall: "I call the court to order. Ladies and gentlemen of the jury, what is your verdict?"

"GUILTY!" Each said in unison, being the members of the jury. Their verdict echoed and echoed off of Grace's bedroom walls.

"How shall his punishment be served?" asked Dockie.

Lillie, still holding the reins, responded: "We could turn Tommy over to the local authorities tonight,: drive him down to the jail and press charges. Once that's done, Tommy will be shipped to California and, if found guilty by California law, Tommy Twinkle will get the gas chamber. The gas chamber is a pretty awful death, Tommy."

Tommy cried: "Please don't do that to me. I didn't mean to do it. My parents were so mean to me. I hated what they did to me." Sobbing, he continued: "Only monster parents would treat their child as I was treated. Nobody has ever loved me. Nobody. I have been used since the day I was born. I was never treated as a human being. I was only a thing—a commodity to be manipulated by my parents. Arthur could have called in the authorities on my parents and told them what was happening to a child. He could have put my parents in jail. He didn't. Instead, he called the police on me. He hated me. Heidi used me, too. She made me help her get the goods on people . . . but after I killed Arthur, I had become too dangerous for her to have me around as a friend. Please, understand me. I just wanted to be loved. I never wanted to be a freak."

"We hear you, Tommy," said Grace, taking back the reins, "I hear you, and because of that, we are giving you a second chance— another choice of punishment. Kauai is a special island . . . some say it is one of the most powerful, mystical spots on earth. All of us would be willing to let nature take care of your punishment. There is a valley on this island—I call it Shanghai-La; others call it the Valley of Karma; Hawaiians call it the Valley of Lono. It is a hidden valley . . . very small, hard to find, difficult to get into, and even more impossible to get out of because of the sharp, impassible cliffs that surround it. There is plenty of water and food there. It is a place where the force, the *mana*, of the island is so powerful that, in this valley, you will have to face yourself and face all the evil deeds you have done to others. You will be forced to discover your inner self. What will be given to you in this valley is where the punishment fits the crime. You will face unspeakable horrors but, in the end, it is said by the Hawaiians, you will be able to forgive yourself. Here in this valley karma meets karma head on in the most profound, most powerful, and most unknown ways. You will be taken to this valley, blindfolded, and, after you have completed the many years of punishment given to you and if you can find your way out of the valley, which is doubtful, you can head for the City of Refuge—a *heiau* (a Hawaiian temple) by the Wailua River, Once there, your sins will be forgiven, the three of us will forgive you, and so will the authorities. What is your pleasure?"

Without hesitation, Tommy whimpered, "Take me to the valley."

"That is your decision?" Grace asked.

Tommy nodded.

"The valley is full of centipedes, scorpions, and hidden dangers abound in the steep cliffs that surround you; and most importantly, you are far, far away from the ocean. You will be completely alone and no one will ever come for you. It will be up to you to find your way out, which, to my knowledge, no one has ever escaped from the valley—ever. You will have to learn to feed yourself, protect yourself, shelter yourself, and, worst of all, face yourself every day while you live in that valley. There is no greater punishment that I can think of than having, day after day, year after year, look inside your soul and see all the horrors you have created.

Speaking in a strong and determined voice, Tommy replied, "That is my decision."

"Tonight, Big John will take you and lower you in a basket down into the valley. And when the sun comes up the next morning, you will find yourself in your new home and begin your life anew."

"What may I take with me?"

"Your personal belongings will be placed in a duffel bag along with the Charlie McCarthy doll as your only companion."

Tommy closed his eyes and cried as Big John lifted him off the bed. Big John carried Tommy gently, cradling him in his arms like a newborn baby—a baby who had just been born in Grace's bedroom.

Grace gave the benediction before Tommy left the room. "Justice is done . . . though justice is never a pleasant task to exact, but in a world that believes in goodness and mercy, it must be done here. Let us remember, everybody living on this planet wants and needs to be loved."

CHAPTER TWENTY-TWO

May 10, 1960 – Bono (lead singer for Irish rock band U2) is born.

The next morning, while breakfast was served in the Blue Hawaii Palms suite, the usual suspects gagged on their coconut pancakes when a very much alive Lillie and Alice walked in, arm in arm with Grace. The most surprised of all was Eric the Hun.

Lillie, standing in front of them, looking unbelievably beautiful, scanned all the faces in the room. It was if an invisible hand, seeing Lillie, sculpted them into marble statues. Each one of them speechless, believed they were seeing ghosts standing in front of them.

Lillie smiled, "Boo, everyone. Darling Lillie has arisen from the grave." Saying that, amused at their reactions seing her, Lillie tinkled a laugh that sounded as delicate as a Japanese wind chime.

"Don't be scared, my darlings, I'm real. Everyone, join me downstairs. Let's get the hell out of this awful room and that skimpy breakfast you're eating and follow me. The buffet breakfast is serving Loco Moco Eggs Benedict in the Main Dining Room and breakfast is on me."

Lillie twirled around in a cloud of blue-and-pink chiffon and, as she had planned, before she left the room, pinched Eric hard on his cheek. By her touch and Eric's scream, she had changed herself in front of everyone from a ghost into a live human being and exited the room.

Before anyone could react to what they had just witnessed, Alice sat down beside Eric.

Eric's eyes bulged out of his head as he looked stunned at who was sitting beside him. Here was an alive Alice. For the first time in his life, Eric had become speechless.

Alice took his hand and hissed into his ear, "Darling, I am divorcing you and taking you for all you are worth . . . which is probably a big zero."

"Alice, I thought you were dead . . ."

"Don't speak. Just listen." Taking a recording tape out of her purse, Alice looked him square in the face and hissed again, "I repeat, my darling, in case you didn't hear me the first time, I am divorcing you and taking you for every cent that you have in the bank, which isn't much considering you have lived off of me and my money for years."

She shoved the tape recording in his face. "On this tape, I've got the goods on you and you won't be suing me or anyone around here for anything. You'll be lucky to find a job directing porno films after I drag you back and forth through the courts."

Eric sputtered, "but . . . but . . . don't do anything rash until we can talk together alone, darlink. Remember what I have!"

"Listen Eric von Bismark, darlink, you will never be alone with me ever again." Rising from the chair and reaching for Grace's hand, she said: "Miss Buscher, I am having my breakfast in the restaurant below with the others. The air in here stinks. Join me, anyone?"

Hearing Alice speak, the former suspects followed the lady who had risen from the grave—all their heads filled with many unanswered questions. Playing follow the leader, they scrambled out of the room, leaving behind a stunned Eric. He sat at the table sobbing. It should be noted, that morning, the most alert, sober-acting person in the group was called Dockie Wockie and he hadn't even spoken one word.

Gretchen, last in the line, grabbed Miss Buscher's hand and asked, "Please, explain to me what is going on."

"Gretchen, this is Lillie's birthday party. Let Lillie explain everything to you at breakfast. Hurry it along as your limousine will be at the lobby to take you to the airport in half an hour. You'll be wanting to return home to your husband."

Running down the hall, waving papers, appeared a beefy man without a mustache, who called out, "Miss Buscher! You have to sign these papers. They have to go to Honolulu on the late morning plane."

Grace grabbed the papers out of his hand, and scrawled her name at the bottom of each paper as he thrust the documents to her one by one.

Taking back the papers, he nodded, "Thanks, Miss Buscher. I'll see they get to the airport in time to reach our home office by noon."

Grace called out: "Don't forget to send a box of mangoes along with them. Let's sweeten the pot with those crooks in Honolulu."

He galloped two steps at a time down the backstairs to the front office. Gretchen looked dumbfounded as she asked Grace, "Wasn't that Sheriff Rice?"

"Oh no, my dear," Grace responded as she gently pushed Gretchen toward the elevator. "That's my accountant, Harold Hargrove. He's a transplant from Madison, Wisconsin. I keep him hidden in the back office. After all, it's Hawaiians that our guests want to see at the Coco Palms."

"I am sure that was Sheriff Rice!"

The elevator door opened and, as Gretchen stepped inside, Grace winked at her, "Yes, he has a strong resemblance to Sheriff Rice. But Sheriff Rice passed away a number of years ago. He was quite a legend on Kauai. There is so much in life that can't be explained—not everything is always what it seems to be and so it is at my Coco Palms. Don't you agree? You see, my dear, here at Coco Palms, time stops because our grounds are sacred. Coco Palms is a fantasy come true—a Hawaiian fantasy where forgotten dreams once lost are now found again. Anything you can imagine can and does happen at the Coco Palms Hotel. It's all because the good angels watch over us and protect us. And now, our good angels will protect you."

As the elevator doors closed, Gretchen felt she had just been touched by Coco Palms' magic. Grace's words had morphed into her and Gretchen once again felt as beautiful as she once had been. Many who visited the hotel, and those who drank the sacred, magical waters of Mt. Waialeale, the wettest spot on earth, and believed in the magic of the Coco Palms Hotel, were never, ever the same again.

The half hour before Lillie was to leave with her guests for Lihue airport, Grace's coconut wireless had summoned me into her office. Standing in front of her, and because my head was filled with so many unanswered questions, my brain cells had turned to mush. My mind unplugged the moment Lillie and Alice rose from the grave.

"Percy, my boy, I want to thank you for playing your role to the hilt," Grace spoke, sipping her coffee. "You were magnificent and lived up to all my expectations. One of my worries was that you couldn't resist being a nosy Parker—which you were and are—and a teller of tales when they should not have been told—which you did—but I have to say, you did keep a confidence when I asked you to. You have become a man, my boy."

Pretending—no not pretending—wishing I had a double Cary Grant martini in my hand, I pleaded: "Miss Buscher, please tell me . . . tell me . . . what happened? Nothing was what it seemed. And remember that I didn't give your ruse away about Sheriff Rice."

"Not much of life is what it seems, my boy." Grace nodded to me and nibbled on a piece of burnt toast.

I noticed Grace had won her bet with Kathryn Hulme, her favorite author, because on the desk, prominently displayed, was a stack of Hulme's first edition books. Grace, with her piercing, blue eyes, which made lying to her impossible, proceeded to tell me what I thought I had lived through but was totally different from what I thought had happened. All I knew was that another Coco Palms legend had been created by Grace Buscher.

Nothing at Coco Palms was ever ordinary.

Savoring the moment, Grace began her tale. "Lillie Russell got my name through Mitzi Gaynor and Jack Bean."

I interjected, "Mitzi Gaynor my favorite *South Pacific* movie star and Jack, her husband. The guy who could have been another David Niven, debonair movie star."

"Stop talking, Percy. Do you want to hear the rest of the story?"

I nodded.

"Pay attention."

Finishing her coffee, Grace picked up a pencil from her desk and wrote something on a pad of paper wanting to remember a thought that had just popped into her head. After writing a word down on her pad, Grace said: "Lillie, on the phone, became an instant friend. Speaking from Hollywood, she told me that she wanted to come to Coco Palms to celebrate her birthday, but there was more to it than merely a birthday celebration. Lillie asked me if I liked mysteries. Well, that got me and I said, 'Yes.' And she asked if I wouldn't mind being part of a charade she would like to perform on the night of her birthday dinner. That was too much for me to resist. In a few sentences, Lillie explained that her father had been murdered and felt that one of the guests that she was bringing had killed him. Well, Mr. Nosy, you know how much I love Agatha Christie mysteries, and I have always felt I could have been an excellent Miss Marple. But, knew, that all of this had to be kept a deep dark secret from Mr. Guslander. Because if Gus knew what I was up to, he would have fired me—especially if the whole thing had backfired on me. However, I just couldn't turn down the adventure. There would be four people who would know the entire script: myself, Lillie, the doctor, and Alice. The doctor was included because he had become suspicious of Tommy. Lillie added Alice to the mix, because the unhappy Alice wanted to get the goods on Eric who had recently ruined Lillie's career. My supporting players were to be: Mrs. Nakai, you, and Big John. Mrs. Nakai was my biggest support, because she knows to the minute, always, what goes on in the front and in the back of the hotel. Big John knew more than you did about what I was up to because, well, Percy, you can be a little too dramatic at times. The reason I chose you three to assist me in exposing the killer is because I knew I could trust your loyalty—and you three didn't let me down. On the night of the party, Lillie pretended to be poisoned, but not before pointing out clues about the death of her father. Then, as planned, after the doctor pronounced a very much alive Lillie dead, we were off to catch our killer. Lillie placed the dolls in the chairs to intimidate Tommy, because he would have been the only one at the table who understood the meaning of the Charlie McCarthy doll. It was Big John's idea to twist off the doll's heads. Tommy couldn't understand the killings because he had nothing to do with them ... yet, I felt that Tommy deep down knew that he was a party to it all. The two murders, Lillie's and Alice's, really threw him off—and that, Percy, was our whole intent and it worked. We wanted to unhinge Tommy so that he would make a mistake. Big John kept Alice and Lillie hidden in a house off property until they made their final appearance last night in my bedroom. Remember, it was only Big John's description and my description of Alice's fake grisly death that you and the suspects heard. Also, before Alice went into hiding, she concealed herself in the next room and taped Eric when he went off on her."

Clapping her hands and chuckling to herself, she offered: "I would say it was a job well done by all of us. Now, young man, Lillie's party is about to leave the hotel in a few short minutes. Get out of here NOW. We have Elvis and Paramount Studios arriving in minutes. They fly in on the same plane that Lillie is leaving on. Out of here, I want go to my room and freshen up."

I knew what freshen up meant: a spray of Chanel No.5, a dab of fresh pink lipstick on the lips, and a hoist up on the girdle.

Out in the lobby, Lillie was surrounded by her guests . . . except for Eric, who sulked behind a potted palm.

I heard a familiar voice say: "Lillie, finish telling them everything on the plane. Looking back on these past few days has been a magical time for me." Alice, wearing a colorful red *muumuu* and a purple Vanda orchid behind each ear, spoke to Lillie who now appeared not so lizard-like but more like a sweet, cuddly little gecko.

Lillie broke from Alice and put her arm through Raul's. She squeezed his arm as I heard her tell him, "Raul, the ranch is yours and I want you to divorce me. I will give you alimony for everything that you have had to put up with me these many years. But you must promise me that you will marry Conchita and make your two children legitimate."

Looking into his big beautiful, blue eyes, Lillie whispered, "Don't say anything to spoil my magnanimous moment. Right now, I want to feel good about myself." Raul kissed the top of Lillie's head as they parted in silence.

Then Lillie took Gretchen's face in her two hands. "Honey, I promise that we'll get your face fixed good as new."

I stood back in the lobby and watched the Russell party departure from a distance. How different they all were from a couple of days ago. Their stay at the Coco Palms had changed all of them. Dockie Wockie presents himself now as the sober, respectable Dr. Trescutt from Boston. His white seersucker suit was spotless and pressed. Raul and Lillie were very companionable, laughing at some past remembrance. Tilda and Tony were Romeo and Juliet. Through Tony's influence, not one swear word was uttered out of Tilda's pretty, little mouth. I could say honestly at that moment that Tilda and Tony were the best-looking couple on Kauai . . . better looking than Duke Wayne and Doris Day.

Gretchen, thinking of Lillie's promise, and of being reunited with her husband, glowed with a beauty all her own.

Granny was head over heels in love with one of the maintenance fellows out in the coconut grove. Granny, after she had locked the bathroom door, pushed herself out the window and shimmied herself down a coconut tree, hit the bars in Kapaa, and danced until dawn with Mutt. Mutt was a pure Hawaiian—the same age as Granny. He filled the #3 cans in the coconut grove with kerosene. Both shared the same passions: beer and sex. Granny had already moved in with Mutt and Kauai was about to add another legendary character to its roster. Grace, Mrs. Nakai, and the maids had been well aware of Granny's adventures.

The other miracle: since the day Lillie arrived at the Coco Palms, she never lisped once. Even Eric had changed—he was a crying mess.

As Lillie was about to step into the limo, Granny embraced her. "Honey, thank you for giving me a second chance at life."

"When you and your native friend get married, I'll fly over and give you away."

"Ah honey, living in sin is much more fun. I ain't the married-kind anymore. Anyway, I've been married too many times to count. This time I want it to work out," Granny cackled with the joy thinking about her new life.

"Does he know you snore like a locomotive?"

"Honey, he knows everything about me and what's more . . . he's deef!" Giving Lillie another hug, she said, "Tell, Hollywood, I ain't ever coming back. Ever."

Lillie slid into the backseat of the limo and Big John closed the door. In the distance, the sound of a plane could be heard flying to Kauai from Honolulu. The Lillie Russell party left the hotel with little fanfare.

CHAPTER TWENTY-THREE

November 16, 1960 – MGM film star Clark Gable (star of the 1939 film Gone with the Wind) dies.

Within the hour, conch shells blew at the entrance of the hotel. Led in by a parade of loin-clothed, bare-chested Hawaiian warriors, and swaying hula dancers, seven white limousines drove down the driveway into the hotel porte-cochere. Out of the first limo stepped the King of Hollywood, the rock n' roll, Elvis Presley. He appeared the same as he did in his films: tall, slim, chisel-faced, a long-lashed, blue-eyed, handsome, young star. He gave everyone the smile that had melted the hearts of all the women in America.

Grace stepped daintily down the steps to welcome Elvis. Lowering his head, he received a double red carnation lei and a kiss from Grace.

"Mr. Presley, Coco Palms welcomes you to Kauai. I'm Miss Buscher, manager of the Coco Palms Hotel."

"Ma'am, it is my pleasure to be with you all." With that, he took her hand and kissed it. The teenyboppers in the crowd, who had gathered at the hotel since four in the morning, swooned—one fainted.

A distinguished white-haired man, whose features were as chiseled as those on Mount Rushmore, stood beside the King.

"Miss Buscher," Elvis said, "this is the producer of our film, Mr. Hal Wallis, and his beautiful friend, actress Miss Martha Hyer. Behind them is the sensational Joan Blackman, who I am fortunate to have co-starring with me."

After the stars and producer received their leis, they were whisked away in electric carts to their King's Cottage suites as the Paramount contract had requested in large print. "As soon as Elvis Presley arrives," the contract stated, "the studio wants him to be far, far away from the madding crowd as possible."

From that moment on, and for their entire month-long stay at the Coco Palms, crowds of giddy girls blocked the entrance to the hotel looking for a glimpse of the star.

Out of the second limo stepped the film star that Grace had been most anxious to meet—Angela Lansbury (the comely MGM star.) Standing alone, Miss Buscher approached the actress, holding out a single white ginger lei that she had especially ordered from Honey's lei stand in Honolulu.

"Miss Lansbury, welcome to Coco Palms. I feel so honored that you will be staying with us during the shooting of *Blue Hawaii*.

"Thank you," Miss Lansbury replied in a voice tinged with British-sounding vowels.

"I have been a fan of yours since you first appeared in *Gaslight*."

"Thank you. I love those juicy roles that have a touch of evil in them . . . sometimes more than a touch. I am much too nice of a woman in this film—a lady who speaks with a southern accent to boot . . . Sarah Lee Gates. Can you imagine that? A boring role, darling, but it pays the bills." The last four sentences she spoke not as a Londoner but as if she was born in "Scarlett O'Hara" country.

Grace smiled. "While you are here with us at the Coco Palms, if there is anything you need, you just holler out for me, *y'all*. I'll see to it that one of the boys will get you whatever you want or need."

Angela seemed delighted in her new friend and chirped: "I think we are going to be great friends. I have a distinct feeling that you like to have fun. You know, there is one role I'd love to play: I'd like to be a character out of an Agatha Christie mystery novel—a woman who writes mysteries and solves them at the same time. Call it something like, 'She Wrote Murder Mysteries' or 'Murder She Wrote.' Wouldn't that be the most delicious fun?"

"I own every book Agatha Christie ever wrote. I have them stashed under my bed. I'd be glad to send all of them over to your cottage."

With a wink of her eye, Angela said laughingly: "That would be most delightful. Perhaps, while here, we two could solve a mystery together."

"That would be fun, Angela. Staying at the Coco Palms, you're going to find magic. And when you leave, many good things will have come into your life. You will be changed, trust me, and someday, I am sure, you will get your wish. I have a feeling that one of your greatest roles will be that of a woman detective-writer who solves mysteries."

Then Angela took hold of Grace's arm, squeezed it, and they walked down a sandy path into a bright Technicolor sunny Hawaiian morning.

———◆———

The night Elvis Presley arrived at the Coco Palms, Gus phoned at his usual time and screamed: "How many rooms did you comp and for what! What the hell is going on at your Goddamn hotel?"

Not waiting for an answer, Gus continued "And I got a call today from the Beverly Hills Police Department with some cocka-mamie story about a killer staying at the Coco Palms . . . I told them they were out of their minds, because no killer would dare to come to Coco Palms. Because, if a killer met my manager at my hotel, he'd head for cave in Kathmandu and hide. I told them, when my manager, Miss Buscher, is on the war path, I have often had the thought of joining the French Foreign Legion myself."

Gus was back in the saddle again; Elvis was filming at the hotel; Grace was creating new projects; God was back from Maui and watching over Kauai; and all was right again at the wonderful, miraculous Coco Palms Hotel.

Postscript: In the next issue of the *Garden Island* newspaper, there were two small squibs at the bottom on page three and four.

Page Three. Film star, Miss Lillie Russell of Hollywood, celebrated her birthday at the Coco Palms Hotel. Her party of seven left Kauai on the same plane that Elvis Presley arrived on to film, *Blue Hawaii.*

Page Four. Two pig hunters shooting goats near the source of the Wailua River, directly below the cliffs of the impenetrable valley of Lono, swear they heard someone singing, "Give My Regards to Broadway." They also swore that the singer tap danced while he sang. The pig hunters' wives have strictly forbidden their husbands to drink beer, shoot goats, or hunt pigs for the next month, and threatened to dry them out at the Montgomery Hotel.

A further postscript: I was bemused because not one person asked about Tommy Twinkle. I wondered how or if Lillie or Dockie would ever explain what happened to Tommy at the Coco Palms.

The murders of Lillie's father and Heidi were written off in the Beverly Hills police files as unsolved mysteries.

August 23, 1960 – Oscar Hammerstein II (South Pacific lyricist) died.

[FADE OUT]

David Penhallow-Scott is a Hawaii-born writer and author of *After the Ball*, *The Betrayers*, and the *The Story of the Coco Palms Hotel*, and has written the plays *The Eudora Quartet*, *The Dark Side of the Moon*, and *Listen to the Stars and Lights Out*.

Penhallow-Scott presently resides in Hilo on Hawaii Island. *Murder with Aloha at the Coco Palms Hotel* is another "Percy" story.

Grace Guslander and Author